MW00626197

ANOMALIES
IN
BLUE

ANOMALIES
IN
BLUE

GLENN
KAMMEN

Boffin Press

Copyright © 2020, 2019 Glenn Kammen

All rights reserved. No part of this publication may be reproduced, distributed, or transmitted in any form or by any means, including photocopying, recording, or other electronic or mechanical methods, without the prior written permission of the publisher, except in the case of brief quotations embodied in critical reviews and certain other noncommercial uses permitted by copyright law.

ISBN: 978-1-7340195-0-6 (Paperback)
ISBN: 978-1-7340195-1-3 (E-Book)

Library of Congress Control Number:2019918015

This book is a work of fiction. Any references to historical events, real people, or real places are used fictitiously. Other names, characters, and places are products of the author's imagination.

Quote from p. 286 (used three times) from Possible Worlds and Other Essays by J.B.S. Haldane. Copyright © 1928 by Harper & Brothers. Copyright © renewed 1956 by J.B.S. Haldane. Used by permission of HarperCollins Publishers.

Cover Design and Formatting by Damonza.com

Printed in the United States of America
First printing, 2020

Published by Boffin Press
200 Windtree Avenue
Thousand Oaks, CA 91320

www.glennkammen.com

For Alexandra and Elizabeth, who will always be at the center of my universe.

CHAPTER 1

His CURRICULUM VITAE was impressive, even in a city teeming with overachievers. University President. Award-winning author. And most recently, Deputy Secretary of Education. But Simeon Marshall's dream had always been to create a neighborhood school that would develop curious, well-rounded young men and women of all backgrounds, regardless of their financial circumstances. So, when his time in Washington, DC came to an end, this renowned African-American educator with a penchant for bespoke Italian suits returned to his home state of California and assembled a group of financial backers to help make that dream a reality. Two years later, he had founded the Benjamin Banneker School, named for the eighteenth-century writer, scientist, and mathematician, who believed that free schools should be established in every city, town, and village in the United States. There were other educational institutions that had been named after this African-American Renaissance man, but this one offered something that none of the others did: a comprehensive K-12 solution on a single site.

I was honored and somewhat intimidated when Dr. Marshall recruited me to teach high school science at Banneker. We met in his office one morning in early June before departing on a walking tour of the campus, located in a Pasadena, California industrial park that had been abandoned following a protracted economic downturn. After years of neglect and decay, the dusty bungalows and ranch-style buildings were undergoing a major renovation that was still in its early stages. Chunks of wood, rusted-out pipe, and enough nails to stock a home-improvement store littered the site, which looked more like a beaten-down junkyard than the future of education. But after a dozen years in the Los Angeles Unified School District, I was ready for a change. A few cosmetic blemishes weren't going to stop me from signing on to what local media had dubbed "The Marshall Plan."

Over the course of that summer, Dr. Marshall and I crafted the curriculum for Integrated Science Studies, an innovative, multidisciplinary tenth-grade course that we both believed could be the centerpiece of Banneker's science department. I would also teach more traditional, single-subject science classes, but ISS 100, as it would be known in our online catalogue, embodied Banneker's balanced approach to education. Sadly, four weeks before the beginning of the school year, Simeon Marshall suffered a stroke that left him paralyzed on the right side and unable to speak. In an interview with the *Los Angeles Times*, his neurologist explained that the road to rehabilitation would be long and the outcome uncertain.

Given that murky prognosis, the school's board of directors launched a national search for an interim principal to take Dr. Marshall's place for at least the coming year. They settled on Janet Del Rio, a gangly woman with squinty eyes, who shared Dr. Marshall's preference for imported fashion but little else. She had earned an EdD from a small, private university after working for several years in the wealth-management division of a Wall Street investment bank. This followed a brief stint as chief of staff for a Texas congressman who had been forced to resign in the wake of a well-chronicled ethics scandal. There was no official explanation for the board's decision to choose someone outside the field of education, although many speculated that board members had been swayed by Del Rio's political connections and reputation for efficient management.

Regardless of why she had been hired, the contrast in academic philosophy between Dr. Del Rio and Dr. Marshall could not have been more pronounced. Marshall wanted to develop active young minds through a curriculum that placed equal emphasis on academic rigor and intellectual curiosity. Del Rio's primary focus was on pushing test scores as high as possible to spur donations from corporate sponsors, which she felt were especially important given that Banneker offered financial assistance to many of its students.

But none of that was on my mind as I stood in front of the demo table in my Integrated Science Studies classroom on the morning of the first day of school and awaited the arrival of my students. The flexible space, with lab counters and sinks lining its perimeter, was large enough for the instructor to deliver lecture content or to work individually with students seated in small groups at modular workstations. The room was outfitted with the kind of equipment found in most high-school science classrooms: an LCD projector for PowerPoint presentations or the occasional overhead transparency, electrical outlets suspended from the ceiling to give students access to real-time data-collection probeware, and high-density storage systems with removable bins and tote trays for tools and supplies.

There was, however, one thing in the combination lecture room and lab not found in science classrooms everywhere: a seven-foot-wide, interactive SMART Board that could display ultra-high definition visual content, like that morning's television news coverage of mysterious booming sounds that had been reported the previous two nights in Wisconsin. I stumbled upon the story while giving the SMART Board one last run-through before the opening bell. Unfortunately, I didn't have time to watch the entire piece because I wanted to take a final look at the school records of the fifteen students who were about to walk in the door. According to evaluations from previous instructors, only eight of them found science even remotely interesting, meaning the other seven were likely taking the course because of schedule problems or to satisfy school requirements. It was no surprise, then, that when my future scientists began drifting into the room, some appeared glad to be there, while others looked like they wished summer vacation could have lasted another week or two.

"Welcome to Integrated Science Studies, or ISS 100 as it's also known. Not to be confused with the International Space Station." I hoped a little nerdy humor might help settle everyone's first-day nerves—or at least let them know they were in the right room. Most of the students found seats right away; a few wandered around for a while, looking lost.

"You can sit wherever you like for now. We'll figure out something more permanent later. I'm Andrew Siegel. You can call me Mr. Siegel, Andrew, Fearless Leader, or whatever you like, within the reasonable bounds of good taste."

"How about we just call you Andy?" asked Victor Esparza, a quick-witted student of Mediterranean descent, who had consistently underachieved in school.

"I said within the bounds of good taste, Victor. Andy is a nickname I've always hated, so calling me that would constitute exceptionally bad taste."

"Wait, you already know my name? It usually takes at least ten minutes."

With his slicked-back hair and sharp leather tie, Victor looked like the doorman at a trendy club. He had made a name for himself in middle school by commandeering classroom exchanges with sharply drawn but disruptive comedic observations. School psychologists explained Victor's sarcastic humor as a coping mechanism devised to help him endure the abusive behavior of his stepfather, an occasionally employed semi-functional alcoholic. His mother, the one constant in Victor's life, worked three jobs to keep the family afloat financially, while at the same time trying to protect her son and herself from her husband's increasingly frequent alcohol-fueled tirades.

"Actually, I know all of your names, as well as quite a bit about each one of you."

"Awesome," said Tanya Riddell. "Our science teacher is a stalker."

Nearly six feet tall and rail thin, with the unflinching focus of a laser, Tanya was the only child of retired tech billionaire Martin Riddell and his trophy second wife, Delilah. She was also reputed to have a rare form of eidetic memory that gave her the ability to remember virtually everything she read or heard. But while her retention skills were remarkable, the rest of Tanya's life was far from perfect. She struggled with a multitude of demons, including a bulimia problem that even the most exclusive treatment programs in Palm Springs and Malibu had been unable to solve. Along with her dietary issues, Tanya battled depression. She had tried on two occasions to take her own life—once with a handful of her mother's OxyContin pills and another time with her father's imported Tunisian letter opener, which she had used to nearly sever the radial artery of her left wrist. Tanya's parents spent the majority of their time cruising the world's oceans on a two hundred-foot-long super yacht, so child-rearing duties fell primarily to nannies, extended family members, and assorted staffers within the Riddell technology empire.

I walked behind the demo table and felt fifteen pairs of eyes following me. A quick keystroke later and the SMART Board sprang to life with a string of white letters that stood out crisply against the dark background: "Now my own suspicion is that the universe is not only queerer than we suppose, but queerer than we can suppose."

"Anybody familiar with that quote?"

"I think I might've heard it on an old *Twilight Zone*," said Chad Osterhaus, a chiseled surfer with the quiet confidence that came from knowing he was the closest thing to a jock the Benjamin Banneker School might ever have. Chad had been diagnosed years earlier with moderate learning disabilities, which may have been why academic excellence was not something he chose to pursue.

"Actually, it goes back even farther than that. It was written by British geneticist J.B.S. Haldane and published in a collection of his essays in 1927."

"Excuse me," Tanya blurted out.

"Yes?"

"Are you aware that you say *actually* a lot?"

"I do what?"

"You say *actually* a lot. You said it a minute ago when you were talking about how much you know about us. And now you just said it again. I didn't know if you were aware of that."

"Actually, I was not aware of that."

"No worries," Tanya said with a wry smile.

Lawrence Halloran, a pudgy student with a shock of red hair and thick glasses, raised his hand.

"Yes, Lawrence. Or do you go by Larry?"

"You can call him Larry if he can call you Andy." Victor's comment drew skittish laughter from several of the students. It was already apparent that his reputation for smart-ass comedy was well-deserved.

"Go ahead, Lawrence."

"I was just wondering. Is genetics part of this class?"

"A small part, but yes."

"And that's related to evolution, right?"

"Right, and that's the point behind this integrated approach to science. Everything is related, which is why we'll be studying biology, chemistry, physics, ecology, astronomy, cosmology. And, yes, genetics and evolution. Kind of a science buffet."

Lawrence looked confused, which, considering his past educational experience, was not altogether surprising. His mother, a staunch social conservative, had previously home schooled her son according to her strict religious beliefs and had expected to continue doing so during his high school years. However, Lawrence's father, a successful commercial builder and founder of Halloran Industries, had other ideas. He was so impressed by Banneker's STEM program that he made the unilateral decision to enroll Lawrence—over the strenuous objections of Lawrence's mother. Mrs. Halloran eventually relented but only after satisfying herself that Lawrence understood her instructional preferences and could articulate them to his teachers as necessary.

"Okay, I was just asking because my mom wanted to be sure that we talk about evolution as a theory and not like it's a fact."

Class had been in session for less than ten minutes, and we were already steeped in controversy.

"Well, Lawrence, you can assure your mother she has nothing to worry about. Whether we're studying the laws of motion, the anatomy of the cell, or genetics and evolution, we'll do our work in a fair and objective manner."

"Okay, I'll let her know."

One crisis averted, at least for the moment.

"So, back to J.B.S. Haldane. His perspective on the universe touches on something very fundamental—that we are not only limited by what we know but by what we *can* know. In other words, this place we call the universe is probably much stranger than we can even imagine. But I can tell you this—we will know a good deal more about it by the end of the semester. Which is a sneaky way of telling you that we have lots of work ahead of us, and I hope you're as excited about diving into it as I am."

The blank looks on the faces staring back at me did not exactly scream excitement.

"One other thing I'd like to add—we'll do a lot more than just memorize names and dates in this class. I'm more interested in introducing you to the scientific method and the *process* of science than cramming a bunch of facts into your heads that you'll forget the minute you walk out that door at the end of the year."

"But we are going to learn enough facts to pass the tests we need to move on to other science classes, right?"

I had wondered when we would hear from Charley Harper. With his baggy corduroy pants, flannel shirt, and suspenders, Charley could have been plucked from the pages of *Field and Stream*. He was not only short for his age but, owing to chronic digestive problems, somewhat gaunt, with a grayish pallor despite his African-American heritage. Mychal and Keeshana Harper had adopted Charley as an infant, not long after his teenage birth mother abandoned him in the bathroom of a Chicago area bus station. By the time the Harpers moved to Pasadena, Charley had already begun to display an unusual array of talents, including the ability to play concert-level classical piano at the age of seven and code in multiple programming languages by eight. He had also begun to struggle with social anxiety issues and was becoming a serious worrier, which likely explained his concerns about exam prep.

"No question about it, Charley. Anyone in this class who puts in the time will pass those exams. But there is more at stake here than just passing a test. If we have any hope of solving the mysteries of the universe, we need to go beyond memorizing answers. We also need to learn how to ask the right questions."

"Like what kind of questions?" Tanya asked.

"Mostly questions pertaining to life," I said, pacing back and forth behind the demo table, "which will provide the context and connective tissue for everything we study. How and why did life begin? What are the conditions necessary for it to flourish? What are some of the challenges that threaten it? In the process of answering those questions and others, we'll explore multiple areas of science, all of which are related in some way.

"You might not see how they fit together at first because we won't always follow a linear and predictable path. Eventually, though, you'll begin to recognize the patterns and connections that underlie everything we're learning. And at that point, you'll be thinking like real scientists, with your own ideas and new ways of looking at this thing we call life."

I scanned the room and noticed that the only thing Krista Hollingsworth seemed to be looking at was her own reflection in the compact mirror she had pulled from her purse. Krista's platinum-blonde hair framed her heavily made-up face in a flawless bob that terminated just below her ears. I wondered how much time was needed to pull all that together every day. I also wondered whether she had the slightest interest in anything beyond herself. Although she'd scored well above average on standardized tests, Krista had demonstrated little curiosity, intellectual or otherwise, to that point in her young life.

Undeterred, I walked out from behind the demo table to make my final appeal.

"What I am challenging you to do, in other words, is to go beyond the limitations of conventional thinking and prove J.B.S. Haldane wrong. All it takes is a sense of adventure, a willingness to explore, and some hard work." I realized I'd thrown a lot at these kids, who probably had no idea what they were getting themselves into when they enrolled in my class. "Alright, I've said enough for one day. Anybody have any questions?"

"Can you talk about grades?"

"Do you give extra credit on homework?"

"Can we drop a test if we mess up?"

"What's your policy for unexcused absences?"

I was talking about pushing the boundaries of scientific inquiry; they were obsessing over grades and homework.

"Look, I understand your interest in those administrative sorts of things. But I wanted to at least introduce you to the approach we'll be using in doing our work. We can talk about the other stuff later."

Maybe it was just my imagination, but I could have sworn I saw a couple of students roll their eyes.

"I'm sure everyone appreciates that you wanted to tell us about the class," Krista said, tapping her perfect acrylic nails on the tabletop, "but it's the first day of school, and most teachers talk about grades and tests and attendance on the first day."

"Well, Krista, I'm not necessarily like most teachers. And this might not be like most classes."

In the time it took to utter that single confrontational

statement, the climate in the room shifted from pleasantly temperate to unmistakably chilly—and any hope of enticing those youngsters with the lure of science was swept away in a tidal wave of anxiety.

It was not the first day I had expected.

CHAPTER 2

THE WORDS *CASA del Mundo* were etched into the alder wood sign that hung above the front porch of my parents' Spanish Colonial hacienda, located a few miles northwest of Pasadena in the affluent community of La Cañada Flintridge. The estate was built around a central courtyard dominated by a massive fountain and enough wrought iron to outfit a medieval dungeon. But more than anything, it was a shrine to my older sister, Katie, who died at the age of sixteen when a pickup truck that had run a red light broadsided the van she was riding in with her high school volleyball team. The walls throughout the house were covered with photos of her, along with trophies, medals, certificates, framed report cards, and other memorabilia.

Our parents, Arthur and Barbara, had always been obsessed with Katie. My father had plotted out her entire career by the time she was three, when he nicknamed her "the Goddess." According to his master plan, she would be the valedictorian of her high school and then attend an Ivy League university, from which she would graduate summa cum laude. Following that, she would be crowned Miss Universe and go on to earn a gold medal playing volleyball in the Olympics, before enrolling in a top law school. Finally, after a sterling legal career, Katherine Siegel, JD, would become the first female Chief Justice of the United States Supreme Court.

Unfortunately, none of that actually happened.

For all practical purposes, the accident that took Katie's life ended the lives of our parents as well. Prior to that, my father had been a strapping middle-aged man who lifted weights, followed a strict diet, and prided himself on his rippling physique. Within six months of Katie's death, he had packed on forty pounds of non-rippling fat after replacing his nutrition and exercise regimen with massive quantities of chocolate peanut butter cheesecake and deep-fried everything else. He also gave up his practice as one of California's top criminal-defense attorneys and discontinued the pro bono legal work he had donated to progressive causes on a routine basis. Fueled by equal amounts of rage and bitterness, he focused all his attention on making obscene amounts of money as a rapacious slumlord, as if unbridled financial success might somehow insulate him from his loss.

Mother, on the other hand, shed thirty pounds, along with much of her salt-and-pepper hair, which began falling out in large clumps. She also went from enjoying the occasional glass of pinot grigio to living life as a closeted alcoholic, dependent on the anesthetizing properties of hard liquor to make it through the day. Her drink of choice was vodka, although gin would do in a pinch, concealed behind the masking properties of iced tea, juice, or any other potable liquid that might be available.

My wife, Joanna, and I were at my parents' house for dinner to celebrate her recent promotion to partner at her law firm, as well as an invitation to write an article for a prestigious legal journal. The evening began on the veranda with champagne and hors d'oeuvres served by Carlotta, who had worked for our family as housekeeper, chef, designated driver, and unofficial therapist for more than thirty years.

"To Joanna," Mother said, her right hand trembling as she raised the first of several glasses of Louis Roederer Brut Rosé she would down that night. "Not only a wonderful wife to our son, but an amazing woman in her own right and now the first female partner at . . . Oh shit, I'm drawing a blank." She snapped her fingers, as if that might jumpstart her brain. "Help me, Andrew."

"Harrison, Kearns & McMillan."

"Right, right. May you know nothing but the most beautiful—sorry, the most bountiful amounts of happiness and success."

Everyone clinked glasses and took a sip of champagne, which in Mother's case was more of a gulp.

"Thank you both so much for all your love and support," Joanna said. "It means the world to me, especially with my parents so far away." David and Annabeth Robbins had retired years earlier and moved to Hawaii, where they bought a small home in the upcountry area of Maui. Although Joanna never said so explicitly, I always sensed an undercurrent of resentment when she joked about how her parents had abandoned her.

"And if I might add a thought, or a couple of thoughts, actually . . ." My father lifted his glass for toast number two. "Here's to my son for recognizing the wisdom of marrying up."

"Ain't that the truth," I agreed.

"And here's to his parents, who were at least partly responsible for him meeting this lovely lady in the first place."

I hated to give my father credit for anything, but in this case he was right. My initial interest in science had been sparked at the age of six when Katie invited me outside one night to look at Mars, which was making one of its periodic, closer-than-usual approaches to Earth. My love affair with astronomy eventually expanded to include chemistry, physics, and biology. When the time came, the choice of attending a university that emphasized science was an easy one.

By the time I started my junior year, when most of my classmates were making plans for summer internships and graduate school, I still had no idea what I wanted to do after graduation. Toward the end of the semester, I allowed my parents to manipulate me into applying to law school, probably because I felt it was my duty to give them the attorney they lost when my sister died. I rationalized the decision by vowing to specialize in some aspect of the law that involved science.

I attended the UCLA School of Law for all of four days before the stupidity of what I'd done became obvious, and I dropped out to pursue a career in science education. There was, however, one positive by-product of my brief stint in Westwood: I met my classmate and future spouse, Joanna Robbins, who actually stayed in law school beyond the first week. Joanna had all the qualities good lawyers are supposed to have. She was logical, articulate, and could deliver a withering rebuke at the slightest provocation. But she had more going for her than just her intellect. Her jutting cheekbones and indigo eyes fused the best of East and West. Had she not decided to pursue a career in law, Joanna could have been a supermodel who owned both the runway and the agency. Instead, she went on to become an intellectual-property attorney specializing in copyright law, and now was a partner at her venerable Los Angeles law firm.

"If only she were also an accountant, so I had someone I trust to take care of my taxes," my father said.

"Arthur, please," said Mother. "You have an army of people doing your taxes."

"I said someone I trust."

Joanna managed a tortured smile and slipped a bacon-wrapped scallop in her mouth.

"Well, in any case, Joanna, darling," Mother continued, "we are beyond proud of you." She gazed off at the sun as it ducked behind the San Gabriel Mountains, and downed what remained in her gold-tipped crystal flute. "In some ways, it's almost like having a daughter again."

We weren't even to the main course, and Mother had already slid from celebratory to morose.

"The salmon's ready, Mrs. Siegel." Among her other talents, Carlotta always knew when to rescue Mother from herself.

We took our seats in the dining room, and Carlotta began serving. "I hope they're giving you a larger office with a nice big window," Mother said.

"No, not right away at least. We're going to be moving to a new building in the next year, so we'll probably keep things as they are until then."

"There's plenty of time for perks and rewards later," my father said.

"I know that. I just meant that Joanna ought to get the—"

"She's a partner now, Barbara," he bellowed. "She has to think about running a business. Something you wouldn't even begin to understand."

Maybe she didn't understand it that night, but she certainly would have at an earlier time in her life, when she was capable of doing more than emptying a bottle of Grey Goose at a single sitting. That seemed like a hundred lifetimes ago as I sat at the dinner table and listened to my father reduce her to dining-room roadkill.

"And what about you, dear?" Mother asked, wincing slightly as she turned to me. "How are things going at your new school?"

"Well, today was only the first day, so the jury's still out."

"I appreciate the legal metaphor," my father said with a thin smile. "You know, Andrew, we're breaking ground soon on an outdoor mall in Palo Alto. I'm working with some major VC players up there."

Mother dabbed her lips with her napkin. "What kind of players, Arthur?" she asked.

He glowered at her in contemptuous silence.

"Venture capital," Joanna said quietly.

"I could make a call or two. I'm sure they'd be willing to talk to you."

"Talk to me about what?" I asked, although I knew exactly what he meant and where this was headed.

"Hopefully, gainful employment. All of them are well-connected with Silicon Valley technology firms. Some of those have offices in the L.A. area."

I offered a vacant smile. "I already have a job, but thanks."

"Andrew, I'm not talking about a job. I'm talking about a career."

"Last time I checked, I believe teaching was considered a career."

"And at least you don't have to worry about getting a corner office," Mother added with a laugh.

Nobody else was laughing, least of all me. "I wasn't worried, but thank you for the reassurance."

"I just meant, with Joanna making partner, you don't need to think about fancy offices or making a ton of money."

At that point, the only thing I was thinking about was getting the hell out of there.

"Carlotta, these au gratin potatoes are amazing," Joanna said, making a valiant but unsuccessful effort to lighten the mood.

"Thank you, Miss Joanna."

After a few seconds of strained silence, my father leaned forward and clasped his hands. "Andrew, I'm sorry if you took offense at my offer. All I meant was that you had a stellar academic record. You could write your own ticket."

I looked directly at him for the first time that night.

"I am writing my own ticket. It's just not the one you had in mind."

❧

We peeled away from the circular driveway, kicking up a small mountain of gravel in the process. I ripped through the gears like we were fleeing a crime scene.

"Can you slow down, please?" Joanna asked, as we barreled toward the Foothill Freeway. "Why are you so angry?"

"I'm not angry," I said, winding out the revs close to redline with each throw. Joanna knew I was bullshitting but didn't press the point. I turned on the radio and tore through the presets until some abstract jazz poured over us like a blast of cool air. Neither of us liked jazz all that much, but I needed something unexpected to get that soul-crushing dinner out of my head. I cranked up the volume to somewhere between deafening and painful.

Joanna turned it down and changed the station to what that sounded like background music at a day spa.

"I hate that New Age shit," I said, punching up an all-news station.

"Look, I know your dad can be a little condescending at times."

"Really? I hadn't noticed."

"And obviously your mother was a bit off her game."

"I thought she was totally on her game. Wasted as usual."

After wrapping up a story about the California drought and tensions in the Middle East, the news reader teased the same mysterious booming sounds story I had heard about at school that morning. That was followed, just as we pulled in the driveway, by an ad explaining how to make a fortune working part-time at home. Joanna turned the radio off before I could get further details.

"Hey, I wanted to hear that."

"You're thinking about working from home?"

"No, I wanted to hear about the booming sounds in Wisconsin."

We walked into the house, and before I could flick on the light, a 135-pound beast knocked me backwards with a perfectly timed leap.

"Largo, no! Get down!" I shouted, pushing our overeager Newfoundland away with more force than I had intended.

"You don't have to take it out on the dog just because you're in a nasty mood."

"Sorry, boy," I said, overcome with guilt. "Treats are on me."

We lived only fifteen minutes from my parents, but it felt like another planet. Our aging Craftsman bungalow—all 1,225 square feet of it—looked out on the world through a tangle of misshapen cactus plants and succulents. It was located in a diverse, unincorporated appendage of Pasadena called Altadena. Or at least it had been called that. A group of enterprising property developers had recently been lobbying local politicians with plans to "restore the original luster" of the area by turning it into a master-planned community to be known as Parkway Grove.

As far as I was concerned, the area was fine the way it was and didn't need any transparent gentrification gimmicks to make it more desirable. Our two-bedroom, one-and-a-half-bath home was likewise just right, despite its modest size and occasionally cranky plumbing. What it may have lacked in modern amenities, it made up for with hardwood floors, built-in bookshelves, Mission-style wall sconces, and an original Arts and Crafts tile fireplace. But my favorite part of the house was the garage, which I had converted into an air-conditioned, fully-insulated home for my growing army of vintage Fender Telecaster electric guitars. Joanna and I did, on occasion, have to play the car shuttle game, moving our vehicles between the carport and the street. But that was a small price to pay for what my wife referred to as my guitar shrine.

I fed Largo his extra treats and attached his leash for our nightly stroll through the neighborhood. We were about to duck out the front door when Joanna called to me from what we charitably referred to as the master bathroom, located off the hallway that connected the two bedrooms. When I walked in, she pointed to a calendar she had tacked on the wall and decorated with pink and blue circles around select groups of days over the next few months.

"So, what do you think?" she said, stepping back to admire her handiwork.

"Very colorful."

"That's it? Very colorful?"

I couldn't tell if she was angry or just disappointed in my descriptive skills. "Okay, how about, 'It's nice to have a calendar in the bathroom.'"

"It's not just a calendar, Andrew. It's got all my menstrual dates on it."

"Alright. That's good to know, I guess."

"Oh my God. You are so—" It was one of the only times I had ever seen Joanna at a loss for words. Largo chimed in with a volley of barks from somewhere near the front door.

"I should probably take him out."

"Do you not remember what we talked about?"

"We talk about a lot of things."

"I'm aware of that. I was referring to the calendar."

"Can you maybe give me a hint, or should I just start guessing?"

What had been a mostly civil discussion was on the verge of descending into all-out verbal combat. "We were saying, now that I'm a partner, this would be a good time to work on starting a family. Hence the calendar. Hello?"

I did recall a couple of conversations about that general topic, but as far as I knew, it was still in the theoretical stage. "Are these circles what I think they are?"

"I have no idea what you think they are, but they're the days I should be ovulating if I'm not taking my BC pills."

I looked at the circled dates more closely.

"So, you're really serious about this."

Largo barked again, louder, and with added urgency.

"Uh, yeah. Aren't you?"

"I guess. I don't know."

"You don't know what?"

"I mean, I know we talked about it. I just didn't know we were going to try to do this so soon."

"Andrew, I'm thirty-seven years old. How much longer did you want to wait?"

I didn't have an answer to the rhetorical question, nor did Joanna stick around to wait for one. Our bedroom door slammed shut about three seconds later, which I took as my cue to escort Largo through the mean streets of Altadena or Parkway Grove or wherever the hell we lived. As he sniffed and piddled his way through the neighborhood, I thought about the absurdity of my domestic situation. Joanna could not have been doing any better professionally. For a woman to become a partner at Harrison, Kearns & McMillan was not only unprecedented—it was tantamount to overturning the fundamental laws of the universe. Yet all she seemed to care about was what she relentlessly referred to as "starting a family." Always in those exact words. Further complicating matters, she had convinced herself that I didn't want to have a kid because I was unwilling to give up even a sliver of my personal freedom. In fact, my hesitation about becoming a parent had nothing to do with that.

The door to the bedroom was still shut when Largo and I returned from our walk. I thought about marching in and repleading my case but didn't want to do anything that might trigger another blowup. Instead, I decided to follow up on the news story I'd heard about in the car and had seen that morning on TV. A couple of taps on my phone, and there it was: "Mysterious Booming Sounds Rattle Nerves and Windows in Wisconsin." According to the article, dozens of Eau Claire, Wisconsin residents had called the police and local media after hearing loud booms for the third night in a row. From what I could tell, it didn't seem all that different from the usual wacked-out things people claim to see or hear on a daily basis, although there usually aren't that many of them seeing or hearing the same thing. Before I had a chance to read any further, the bedroom door opened, and I put my phone away. As much as I wanted to find out what was going on in Wisconsin, there were more important issues for me to deal with in my own house.

CHAPTER 3

THE NEXT MORNING, I threw together my standard weekday breakfast of plain yogurt mixed with any available fruit hovering between ripe and rancid. While I ate, I scrolled through the news app on my phone, looking for science stories that my students might draw from for their upcoming independent research projects. The first of these concerned a recent study about whether animals have a sense of time. Based on the behavior of one goofy Newfoundland in the Robbins-Siegel household, the answer was a definite yes. Largo always greeted us much more enthusiastically when we came home at the end of the day, as compared to, say, when we walked in after taking out the trash. Not sure why I'd noticed that, but it was good to know that if the whole teaching thing didn't work out, I could always fall back on a career as a canine behaviorist.

Maybe that would make my father happy.

Further down the page were the non-canine-related articles covering topics like the evolution of birds; the demise of woolly mammoths; and the unexpected abundance of bacteria at the deepest point in the ocean, more than thirty-six thousand feet below the surface in the Mariana Trench. While I found those subjects riveting, I doubted any of them would ignite my students' curiosity. I continued to scroll until I got to what looked like a recap of the Wisconsin booming-sounds story from the previous day. Once again there were descriptions of nervous residents, puzzled authorities, frayed nerves, et cetera. But there was one difference: the city in question was Greenwood, South Carolina. I glanced up at the top of the screen just as the numbers on the clock were changing from 6:59 to 7:00 a.m. The mysteries of South Carolina and Wisconsin would have to wait; I had a date with a squadron of cranky tenth graders.

∽

I was bracing for the worst in my Integrated Science class, which is probably why I positioned myself behind the demo table as my students filed into the room.

"Glad to see you all made it back. I thought I might have scared you off yesterday."

"Every other science class is full," Victor explained.

"Nothing personal," said Tanya. "You just seemed a little overenthusiastic for the first day."

"Except about cutting us a break on grades and homework," Krista added, while touching up her lip gloss.

"Look, Mr. Seagull or whatever your name is," Victor said, "if we were that into science, we wouldn't be taking Integrated."

I ventured out from behind the demo table to face my accusers. "The name is Siegel—S-I-E-G-E-L—and whether you realize it or not, if it weren't for science, your lives would be very different. And not in a good way."

"Really?" Victor challenged.

"Yes, really. Without science, Copernicus might never have

discovered that the Sun—and not this planet—is at the center of the solar system."

"That's it?" Victor asked. "That's all you got?"

"No, there's more. Lots more. Robert Hooke might not have discovered the cell. Isaac Newton might not have figured out the first law of motion. Einstein might have never developed the theory of relativity. I could go on if you'd like."

"No thanks, we're good," Victor shot back.

"So, I've got a question," Krista said.

"Okay."

"Why should we care about a bunch of dead guys who are, like, ancient history?"

"You shouldn't care about them. You should care about their work."

"Boring," Victor said through a fake yawn.

"If it's boring, it's because you don't understand it."

"You do realize we've heard that line before," Tanya said.

It was only the second day of school, and my young scientists were fighting me at every turn—not unlike someone else who kept popping into my head that morning.

"You guys are tougher on me than my own father, and trust me, that's next to impossible."

"What's so tough about him?" Tanya asked.

"Pretty much everything." I pulled up a stray chair. "Last night, for example, he questioned why an MIT graduate would want to teach high school science. And that was before I'd said a word about my apathetic Integrated Science students."

"Whoa, rewind," Victor said. "Who do you know that graduated from MIT and teaches high school science?"

"Other than me, no one."

"Wait, you went to MIT?" Tanya asked.

"Shocking, I know, but yes." The room fell silent. I might not have converted them, but at least I had their attention. "So, here's what I'm thinking. I promise to work with you as far as test scores and homework go."

"I feel a *but* coming," Krista said.

"But I need you to meet me halfway on this."

Charley crossed his arms. "Meaning what, exactly?"

"I won't force-feed you a steady diet of dry facts, and I'll try to keep the dead people references to a minimum."

"And what's our half?" Tanya asked.

"Displaying a modicum of curiosity. Approaching the work we do in here as actual working scientists."

"Define *actual working scientists*," said Charley.

"I was going to ask him to define *modicum*," Victor said.

I stood up and headed back to the demo table. "All I'm asking you to do is work together to explore some of the mysteries of the universe. Doing the same kinds of things that scientists everywhere are doing. Not scientists a hundred years ago. Scientists today. Right now."

Tanya glanced over at Charley, then peered up at me. "Like what?"

I reached for a stack of articles I had printed out and grabbed a few off the top. "Okay, these are just examples. No particular order. A team of scientists grew several hundred different kinds of bacteria in a group of caves. They were able to test about twenty percent of them for resistance to various antimicrobial agents. What these scientists were trying to determine—and what you and your research group would need to address if you were to choose this topic—is what are the origins of antibiotic resistance?"

I pulled out the next article. "Here's a study about a group of monkeys who exhibited higher-level cognitive and social skills, including the ability to plan, organize, and do simple arithmetic. Some have said that, taken together, these capabilities suggest that the line between humans and animals is not as distinct as we've always thought. So, you and your group would need to take a position on that, pro or con, and provide evidence to back up your argument."

I took a third article from the pile. "This one's not focused on life per se, but it poses an interesting question: Is time real or is it just an illusion?"

Chad, who to that point had been the chill embodiment of Southern California cool, jerked back in his seat. "That's like totally ridiculous!"

"Why do you say that?"

"Because it makes zero sense. For one thing, when you play sports—say, if you're a swimmer, like I am—they time you down to like a hundredth of a second. Not only that, my favorite TV show comes on every Tuesday night at eight o'clock. So, how could time be an illusion?"

I doubted that Chad's observations would be cited any time soon in *The American Journal of Physics*, but I appreciated that he was at least participating.

"Let me rephrase the question. Is it possible that time is relative rather than absolute?"

"Maybe so," Krista said, "but even if that's true, everything still has a beginning and an end."

"Like this class, which thankfully is going to end in about a minute and a half," said Victor, triggering a wave of laughter around the room. Even I chuckled a bit.

"What about the universe itself?" I asked. "Did it have a beginning?"

"That would be the Big Bang, duh," Krista said.

"You might be right but consider this—even if we accept that the universe was created in an event we call the Big Bang, many scientists think our universe may be just one in an infinite number of universes that comprise something called the multiverse."

Krista grimaced at the suggestion. "The what?"

"The multiverse. Kind of like a collection of universes. Nobody knows if there really is such a thing, and there's a good chance nobody ever will. But if there is, when did *it* begin? As soon as you start talking about the beginning and end of things like universes and multiverses, time becomes kind of slippery."

"And I get a headache," Victor said.

"We all do. Science can be messy and unpredictable, with lots of wrong turns and dead ends along the way. You might never reach the destination you were aiming for, but the journey can take you places you never imagined." I laid out the rest of the articles on the demo table. "Anyway, there are a lot of unsolved mysteries for us to untangle. These are just a few of them."

My students began sifting through the articles, swapping them back and forth like trading cards. They didn't even notice when an office monitor walked in the room.

"Mr. Siegel?"

"Yes."

"Dr. Del Rio wanted to know if you could stop by her office at some point today."

"Sure. Tell her I'll come by during lunch."

⁓

Within days of being named interim principal at Banneker, Janet Del Rio had ordered maintenance staff to remove anything with even the slightest connection to Dr. Marshall from what was now her office. In place of the warm Brazilian woods and impressionist art, she had substituted an icy assortment of contemporary furniture that could have graced the cover of any corporate brochure. One entire wall was filled with a splashy display of photos and news clippings that celebrated her professional accomplishments.

I took a seat across from Dr. Del Rio, who sat behind a massive glass desk that had nothing on it but a high-intensity lamp and an array of lethally sharpened pencils pointed upward like a fleet of nuclear missiles.

"So, Andrew. How's the first week going in your Integrated Science Studies class?"

"You know, if you'd asked me that twenty-four hours ago, I might have given you a different answer. But I think things are headed in the right direction."

Del Rio looked surprised, as if she had expected a more dire assessment. "I was just curious because the counselor's office said they'd never seen so many students try to transfer out of a class after the first day."

"It was a bit rocky on day one, but it feels like the students and I are on the same page now. Or at least reading from the same book." I hoped that minor bit of wordplay might make a small dent in her armor, but she skipped right over it.

"What also concerned me was that you apparently told the students they wouldn't have to worry about learning facts in your class. You didn't actually say that, did you?"

I shifted in my chair. "No, of course I didn't."

"Well then, what did you say that could have been so misconstrued?"

I knew I hadn't been summoned by Dr. Del Rio to chat about the highlights of my teaching career, but I didn't expect to be interrogated like a third-strike felon with no Miranda rights.

"I think I said something about how important it is to learn about the *process* of science. But I never said they wouldn't have to learn scientific facts. I would never say that."

"I'm glad to hear that, because if these students don't learn the necessary facts, they're not going to do very well on their state assessment tests. And if that should happen, you and I would have a serious problem." The hell with Miranda—I needed a bulletproof vest. "I expect to see test scores go through the roof, Andrew. That's how we're measured. That's how we attract students and their families, not to mention corporate donors. That's not just something that kind of matters. It's all that matters. If you don't think you can manage that, you might want to keep your résumé handy."

∽

I walked into the house that afternoon still smarting from my come-to-Jesus meeting with the interim principal. For a few dark moments, I thought about putting my fist through the wall or at least calling Janet Del Rio and letting her know what she could do with her state assessment tests. Minutes later, I was outside in running shoes and shorts, pounding down the asphalt. At one point, I was so lost in thoughts of retribution that I barreled through a red light just as a three-ton SUV with the right-of-way crossed into the intersection. Had it not been for the quick reflexes of the driver, I would never again have had to worry about my first-week problems at the Benjamin Banneker School.

Once back home, I took a long shower and fed Largo his usual evening meal of deboned turkey and brown-rice kibble. While he was inhaling that, I got a call from Joanna reminding me that my dinner-wrangling duties were not yet complete. I still needed to pick up Italian takeout and meet her at the home of our friends Kim and Danny Adler. Normally, I looked forward to grabbing

Calabrese pizza and antipasto with the Adlers at our favorite local trattoria. But this was not going to be a normal dinner.

∽

Unlike the trendy eateries of Old Town, Osteria Vecchia was a family-owned Italian restaurant that had been a fixture in Pasadena for years. Everything was almost exactly as it had been when I used to eat there with my parents as a kid: the assorted olive oils, colorful bottled sodas, and tempting chocolate confections, not to mention the kitschy trinkets and mementoes depicting the Vatican and the Leaning Tower of Pisa. There was, however, one concession to modern times: a flatscreen TV mounted on the wall behind the cashier. It was tuned to a local news station doing a story—like other recent news reports I'd seen—about booming noises. A reporter standing in front of a shed was interviewing a Bakersfield man, who was wearing camo pants and a military-green hoodie. The sound was turned off, but I could read the closed captions. "It sounded like we were in the middle of a war," the man said. "The house was shaking. Dishes were rattling. Spooked my dogs about half to death. Never heard them make a ruckus like that before."

"And so, the mystery booms continue," the in-studio anchor said over a map of the United States, "with local residents starting to get more than a little anxious. The number of cities reporting these sounds is now up to five." Red dots popped on at each location as the anchor ticked off the names of the cities. "They include Eau Claire, Wisconsin; Greenwood, South Carolina; Kingman, Arizona; Galesburg, Illinois; and now, Bakersfield, California."

I was starting to think that this might be more than just a ragtag bunch of conspiracy nuts chasing their tails. When I got back to the car, I turned on the radio to see what else I could find out, which turned out to be nothing. One of our two local all-news stations was doing a traffic report; the other was in a commercial. I thought about calling Marty Olivo, my old college roommate who ran the emergency room at one of the hospitals up in Bakersfield, but decided to put that off until after the night's work was done.

⤴

Danny Adler and I had known each other since kindergarten, but it was my tenth birthday party at Garfield Park in South Pasadena that cemented our friendship. And what a party it was. Settling on an Olympic Games theme, the obsessed party planner—who also happened to be my mother—micromanaged every moment in chilling detail. But Mother did not work alone. She had a willing co-conspirator in my sister, who created a poster that featured the iconic Olympic rings logo, a schedule worked out to the minute, and a suitably pretentious title: "The Andrew Siegel Tenth Birthday Celebration and Olympiad."

The most memorable part of the day was not the Olympics-inspired athletic competition. It was, instead, an unscheduled activity that Danny orchestrated during the last few minutes of the party. Just before closing ceremonies, my friends and I stuffed packets of salt into our jeans and headed off to the far side of the park. We combed through the parched grass until we came upon a cadre of spiral-shaped, motionless gastropods—better known as snails—none of which had any idea they were about to give their lives for our amusement. I looked on as the other members of our juvenile hit squad dropped saline bombs on their overmatched victims. After strafing the enemy one last time, Danny handed me an opened salt packet.

"Your turn, birthday boy."

"That's okay. I think you got 'em all."

"Don't wimp out on me. That one down there's got your name on it."

My fellow executioners closed in with the menacing inevitability of a lynch mob. Feigning excitement, I glared down at the day's grand prize: a brownish-gray snail, larger than the others and adorned with a distinct pattern of striated markings that imparted the dignity of a village elder. I hesitated a moment, then lowered the ordnance into launch position and emptied my white, crystalline arsenal on the unsuspecting mollusk below. His internal organs were concealed behind a layer of protective armor, which had served him well for a lifetime but was about to give way in a rush of liquid surrender. Once his bodily fluids had trickled out, my birthday guests stomped on his shell and any other organic matter that remained until there was nothing left. Danny pounded my shoulder excitedly.

"You did good!" he said.

One week before Banneker was scheduled to open its doors, Joanna and I drove out to the Beth Israel chapel in West Los Angeles on a sweltering August afternoon and took our place at the end of a long line of mourners waiting to get inside. Two dour gentlemen in dark suits handed each male a simple black yarmulke, the traditional Jewish skullcap, and distributed torn black ribbons to both men and women. This was part of the *Keriah*, an ancient ritual that symbolized the torn hearts of those who have lost a loved one. My mind skipped back to that day in the park when I celebrated my tenth birthday. It was just one of many childhood memories I had of Danny Adler, who was being laid to rest at the age of thirty-seven after drowning off the coast of Cozumel on a family vacation.

Danny and I had survived countless scrapes and adventures over the thirty-plus years we'd known each other. But all that was over. And as Joanna and I entered the sanctuary, working our way toward the only remaining seats available, in a row near the back, I was struck by an inescapable reality: for all who live on this Earth—from anonymous snail on the wrong patch of grass, to old friend in the grip of a seething riptide—death is simply part of life. Another side of the same coin.

❦

I knew that bringing dinner for Danny's wife, Kim, and their six-year-old son, Brian, was something we needed to do, something that Danny would have done for Joanna in a second had the situation been reversed. But it wasn't something I looked forward to doing.

When we finished eating, the name everyone had been dancing around was finally mentioned. Kim, Joanna, and I told all our favorite Danny stories, hoping to find some elusive comfort in our shared recollections. Brian seemed off in his own world during all this and said very little. Just before Joanna and I were about to leave, he showed us a colored-pencil drawing of him and his dad playing baseball—something he said he had planned to give Danny as a birthday present. The adults in the room gushed over the picture and assured Brian that Danny would have loved it. But that was of little consolation to that scrawny kid, who promised through his tears that he would look everywhere around the world—in every country, on every street, in every forest, and in every cave—no matter how long it took, until he found his father and could give him that gift.

On the way to our cars afterward, I put my arm around Joanna and drew her in close. It hadn't been the easiest of times lately, thanks to lingering tensions about family planning, school politics, and my always-grating mother and father. But those were petty trifles compared to the grief and pain that little boy and his mother were living with every moment of every day. I glanced up at the full moon, which was peeking out from behind a ring of gauzy blue light, and reminded myself that Joanna and I were healthy, we were together, and we had a future.

In the grand scheme of things, that was all that mattered.

CHAPTER 4

WHEN WE GOT home that night, Joanna and I both struggled to process what we had seen and heard at the Adler house. She finally decided to take Largo for what turned out to be a much longer walk than usual, and I somewhat randomly started thinking about the booming sounds mystery, which I'd forgotten about over the previous few hours. I had assumed the unexplained sounds were either weather related or somehow connected to military testing. But whatever their cause, when I powered up my laptop, I learned that the five cities in which they had been reported had now become eight, with Ogden, Utah; Muncie, Indiana; and Enid, Oklahoma having joined the list that evening.

There were several videos about all this that had already been posted on YouTube. One in particular stuck out because the reporter's name was laughably catchy, even for a local news personality. But Faraday DuPont had more than just an entertaining name. She also had a verbal tick, like so many others who cover the news, that caused her to begin almost every sentence with the word *now*.

"Now, authorities have not yet determined . . ."

"Now, the latest information we are getting . . ."

To Ms. DuPont and all the other eager reporters who grace our airwaves: When you report from the scene of a breaking news story, no one thinks you're talking about something that happened last month, last year, or during the War of 1812. There's no need to explain that it's happening now.

That minor gripe aside, the perky Pacific Islander with a death grip on her microphone did a good job summarizing what had happened that night in Enid, Oklahoma. Standing outside a convenience store, she explained that local residents had differing recollections of what they'd heard, but that all agreed there had been a series of loud, percussive booms. On his way out of the store, one of those locals, sporting turquoise bracelets and gray braids that jutted out from under his University of Oklahoma baseball cap, told DuPont that he had heard something "pretty damn loud that seemed to come from the sky."

The portly woman next to him—presumably his wife—who was carrying a twelve-pack of light beer, added a brief but vehement postscript. "It was more than *pretty* damn loud," she said. "It was scary damn loud and shook the whole damn house!"

"Now, most of the folks around here believe the sounds were caused by oil-field exploration or an exploding transformer," DuPont said, turning to the camera. "But local authorities told me a short time ago that there's been no oil-field testing anywhere near here, and Oklahoma Gas and Electric say no transformers have exploded recently. And so, for now at least, the mysterious booming sounds that have shaken Enid remain just that . . . a mystery."

I spent the next forty-five minutes hopscotching from one booming sounds link to another, pausing only briefly to greet Joanna and Largo when they returned from their walk. More than a thousand people around the country had now reported hearing these unexplained sounds, but Eau Claire, Wisconsin, the site of the initial reports, was getting most of the media attention. When the city announced an emergency community meeting at a local high school following the third consecutive night of booms, a slew of reporters and camera crews from national news outlets showed up to cover it. Between their coverage and the videos taken by people attending the meeting, I had lots to choose from on YouTube.

The meeting began with a procession of Eau Claire residents speaking one after another at a lectern that had been set up at one end of the gym. They used words like "humming," "rumbling," and "buzzing," in addition to "booming," to describe the sounds. A few people provided more expansive accounts, comparing what they'd heard to someone blowing into a conch shell or a door being kicked in. One person said it sounded like a round of artillery blasting through the side of his house.

Most people at the meeting said the sounds originated in the sky; some thought they came from underground. A number of residents expressed concerns that energy generated by the sounds might cause sink holes that could swallow up nearby homes. Fortunately, there hadn't been any major structural damage in the area to that point, although a husband and wife did report cracks in their basement walls and flooring, as well as a shattered window.

The area emergency-management coordinator, who was serving as the de facto emcee for the event, thanked everyone for what he called their "detailed and helpful descriptions." But the real reason they were there that night, he explained, was to try to figure out what had *caused* the sounds. Someone who identified himself as a local framing contractor suggested that the source of the noises might have been the propane cannons used by farmers to scare away animals that wander onto their property. Several people talked about the possible role of oil exploration and removal, arguing that these activities weakened the stability of Earth's surface—a process that could have played a role in generating the mysterious sounds. A distraught older woman, who underscored her points by pounding the air with a clenched fist, blamed China for the oil-related issues, insisting it was "buying up oil fields left and right" and that transformers were "blowing up all over the place."

As the night wore on, the residents' explanations became increasingly creative. One gentleman attributed the mysterious sounds to the 2011 Fukushima Daiichi nuclear disaster, which he claimed had liquefied Earth's support structure, including its tectonic plates. It shouldn't be a surprise, he argued, that this could cause booms and other sounds. Someone else made the case that the gravitational pull of "Planet X," sometimes referred to as "Nibiru"—a hypothesized planet some say is lurking just outside the solar system—had boosted Earth's seismic activity, which he maintained was responsible for the bulk of the unexplained noise.

Other explanations featured a blend of astronomy and theology. One of these suggested that the sonic activity was a harbinger of future wars between the forces of good and evil. Another insisted that divine beings were causing collisions between Earth and a neighboring celestial structure in an effort to unify their respective universes. The individual who advanced this theory claimed that these cosmic fender-benders were loud enough to be heard over great distances, which was why reports of the booming sounds were coming from all over the United States.

After a brief intermission, the emergency-management coordinator called the session back to order and invited scientists and other experts in attendance to share their thoughts. A local meteorologist ruled out storms or other weather-related events. One of the geologists said that there had been no recent earthquakes in the area that might explain the sounds. An official with the emergency-management department reviewed a range of possible causes that might be linked to human activity, including mining operations, construction work, gas-line leaks, and military testing. He noted, however, that none of these had occurred recently anywhere in the vicinity of Eau Claire.

And that was it. Everyone with a description to share or an explanation to offer had weighed in, their observations and theories duly noted and respectfully considered. The one thing they all agreed on was that the sounds were frightening and needed to stop. But other than that, when the meeting wrapped up just after nine o'clock, nothing even close to a consensus had emerged. The emergency management coordinator reminded everyone as they headed to the exits that they needed to have a plan in place in case an emergency prevented them from getting home or reaching family members. It was certainly a good idea but hardly what those who had trudged out to the high-school gym that night had hoped to come away with.

Despite all the vivid descriptions, I hadn't yet heard audio of the actual sounds themselves—until I stumbled on something a Kingman, Arizona resident had recorded earlier in the evening. It began with the sound of a truck driving by and a dog baying in the distance, with chirping crickets providing a running commentary in the background. This was followed by a volley of deep booms and the scream of emergency sirens. But it was the sound that came next that was more disturbing than anything I'd heard to that point. Our normally mild-mannered Newfoundland charged in and unleashed a torrent of seething, snarling barks. I muted the volume on my laptop, but Largo continued to howl until Joanna came in to investigate the racket and talk him down.

"Has anybody considered the possibility that these are just sonic booms?" she asked, after I explained what I'd been watching.

"Yeah, lots of people. But that's been ruled out."

I shut down my laptop and closed the lid.

"And all this stuff is happening at night?"

"Mostly, or very early in the morning."

"Why is it these things always happen when it's dark, in small towns?"

"Actually, some of these places are good-sized cities."

"All I know is, whenever anybody claims to see flashing lights or hear strange sounds, it's almost always late at night, in some out-of-the-way place. And there's usually aliens involved. My question is: why don't these aliens ever show up in midtown Manhattan at rush hour?"

"I don't know. Maybe aliens hate traffic."

CHAPTER 5

WHEN I ADDED "Mysterious Booming Sounds" to the list of possible research project topics the next morning, I assumed that most of my Integrated Science students would make that their choice. But as it turned out, most did not. A few chose to investigate climate change through the prism of Earth's ancient climatic past. Others picked less politically charged subjects, like sleep disorders and animal communication skills. In fact, only three students—Victor, Tanya, and Charley—elected to do their research projects on the booming sounds mystery. But because it was such a timely topic, I suggested they might want to do a joint project and share their initial findings with the class later in the week.

On Friday morning, the booming sounds trio transformed the SMART Board into a full-color digital map of the United States. With Charley and Tanya standing on either side of the display, and Victor roaming the room like the host of an afternoon talk show, the three of them led the class through a summary of recent sonic events.

"So, as of this morning," Victor said, using a hand-held controller to insert red dots on the map, "booming sounds have been reported in four more locations: Burlington, Vermont; Meridian, Mississippi; Gadsden, Alabama; and Utica, New York—which brings the total number of cities to twelve."

"We should also probably point out that some people are now calling these sounds *Unexplained Acoustic Events* or *UAEs*," Charley said, "since they haven't all been booms."

I mentioned the Wisconsin community meeting I'd seen on YouTube and some of the descriptions that had come up that night. My students jumped in at that point with personal accounts they'd read and heard about—not only from residents of Wisconsin but from people all over the country.

"Yeah, I saw where one person claimed they heard thunder or at least what sounded like thunder," Tanya said. "Only it was a dry, sunny day."

"And somebody else said it sounded like a train going by," Krista noted, "except there's no train where they live."

Victor strolled up the aisle and joined Charley and Tanya at the SMART Board. "Okay, so, thunder, phantom trains. Anything else?"

"I was reading in a blog where someone said the sound was shrill and metallic," Tanya said, "like something heavy, maybe a stove or a big metal desk being dragged across a cement floor. And a couple people said it was like a jumbo jet hovering over their house."

"One person said it sounded like the Earth was groaning, whatever that means," Charley said.

"And then there was the guy who said it sounded like a trumpet," Victor added.

"A trumpet?" Krista asked.

"Yup, he swears he heard a blast from a horn."

I walked to the back corner of the room, so I could be part

of the discussion but not at the center of it. "What's interesting is that people in different places seem to be hearing different things," I said. "Does that suggest anything?"

"It could mean that differences in local topography or atmospheric conditions could affect what people hear," Tanya said.

"Or that the sounds haven't all been caused by the same thing," said Charley.

"So, yeah, there are lots of possibilities as far as what might be causing all this," Victor said. He pointed the controller at the map, and a list of options populated the screen. "Anyway, here are some of the ones people are talking about."

Tanya pointed to the controller in Victor's hand. "May I?" she asked.

"Knock yourself out," he said, handing it over.

Tanya scrolled down the on-screen list. "One of the possibilities I keep hearing about are explosions," she said, highlighting that word. "Some people say these sounds could be spontaneous explosions of methane, which happen from time to time in landfills. Obviously, there are landfills all over the country. I've also read that the Bureau of Alcohol, Tobacco, and Firearms in Alabama detonates explosives in stone quarries for training purposes. We know there have been reports of booming sounds in that area. So, whether it's due to methane or something else, maybe the link between these sounds is that they're all explosions of some kind."

"Yeah, maybe," Charley said. "But it seems pretty unlikely that there would suddenly be explosions happening in every one of these places. Even with all the landfills."

Krista raised her hand. "No need for hand raising," I said. "We're just a bunch of scientists bouncing ideas off each other. What did you want to say, Krista?"

"Just that I've heard the military is doing a lot of secret tests these days. I mean, I don't know if that's true or not. But if it is, maybe that's what's making all the noise."

"Can I have the controller for a second, please?" Charley asked. Tanya gave it to him as requested, and he highlighted *Military Tests* on the screen. "So, just to piggyback on what Krista just said, I've read some reports that say the military has been secretly testing planes that can fly at hypersonic speeds. That could definitely cause sonic booms."

"Although the Air Force says it hasn't conducted tests recently in any of the places that have reported these sounds," Victor pointed out.

"Right, but what if they're not telling us everything?" Charley asked.

Lawrence perked up at the suggestion that covert military operations might be involved. "My mother says the government is preparing for the breakdown of civilization by building a secret underground tunnel system for the elites. She told me that the sounds are most likely coming from the excavation work."

Several of the students snickered at Lawrence's comment. "Laugh if you want to," he said, "but the government does a lot of things they don't want us to know about."

I walked up the aisle until I was standing directly opposite the SMART Board on the other side of the room. "What about natural phenomena?" I asked. "Is there anything in nature that could explain what's been going on?"

"How about earthquakes?" said Tanya.

Charley clicked to the next page and highlighted that word.

"A lot of people say the ground shook when they heard the booming sounds," Lawrence said.

"If it did, it wasn't because of earthquakes," Charley countered.

"Seismologists have said there haven't been quakes in any of these cities recently."

"Maybe not in those exact cities," said Tanya, "but that doesn't mean quakes aren't involved. And there is historical precedent that links booming sounds and earthquakes."

"There is?" I asked.

"Yeah, think about the New Madrid earthquakes in late 1811 and early 1812. They had magnitudes estimated at between 7.5 and 7.9, although some say they might have gone as high as 8.1."

"Wait, isn't Madrid one of those places in like Europe or something where they have bullfighting?" asked Krista.

"Yes, it's the capital of Spain," Tanya said. "But the quakes I'm talking about happened in the U.S. They were named after New Madrid, Missouri, which was destroyed on February 7, 1812 by the third and final earthquake in that cluster of quakes. Prior to that time, it had been the largest settlement on the Mississippi River."

"As far as I know, there haven't been any booming sounds or earthquakes reported anywhere near there," I said.

"That's true," Tanya acknowledged, "but keep in mind that those quakes were felt far beyond that area. From Cairo, Illinois, to Memphis, Tennessee, and from Chickasaw Bluffs—also in Tennessee—to Crowley's Ridge in northeastern Arkansas."

I should have been used to it by then, but Tanya the human Wikipedia never ceased to amaze me.

"According to the U.S. Geological Survey," she went on, "the shaking from the quakes generated waves on the Mississippi that were so high, people thought the river was flowing backwards. And supposedly, one of the quakes was powerful enough that it made church bells ring as far away as Boston."

"Yeah, I've heard that too," I said. "And there's no question that a large earthquake can be felt a long way from its epicenter. But I'm still not sure what that has to do with booming sounds."

"Oh, I guess I forgot to mention. A lot of people back then said they heard booming sounds just before those quakes hit."

I didn't know what was more surprising: the link between the New Madrid quakes and booming sounds, or the fact that Tanya had forgotten something.

"The USGS says that area is overdue for another major seismic event," she continued. "So, maybe the booms are a precursor of some kind."

"Except why should we believe the USGS?" asked Lawrence.

"Why would they lie about something like that?" Victor questioned.

"Because they're part of the government," Lawrence replied, as if the answer were self-evident.

I headed down the aisle toward the demo table. "Putting aside government conspiracies for the moment—and the possibility that these sounds might portend a coming geologic event—is there anything underground that could mimic the shaking or rumbling of an earthquake?"

"Possibly," Tanya said. "Charley, if you don't mind . . ." She reached for the controller, which Charley handed her. "There's something called *rock bursts*," she said, highlighting that option near the bottom of the screen, "where mining work triggers underground rock to release stress, which can cause a seismic event just below the surface. There's also another methane-related explosion possibility, where methane deposits in coastal areas are under super high pressure underground. If waves created by offshore storms disturb those deposits, the gas can explode."

"That might make sense for cities near the coast," Charley

said, "but I don't see how it could explain what people are hearing in the middle of the country."

"I'm just telling you some of the theories that are out there," Tanya answered, scrolling down to the next possibility. "So, another one is something called *booming sands*, where sand dunes generate rumbling or thunder sounds that can be heard from miles away."

"Again, that might explain sounds in the Mojave Desert," Charley said, "but how could it cause acoustic events in the middle of Wisconsin?"

"And again," Tanya said, sounding more annoyed by the second, "These are just some of the things people are talking about."

"That's fine," I said, trying to tamp down the tension between Tanya and Charley. "No need to edit ourselves at this point. Let's just get all the different theories out on the table."

Tanya clicked forward to the next screen. "Okay, so another possibility is that all of this is coming from changes in Earth's core. We may be in the process of a magnetic pole reversal, something that's happened on a regular basis over the history of this planet. Who knows what kind of sounds that might cause?" She scrolled further down the screen. "It's also possible that changes in the core are causing something called *sky quakes*."

"Sounds like a breakfast cereal," Chad said.

"Actually, they're acoustic events that sound like cannons or sonic booms. They've been reported under a variety of names in locations around the world, including India, parts of Europe, Japan, and the Finger Lakes area of New York. There are several theories about what might cause them. One is that geomagnetic changes in the core create electrical energy, which travels to the surface and up to the sky. From there, it's reflected back and, in the process, gets transformed into booming sounds."

"Whoa," Chad said. "That's intense."

Tanya had been tossing out all sorts of exotic theories, but her ricocheting energy idea seemed even more fantastical than the others.

"I'm sorry, but does anybody actually believe all that mumbo jumbo?" Krista asked. "I mean, seriously?"

"I don't know that I believe it," Charley said, "but at least geomagnetic changes might explain why people thousands of miles apart are hearing all this stuff. Most of the other possibilities we've talked about could only have local impact. They don't make any sense if we're trying to come up with a single explanation for everything that's been going on around the country."

I stepped in front of the demo table. "And it could be that there is no single explanation. We can't subscribe to a unifying theory just because it's convenient. There has to be real evidence that supports it."

"And even if there is a single explanation," Tanya said, clicking to another screen, "it might have nothing to do with anything going on underground."

"Wait, aren't you the one who said these underground bursts or explosions or whatever could be causing all this?" Krista asked.

"Yes, they could be," said Tanya. "But that doesn't mean they are." She highlighted the words *Outer Space* on the SMART Board. "Maybe something beyond our atmosphere is responsible for what people are hearing."

"Like aliens," Chad suggested.

"Or, more likely, meteors," Tanya said. "We know they can produce sonic booms when they enter Earth's atmosphere."

"We know that they can and that they have," I said, "but as you just said to Krista about underground events, there's no evidence meteors are doing that now." I joined Tanya, Charley, and Victor at the SMART Board. "The fact is, at this point, we simply don't know what's causing all these sounds. Although a lot of people seem to know what's *not* causing them."

"So, where do we go from here with our research?" Victor asked.

"Well, I was thinking that we could go on a field trip up to Bakersfield this Saturday."

"Bakersfield?!" Krista blurted out, as if I'd just suggested a weekend getaway to Ethiopia. "Isn't it like super hot up there this time of year?"

"It is pretty hot there," I conceded, "but it's also much closer than any of the other places where these sounds have been reported. If we drove up there and did some field work, maybe interviewed a few of the locals, we could get some firsthand information instead of just depending on what we read online."

"Wait, do you mean just Charley, Tanya, and Victor, or all of us?" Lawrence asked.

"I was hoping everyone might want to go. I mean, I know this is not the topic most of you have chosen for your research projects. But it is very timely and might be a good way for all of us to learn about the process of doing science."

"That makes sense," said Charley.

"Yeah, I'd be up for that," Tanya added.

"Wow, you two actually agree on something," Victor said. "Okay, I'm in."

"Me too," said Chad.

"I think I have to check with my mom," Lawrence said. "But if she says okay, then sure."

Several of the other students also expressed interest in going. Krista raised her hand just as the bell tone sounded.

"Yes, Krista."

"Quick question."

"Okay."

"Since, like you said, most of us aren't doing our projects about this—any chance we might get extra credit if we go?"

Scorching temperatures or not, Krista wasn't going to pass up an opportunity for self-advancement.

CHAPTER 6

I WAS UP early Saturday morning, determined to recreate my students' SMART Board map in our second bedroom, which doubled as a study. If I couldn't come up with a plausible explanation for these strange sounds, I hoped to at least identify common elements that might link the places where they had been reported—which as of that morning also included Grand Junction, Colorado and Amarillo, Texas. In place of the seven-foot electronic display at school, my working resources included: a warped corkboard nailed to the wall, a few hundred index cards, a map of the United States that had been folded up and stuffed in the closet for the last ten years, a lifetime supply of push-pins, and enough Post-It Notes to paper the room from floor to ceiling. But after two and a half hours online, I was no closer to understanding what was going on than my students had been the day before. And with scraps of paper containing random bits of information tacked up everywhere, the study had begun to look like a deranged scientist's lab—which Joanna noticed when she ventured in a short time later.

"Okay, now you're scaring me," she said, her eyes scanning the room.

"I am?"

"This looks like something out of *A Beautiful Mind*."

"I swear I haven't written on a single window pane during this renovation."

"Speaking of home improvement, you think we could pick up some paint chips later?"

"I didn't know we were planning on painting."

Joanna peeled several Post-It Notes off the wall and stuffed them in the top drawer of the desk, which was open.

"Not that I don't like the shabby-chic look, but I thought it might be nice if the baby started life with its room painted."

"There's not even a baby yet, and it already needs its room painted? Seriously?"

She shut the desk drawer sharply. "What is your problem? If I even mention the word *baby*, you get defensive."

I'd started the day trying to figure out why half the country was hearing things. Now I was arguing with my wife about Post-It Notes and paint chips.

"I don't know. Maybe I just don't want to end up like David Corrigan."

"Who?"

"He's a guy I went to high school with."

"Okay."

"Who dropped out in the eleventh grade at the age of seventeen."

"Uh-huh."

"Because he knocked up his girlfriend and needed a full-time job to support his new family."

"Sorry to hear that his education was cut short, but why are you telling me about this?"

I followed Joanna's lead and began peeling Post-It Notes off the wall.

"He said that having a kid changed everything. That it was like going to live on Mars."

She looked baffled. "So, you equate starting a family to living on another planet?"

"I'm just telling you what David Corrigan said."

The expression on Joanna's face went from quizzical to irritated.

"Andrew. He was seventeen. You're almost thirty-seven."

She was shaking her head as she walked past me on her way to the door. "Hey, wait a second—" She stopped and scowled at me. "I don't know why I told you all that. David Corrigan and I are not the same person."

Joanna thought for a moment. "Yeah, well, hopefully, he's grown up over the past twenty years. Even if his high school buddy hasn't."

❧

On Sunday, with a somewhat shaky domestic truce in place, Joanna went on a scouting trip to some high-end baby furniture emporium in Santa Monica, while I put together the details of the class trip to Bakersfield. I had long known that everyone's personal information is available to almost everyone else online, but I'd never realized how easy it is to get in touch with total strangers. I reached eight Bakersfield residents that day, all of whom had been quoted on various websites talking about the mysterious sounds they'd heard. Much to my surprise, five of the eight agreed to meet with members of my Integrated Science class. I didn't know if my students would learn anything or not, but I wanted them to at least have the experience of formulating questions and conducting interviews.

When school reconvened that Tuesday following Labor Day, I handed out permission slips. By the next morning, ten of my students had brought them back, filled out and signed. Even Krista had decided to go, with no further mention of extra credit or other preconditions. After sending those forms to the main office, I explained to the class that the first step in preparing for a field interview is learning as much as possible about the subject under investigation. We then turned our attention to some of the most recent theories about the unexplained sounds, including the Defense Department's HAARP project. Before I'd even had a chance to explain what it was, Chad expressed surprise that "all these sounds could possibly be caused by a harp." This prompted a full-throated guffaw from Tanya, who rarely even smiled, let alone laughed out loud.

"Oh, Chad. You're killing me," she said between fits of laughter. "HAARP stands for High Frequency Active Auroral Research Program."

"Which in English means what?" asked Krista.

"It's an atmospheric research program the Defense Department started in Alaska in the 1990s," I said. "The official purpose was to study how the ionosphere affects radio signals, in order to improve communication with nuclear submarines, among other things."

"But it's become kind of controversial," Tanya added.

"Why is that?" Chad asked.

"My mother says the HAARP program is the government's secret plan to take over the ionosphere and use radio waves as weapons to manipulate the weather and possibly control people's minds," Lawrence said.

"Whoa, that's kind of scary," said Chad.

"That's the government for you." Lawrence said, crossing his arms.

I liked conspiracy theories as much as the next person, and the Halloran family always made sure we were up on all the latest, especially those that involved the federal government. But this was, after all, a science class, and we were focused on theories of a different kind: those that might explain why people were hearing strange sounds all over the country. With that in mind, I ignored Lawrence's warning about governmental excess and brought up some of those theories on the SMART Board.

"Okay, so between last week and today, we've looked at multiple possibilities that might explain these sounds, including earthquakes, meteors, military testing, explosions of various kinds, rock bursts"—I paused and took a deep breath—"changes in Earth's geomagnetic field, booming sands, large waves breaking offshore, sky quakes, and the HAARP project."

"Don't forget the government's secret tunnels," Lawrence said.

"And secret tunnels. Thanks for reminding us, Lawrence. Is there anything we might have overlooked?"

"I think we need to at least consider fracking," Tanya suggested.

"I would be happy to consider it if I knew what it was," said Krista.

"The word comes from *hydraulic fracturing*," Tanya explained. "It's a process where pressurized fluids are injected into shale deep inside the Earth to extract oil and natural gas. Some people say it can cause earthquakes, which might have something to do with all these sounds."

"Although, as I've said about most of these so-called theories," Charley noted, "it seems pretty unlikely that fracking could be going on in every one of these places around the country at the same time."

Charley had made that same basic point so many times that no one in class, including the instructor, wanted to challenge him on it.

"Okay, so other than fracking, anything else?" I asked.

"There's been a lot more solar activity than usual lately," Tanya said. An office monitor walked into the room and handed me a note, which I read quickly. "It's possible that might be causing electrical activity in the atmosphere," Tanya continued, "which could produce sounds that are similar to thunder."

I read the note a second time in hopes that I had misunderstood something. Unfortunately, that was not the case. Our interim principal had determined that science students doing fieldwork would not yield "academically measurable results," which was a fancy way of saying it wouldn't necessarily translate to higher test scores. As a result, she had cancelled the trip to Bakersfield.

I wasn't sure what bothered me more: the fact that my students would be deprived of a valuable learning experience, or that Dr. Del Rio thought nothing of sacrificing their interests in order to focus on her own. I told the class that the trip had been cancelled because of an unexpected shortage of vans at the company Banneker had contracted with for transportation services. It would have given me immense pleasure to tell them the real reason, but I didn't want to risk the wrath of Del Rio.

I tried to make the change in plans a teachable moment, reminding everyone that the process of science is always subject to obstructions and detours. They seemed to get the point, at least in theory, but that hardly eased the sting of disappointment. A couple of weeks earlier, most of these kids had been more interested in scamming their way to a passing grade than learning the first thing about science. Recently, though, that had begun to change. They seemed energized and engaged in the work we were doing in class and eager to do research out in the field. But now, as they filed silently out of the room, they were simply deflated.

⌥

I decided not to tell Joanna that the field trip had been scrubbed. As far as she knew, I would be meeting my students at school that Saturday and driving up to Bakersfield with them in a large commuter van. The truth was, in light of Del Rio's decision, I would be driving up there myself to do the interviews. I thought I owed that to the local residents who had agreed to participate. Plus, I had already arranged to hang out with my former college roommate and good friend Marty Olivo, who had introduced me to the world of old-time country music via the Bakersfield country-music scene.

As the weekend approached, I started to feel guilty about not being honest with Joanna. Years earlier, she and I had established something we called the full-disclosure rule, which either of us could invoke if we suspected that the other one was not being completely candid about something. I knew if I didn't tell Joanna the truth about the field trip, I would be breaking the spirit, if not the letter, of the full-disclosure agreement. But because my intentions were honorable, I convinced myself that this minor transgression was acceptable. I was simply going to Bakersfield to follow through on my commitment to the people who had agreed to be interviewed. Or so I told myself.

That handy bit of rationalizing seemed to work until late Friday afternoon when I realized that the real reason I wanted to drive to Bakersfield, with or without my students, was to get away from Joanna's incessant propaganda about how wonderful it would be to start a family and "begin this new chapter in our lives." I always wanted to ask her: "What about you, me, and Largo? Aren't we a family?" But I never quite worked up the nerve. Good thing, too, because if I had, she would have taken that as an admission that I wasn't all that enthusiastic about the whole child-rearing thing. Which, to be honest, I guess I wasn't.

I was stressed out over breaching the full-disclosure rule, but that didn't stop me from piling one falsehood on top of another when Joanna asked during dinner that night if I'd have time to see Marty up in Bakersfield.

"You know, I hadn't thought of that," I said, lying more easily than I'd ever thought possible. "I'll give him a call and see if he has time to meet up for lunch."

By the time I got in my car early Saturday morning, presumably to meet the kids at school, my head was so full of lies, half-truths, and reminders about what not to say to my wife, that I had stopped talking unless it was to answer a question.

"So, what time do you think you'll be home?" Joanna asked, leaning in through my open window.

"I don't know. Probably around six thirty or seven, depending on traffic."

"Okay. I just want to remind you that despite what that high-school friend of yours said, becoming a parent is not like going to live on another planet. People have been having children for a long time. It's not like their lives come to an end when that happens."

"I realize that. And if I've been kind of negative about the whole thing, it's only because it feels like all of a sudden we're on some kind of timetable."

"The timetable is not something I created, Andrew. The clock is ticking, whether you're listening or not."

We'd been over the same ground so many times, I knew what she was going to say before the words came out of her mouth.

"Yeah, I know. Anyway, I need to get going. They're probably waiting for me at school."

By that point, I didn't even care about lying. I just wanted to get away from the relentless drumbeat of domesticity.

She finally stepped back from the car. "Well, have a good day," she said

"You too."

I tapped the rocker switch on my armrest and watched the window elevate. My much-needed day of freedom was about to begin.

CHAPTER 7

MY EARLIEST MEMORY of Bakersfield—gateway to California's Central Valley, where the temperature is scalding and the air quality lethal—was an old billboard on the outskirts of the city with the words "sun, fun, stay, play" splashed across the top. My family and I were driving up to Yosemite, and I was barely old enough to read, but something about that sign caught my attention. I was thinking about that when my phone rang, and Marty's name popped up on the screen.

"Hey, dingus, what's up?"

"Listen, I hate to do this last minute, but I'm gonna have to bail on today."

"You're kidding me. I'm like five minutes away."

"I know, I'm sorry. It's crazy here. I got maybe an hour's sleep last night."

"Who's the unlucky lady?"

"I was sleeping alone on the sofa in my office. We're totally slammed."

"Sounds serious."

"Yeah, it sucks. Anyway, I gotta run. I'll talk to you later."

"Okay. See ya."

With my schedule now wide open for the next two hours, I drove over to a dusty truckstop diner Marty had once told me about. The menu was dripping with temptation; the food was just dripping. I ordered the "Ranch Hand Special," which consisted of scrambled eggs, sausage, tomato, and fire-roasted chiles—all swimming in massive amounts of an unidentified liquid that resembled iodine. After recovering from my dietary lapse, I drove off to start the interviews. I scribbled down a few notes following each one, so I'd have something to share with my young scientists-in-training the following week.

HOWARD M.

"I work early shift, so I was asleep by eight or eight thirty that night. At some point—I'm not sure what time—I hear this rumbling noise. Kind of far away at first. Then it gets closer and closer, until it feels like it's right outside the house. The floor starts to shake, then the windows. Goes on for, I don't know, about ten or fifteen seconds. Then everything stops, just like that. No sound, no shaking for maybe a minute, minute and a half. I was thinking it was over. Then, all of a sudden, there's four loud booms, one right after another. And then a humming sound for the next three hours."

CARLOS A.

"It was the loudest boom I think I ever heard. Sounded like somebody's house blew up. Our four-year-old, she's in her room down the hall, and she's screaming, "Mommy, mommy!" So, my wife runs down to get her and brings her into our bed. A little while later, it happens again. Another huge boom. And then again, every fifteen or twenty minutes. Seemed like it was never gonna stop."

EVELYN W.

"I was up late. Had trouble falling asleep for some reason.

Anyway, I finally dozed off. Then, there's this bright flash of light that shines through my window and wakes me back up. And then these booming sounds. I'm not sure how many. At first, I thought maybe it was thunder, but it was clear as a bell outside. No more booms after that. Just this low rumbling sound that kept going and going for hours. Crazy thing was, you couldn't tell where it was coming from."

LEOTIS R.

"When I heard the first boom, I figured it must've been some kind of explosion, like a bomb or maybe an electrical accident of some kind. About a half hour later, same thing happens again. Big booming sound. Happened five or six more times. Finally went outside with the wife to see what was going on. Everybody up and down the street was out there."

My final interview took me to a trailer park called the Rocky Peak Estates, where I met a wiry bundle of energy named Charlotte B. Compared to the first four interviews, which contained some interesting tidbits but nothing really unexpected, this one was like a piece of performance art. We started our conversation sitting across from each other at a two-person dining table in her mobile home.

CHARLOTTE B.

"I was in a deep sleep right there on that daybed. And then, from out of nowhere, I hear something that sounds like a pack of wild dogs off in the distance. Look over at the clock on my nightstand. It's got this blue glow that's kind of eerie when you wake up to it in the dark. Anyway, clock says it's 2:30 in the a.m. So, I switch on the light and get myself out of bed to have a look-see." She stood up and ambled over to the window like she was doing a historical reenactment. "I'm lookin' here and lookin' there, tryin' to figure out what in tarnation is going on. Not seeing no dogs or much of anything else for that matter. And the barking's stopped. So, it's back to bed I go." She sauntered over to the daybed and lay down. "Not two seconds after I turn off the light, I hear something I can't say I've ever heard before." She sprang off the bed and scurried back to the window.

"Was it a boom?"

"No, it was a horn. A very loud horn. And then, right after that, there was a crashing sound."

"A lot of people have said they heard a series of booms."

"That came later. There was a low humming sound after the horn and the crash. That lasted for who knows how long. And then came the booming sounds."

"Any idea what might have caused all that?"

"Oh yeah. I know exactly what it was."

"You do?"

"Yes, sir."

"What do you think it was?"

She joined me back at the table.

"It was the chariots of fire."

"The chariots of fire?"

"Yes, sir. No question about it."

"I know there was a movie by that name, but—"

"I'm talking about the arrival of the chariots of fire. Spiritual warfare is manifesting itself here on Earth, just like Scripture said."

"I'm not really familiar with that."

"Well then, you best take out your Good Book and have a look at 2 Kings 2:11. 'As they were walking along and talking together, suddenly a chariot of fire and horses of fire appeared and separated the two of them.'" Her voice rose and began to shake. "'And Elijah went up to heaven in a whirlwind.'"

"What does that mean, exactly?"

"It's a signal right before the gates of hell open and Satan's demons are unleashed from the dimension below."

I had heard all kinds of theories about these sounds, but Charlotte B.'s fiery explanation was unlike any other. By the time we finished talking and she'd given me an unsolicited tour of the trailer park, it was nearly five o'clock. I knew I'd need some sort of caffeinated assistance if I was going to make it home in one piece. On the way to the freeway, I spotted a fast-food place and got in line behind a mid-60s Chevy Impala with a twenty-first-century sound system cranked up to eleven. A few seconds later, a raised pickup truck roared up from behind with its bass thumping so loud that it shook my rearview mirror. I felt like Sonny Corleone in *The Godfather*, when he's trapped between two cars at a tollbooth and gets tenderized in a hail of bullets. In the midst of the sonic mayhem, I vowed that if I somehow survived, I'd swing by the hospital and do a quick check on Marty, just in case things had eased up. When I finally got to the head of the line and secured my thirty-two ounces of liquid fortification, I was primed and ready to go. Freed from the fast-food ambush, I pulled a U-turn and headed off to Valley Memorial.

Based on what Marty had said, I expected that parking anywhere even close to the ER would be problematic. So, I drove around to a remote section of the visitors' lot and hiked over to the main entrance. When the automatic doors opened, I glanced up at the words "Valley Memorial Hospital" posted on the stucco façade overhead. I could never figure out why so many hospitals have the word *memorial* in their name. Like people really need to be reminded of what could happen if things don't go well inside.

As at many large hospitals, photographs of past CEOs lined the walls on the main floor. Trees and plants in colorful pots, and furniture arranged to encourage conversation, made the waiting area as welcoming as possible. There was also an assortment of gift-shop items on display, including a six-foot-tall stuffed giraffe, in case visitors wanted to give something other than flowers or plastic balloons to the sick and infirm.

While the layout of the first floor might have been conventional, what I saw beyond that point was not. Medical personnel were hunched together in small groups every fifteen to twenty feet along the maze of corridors leading to the emergency room. In the area just outside the ER, security people stopped anyone not wearing a badge or nametag. A massive, stooped-over man named Johnny Montez, who looked like he might have been an offensive lineman in a former life, asked for some identification and wanted to know who I was there to see. I produced my driver's license and explained that I was a personal friend of Dr. Olivo. Johnny tapped the metal plate on the wall behind him, and a pair of doors opened. He lumbered over to the triage nurse and showed her my license. While they assessed my credentials, something behind them caught my attention just before the doors closed: four gurneys were lined up along the back wall, each occupied by an unconscious patient hooked up to an IV and tethered to an array of medical equipment.

∽

When the doors opened again a couple of minutes later, an unshaven Marty Olivo, dressed in scrubs and a pair of clogs, walked out and handed me my driver's license.

"Thanks, I'd already forgotten that."

Marty had a puzzled look on his face. "Didn't expect to see you today," he said.

"Joanna would kill me if I told her I came all the way up here and didn't even spend ten minutes with you."

"Let's shoot for five and hope for the best. You want to get a coffee?"

"Whatever you can do."

They were no longer serving food in the cafeteria, but self-service beverages were still available. I grabbed some water; Marty poured himself a cup of coffee and dumped in several packs of sugar. He led us to a table that looked out on a small, well-tended garden.

"Just wanted to see what the outside world looks like," he said. He was about to take a sip of his coffee when his pager had a hissy fit.

"I didn't think people still used those things."

"Cell service is pretty much non-existent in here."

He scrolled through his messages and glanced down at his watch.

"How long since you've been home?"

"Came in late Thursday night. Been here since." He took off his wire-rim glasses and wiped them down with his shirt.

"So, I got a quick look inside the ER when the doors opened."

"You saw the gurneys?"

"Yeah, looked like jets lined up on a tarmac."

"Like I said on the phone. It's been kind of busy."

"Don't all the hospitals in the area work together when one of them gets overloaded?"

"Usually they do, but—" Marty's pager went into attack mode again. "Sorry, I gotta get back. You can stay if you want."

"That's okay. I'll take it with me."

We walked out without a word and started back toward the ER.

"So, you were going to say something about the other hospitals in the area."

"Yeah, it's just been super busy. That's all I can really tell you."

Marty and I had been friends since freshman year in college. This was the first time I had ever felt awkward around him.

"I wasn't asking for anyone's personal medical information. I just meant I've never seen an ER like that." There was a lot I wanted to ask, but his guard was up—way up—and he wasn't about to drop it.

"How's Joanna, by the way?"

"She's doing great. Made partner at work."

"You are the luckiest schmuck on the face of the earth. You know that, right?"

"Joanna reminds me almost daily."

We turned down the final corridor that lead back to the ER.

"Let her know I haven't forgotten she owes me a lemon-meringue pie for my last birthday."

"Why don't you come down for a visit one of these weekends and tell her yourself?"

"Believe me, I wish I could." He tapped the door opener. "Take care of yourself."

"You too."

We exchanged a quick pat on the back, and Marty disappeared through the double doors.

⁓

It was a few minutes after six when I got on Highway 99 headed south. If the traffic gods cooperated, I'd be home by eight. I thought about everything I'd heard that day, including Charlotte B.'s hell-raising interpretation of recent events. But none of that mattered after what I'd just seen. I wanted to investigate further but knew I needed to get home. I switched on my usual country station and caught the last verse of an old George Jones song, which was followed by an even older tune by Lefty Frizzell. On a normal night, I would have slipped into honky-tonk autopilot and enjoyed the ride. Instead, I swerved across three lanes of traffic and got off the freeway. I drove down the frontage road about a quarter mile before pulling over to get directions to the other major hospital in the area.

When I turned into the parking lot, it was obvious that Doctors Hospital was quite a bit older than Valley Memorial and in serious need of updating. But all I could think about on my way to the main entrance was the fleet of ambulances lined up adjacent to the portico in front. I followed the signs toward the ER, taking long, purposeful strides so it looked like I belonged there. Unfortunately, I never made it inside. There were three gurneys just to the right of the emergency-room door, each occupied by an unconscious patient hooked up to multiple machines.

Obviously, something had made me bolt from the freeway and head over to Doctors, but I wasn't prepared for what I saw when I got there. I knew at that point that I had to check out one more hospital. Two with overcrowded ERs might be a coincidence; a third would establish a pattern. I thought about calling Joanna to let her know I was running late but decided against it for fear that I might blurt out something incriminating. I was probably in trouble anyway, given the late hour. A quick trip to one more hospital wouldn't make that much difference. Hopefully, I'd be able to make up the time on my way home.

From what I could tell on my way over to Bakersfield Medical

Center, everyone on the road seemed to be going about business as usual. Maybe this whole thing was nothing more than the paranoid delusions of one stressed-out science geek who needed to get his ass home. That was my hope at least, when I pulled into the hospital parking lot and walked around the building toward the emergency-room entrance.

When I reached the door, two security officers stepped forward to inform me that non-essential personnel were not being allowed inside. The fact that they had two guards at the door should have told me everything I needed to know, but I still felt the need to ask what was going on. All they said was that they were busier than usual. Technically, that didn't prove Bakersfield Medical Center was experiencing the same spike in ER admissions as Valley Memorial and Doctors. But, by that point, I'd seen enough.

Something clearly was not right in California's Central Valley.

I joined the throng of cars on the packed road headed south and tried to figure out what that something might be. According to a local radio station, the only thing close to an emergency in Bakersfield was a broken water main that had flooded a major intersection. About the time I was making the transition from Highway 99 to the 5 South, the volume on my country-music station dropped, and Joanna's ring tone cut through. I started to pick up but didn't want to risk saying something I shouldn't have. So, I let the call go to voicemail.

When I finally made it home just after nine, there was no one there. Joanna and Largo had left behind a dining room table set for two with formal china, fresh flowers, and serving platters filled with chicken and rice—which Joanna knew was one of my home-cooked favorites—and assorted side dishes including a now very wilted salad. A pair of candles had burned themselves out and leaked purple wax onto the lace tablecloth that Joanna's aunt had given us when we got married.

My wife and dog showed up about twenty minutes later. Other than a fleeting moment when our eyes met almost by accident, Joanna didn't even acknowledge my presence. She hung Largo's leash in its usual spot on the coat rack next to the door and walked into the dining room. I followed her in there.

"Hey, if I'd known we were having a fancy dinner, I might've shown up on time."

My clumsy attempt at humor landed with a well-deserved thud.

"It was supposed to be a surprise." She picked up a knife and scraped some candle wax off the tablecloth. "I thought it might be nice to have an unplanned, romantic dinner, since we're now on such a timetable, I think you called it."

"Yeah, sorry I'm late. Guess I kind of lost track of the time."

"I called you hours ago. Did you not get that?"

"No, I didn't," I said, lying shamelessly. "Cell service is pretty spotty up north."

"Did it not occur to you to maybe call and give me a heads-up that you were going to be late?"

"Actually, it did occur to me at one point, but I kind of got caught up in what was going on. And by the way, you won't believe what's happening in Bakersfield."

Not surprisingly, Joanna had no particular interest in hearing about the latest news from up north. She did ask what the students' families had said when we got back so much later than expected. I told her some lame story about how the kids ended up not going because of a last-minute screwup with the van and how I tried to save the day by driving up on my own to do the interviews. Unfortunately, my attempt to paint myself as the good guy was undercut by her skill at cross-examination, which led to one convoluted inconsistency in my story after another. Before long, I had backed myself into a corner so inescapable that I simply gave up and made a full confession. Joanna listened but said nothing as I droned on. I almost would have preferred an angry outburst, but she was past that point. When I finally concluded my sorry soliloquy, she gathered up as many plates as she could manage and piled them on the kitchen counter.

I started scrubbing dishes like my life depended on it.

"Look, I know I should have called, but I didn't think it was that big a deal. I don't know what you're so mad about."

"Seriously, Andrew? You really don't?"

"No. I mean, it's not like I was up there fooling around with someone."

"Am I supposed to be grateful for that?"

"Of course not. I didn't mean it like that."

Joanna glared at me. "We've been together almost fifteen years. We've never lied to each other before this. At least as far as I know."

"You're right. I should have told you the truth. I don't know why I didn't. I mean, I kind of do, and maybe I should have been up front about everything, but that didn't seem like the best idea because I knew if I said—"

"Just stop, okay, Andrew? I really don't care."

I turned off the water and wrung out the sponge. "I can clean this stuff up in the morning. Why don't we go to bed?"

I reached for her hand; she pulled it away like she was avoiding the plague.

"Don't do me any favors."

She stormed past me, walked straight to the bedroom, and closed the door behind her. And just like that, we were in a fight. We'd had our share of marital spats over the years like every couple, but most were minor. On occasion they could get somewhat heated; none had ever escalated to the point where we slept apart.

I was fairly certain that streak was about to end.

CHAPTER 8

AFTER AVOIDING EACH other the rest of Saturday night and all of Sunday, Joanna and I went our separate ways Monday morning without saying a word. This was new territory for us, and it was an altogether miserable experience. I was glad to be going to school, so I could focus on something other than the shaky state of the union in the Robbins-Siegel household.

I knew that my Integrated Science students would be surprised to hear that I had gone to Bakersfield on my own. But I expected that they would be interested, if not utterly mesmerized, when I told them about my trip. In fact, they had a very different reaction: they were resentful that I hadn't said anything about it beforehand.

Apparently, I had broken the full-disclosure rule with everyone.

Once they got past my unintended betrayal, several of my students commented on Charlotte B.'s chariots-of-fire interpretation. Some thought it was creative; others found it comical. Lawrence had his own take, saying he wished he could have been there to explore the biblical perspective with Charlotte in greater depth.

I thought about sharing my experiences at the various Bakersfield emergency rooms I'd visited but decided not to say anything until government and health officials publicly acknowledged what was happening. Instead, I redirected my students' attention from booming sounds in Bakersfield to our course syllabus and the subject of life: its origins, biological expressions, and challenges—like those faced by the most dominant creatures ever to roam planet Earth.

According to the latest research, the massive asteroid that tore into Mexico's Yucatan Peninsula 65.5 million years ago was not the only source of devastation that confronted dinosaurs at that time. There may also have been a loss of diversity that weakened their ecosystem and further contributed to their demise. I had just posted the link to a recent study about that when a pair of loud chirps drew everyone's attention. The no texting rule was one of the few I had insisted upon since the beginning of the semester. To their credit, my students had always complied—until that moment.

"Sorry, it's from my mom," Victor said, looking down at his phone.

"Everything okay?" I asked.

"I'm not sure."

"Do you want to call her?"

"No, she's at work."

"You can text her back if you want to."

"It's okay. I'll talk to her later."

"Alright, well, whatever you need to do is fine." I took a moment to let everyone get their minds back on dinosaurs. "So, let's click on that link and take a look at—"

"Wait, hang on a second," Krista interrupted. "Victor, what's going on? What happened?"

Krista hadn't struck me as the empathetic type, but she seemed genuinely concerned about her classmate.

"Her sister fell during the night. They're thinking she might have broken her hip."

"Is she going to be okay?" Krista asked.

"I don't know. I guess they're trying to find a hospital, but so far, they're all full."

My mind began racing in multiple directions at once. Normally, I would never ask a student about personal matters in front of the class. But there was nothing normal about any of this.

"Victor, does your aunt by any chance live in Bakersfield?"

"No, she lives in Illinois."

"Oh, okay. I was just wondering."

"Yeah, I think it's someplace like Galeston or Galewood or something like that."

"Could it possibly be Galesburg?" Tanya asked.

Victor looked confused. "Yeah, that's what it is. How did you know?"

Tanya glanced up at me, and I knew she'd made the connection.

"Galesburg is a city in Illinois," she said to Victor. "They've reported booming sounds there."

⊰

As of early afternoon, rumors of hospital overcrowding had begun to emerge from several cities that had previously reported unexplained acoustic events, including Eau Claire, Wisconsin; Greenwood, South Carolina; Gadsden, Alabama; and Enid, Oklahoma, in addition to Galesburg, Illinois, and Bakersfield. Hospital administrators and government officials were still trying to keep the story under wraps, both to maintain patient confidentiality and to avoid unnecessarily scaring the general public. But once details started to trickle out, scattered local leaks became a national flood.

By the time I got home later that afternoon, news websites were taking forever to load, and social-media apps were only working intermittently. Fortunately, there were still some old-media options available, including television, which we almost never watched apart from the occasional guilty pleasure on HBO or Netflix. Our TV in the living room powered right up—no waiting, no buffering. But even in the midst of a developing national crisis, local TV news was still offering its tired but profitable blend of traffic, weather, and cats stuck in trees. I switched to CNN, which was already in full-scale disaster coverage mode, with camera crews in or en route to all of the affected locations. Reports from around the country were nearly identical from one city to the next. In each case, a staggering ER load combined with a surge in hospital admissions was stretching local medical resources to a point that was unsustainable.

Following the latest round of live updates from around the country, CNN broke for a string of commercials. Largo, who had been sleeping next to the sofa on one of his many beds scattered around the house, bolted straight up and began barking—which meant that either another dog was within fifteen blocks of our house, or Joanna had arrived.

"Hi," I said to my wife, who walked in without a word. "You're home early." She gave Largo a hug and put her briefcase on the dining room table before taking a seat at the other end of the sofa. "So, they're talking about the hospital overcrowding situation. Have you been following that today?"

"Yes, Andrew, the whole country is talking about it," she

said, avoiding even incidental eye contact. "Did you see anything like that at Marty's hospital?"

It was just a question, but it was the most expansive she had been in almost forty-eight hours. "Yeah, I did actually, but I had no idea it was happening anywhere else."

CNN's coverage resumed with a shot of Valley Memorial in Bakersfield, where a paunchy spokesperson with thinning hair was fielding questions from reporters gathered around the main entrance.

"—that said, we can confirm that the increase is continuing, but no one has been turned away or refused treatment."

"Have you gotten help from other hospitals in the area?" a reporter asked.

"Not directly, no. They're dealing with the same situation we are. All of us are working with regional emergency personnel to coordinate medical and other resources throughout the greater Kern County area. We expect to have additional equipment and supplies online within the next four to six hours." He pointed to another reporter. "Yes."

"We've heard that the overflow of patients is showing no signs of letting up and may actually be intensifying," she said. "Is there anything you can add to that?"

"I don't have exact numbers at this time. Things are happening pretty quickly, as you can imagine. We'll do our best to keep you updated and try to get you whatever we—" The audio cut off, and the picture scrambled for a moment before settling on a wide shot of reporters milling around a Washington, DC briefing room.

"We are awaiting the appearance of Surgeon General Leona Washington," CNN's female anchor said off-camera. "Although most people associate that position with warning labels on alcoholic beverages and cigarettes, the surgeon general oversees the entire U.S. Public Health Service. We can tell you that Dr. Washington is fifty-three years old and is the third African-American woman to serve as the U.S. surgeon general. She graduated from the Johns Hopkins University School of Medicine and did her residency in—here now is Dr. Washington."

The surgeon general emerged from behind a sliding door in her vice-admiral uniform and strode to the lectern.

"Good evening. As most of you have heard, over the past few days there has been a rise in emergency-room activity and hospital admissions in several cities around the country. From time to time, temporary spikes of this kind do occur, so this is nothing we haven't seen before. We are prepared to bring in whatever resources are necessary, including personnel and equipment from surrounding areas. I want to assure everyone that there is no threat to public health or safety in any of the locations affected. We are working closely with state and local agencies to ensure that all medical needs are being met and will provide additional information as it becomes available. I'll take your questions if anyone—"

The reporters surged forward and began shouting questions. A persistent voice broke through. "Based on the information that you have, do you believe that there is a connection between what's going on at these hospitals and the booming sounds and other unexplained acoustic events, or so-called UAEs, that have been reported previously in many of these same cities?"

"There is no indication of any connection, as far as I am aware. Our primary focus at the moment is to ensure that there are medical facilities and personnel available to meet the needs of the communities in question. And we believe that there are." She pointed to another reporter. "Yes, go ahead."

"Isn't it reasonable to assume, though, that there could be some kind of link, considering that these hospitals are located so close to places where the booming sounds or other acoustic events have been reported? Or even that the jump in admissions might be the result of injuries from whatever it is that caused those events in the first place?"

"As I said, we have no reason to believe that there is any connection whatsoever between the increase in hospital activity and the various unexplained sounds that have been reported. But, to answer the second part of your question, to the best of my knowledge, there have not been any injuries that have resulted from whatever may have caused those sounds."

There was a half second of silence, followed by another barrage of questions. Dr. Washington pointed to one of the reporters. "Yes, in the blue suit."

"There's a rumor that there may be an abbreviation—possibly CTE—that government officials are using to describe or identify some of the patients at these hospitals. Can you confirm that, and if it's true, can you tell us if there's some connection with the brain trauma condition known as CTE, or if those letters stand for something else in this case?"

"I don't have any information about that. Thank you all very much."

Before the reporters had even begun to put their phones and notepads away, the surgeon general had exited the room.

"Whatever it stands for, she sure didn't want to talk about it," I said.

The studio anchor began a recap of the day's events. Joanna muted the audio.

"Have you heard anything about that?" she asked.

"No, nothing."

"Some kind of brain-injury thing though, right?"

"Yeah. Chronic traumatic encephalopathy. Better known as CTE. It's a degenerative brain condition caused by repeated head trauma. Kind of a big deal in football these days because of all the concussions."

"What does that have to do with the increase in hospital admissions?"

"I have no idea. This is the first I've heard of it."

Largo picked that moment to go on another barking jag. "Has he eaten?" Joanna asked.

"No, not yet."

"Come on, boy, time for dinner," she said, leading one very enthusiastic Newfoundland into the kitchen.

I pulled out my phone and saw that Twitter and Facebook were both back up and already buzzing with speculation. With half the country working on this little puzzle, I had no doubt that we'd have an answer before long. But it occurred to me that there was someone who might already know. The odds of reaching him by phone at that moment were miniscule, but I figured it was worth a shot, so I placed the call.

"Is Dr. Olivo there? This is Dr. Siegel. Dr. Andrew Siegel."

The on-hold music was loud and obnoxious, but I was enjoying my new title so much that I hardly noticed. Marty had needed years of training to become a physician; it had only taken me an inspired moment on the telephone.

To my surprise, when the operator came back on the line, she informed me that Marty would return my call in "just a few minutes." That was a much more promising response than I had expected, given everything that was going on at Valley Memorial. Since I was on somewhat of a roll, I decided to take one more flying leap into the great unknown and join my wife in the kitchen, where Largo was wolfing down the last of his dinner.

"Somebody sure was hungry," I said.

"Pretty much like every night."

Joanna still seemed a bit prickly, but I figured this might be my best chance to break through the deep freeze.

"So, I was wondering. You think we could possibly call a truce?"

"I didn't know there was a war."

"A cold war maybe, but a war just the same. You basically haven't talked to me for two days."

"What did you want to talk about?"

"Can we sit down for a minute?"

"Okay."

We ended up in the dining room, where I hoped we might find common ground and hammer out a settlement. Grant and Lee had Appomattox; Joanna and I had our old maple table with a wobbly leg. We took our seats at opposite ends.

"I'm sorry about Bakersfield," I said.

"What is it you're sorry about?"

"Well, I'm sorry that I didn't tell you the field trip had been cancelled. And after I decided to go anyway, I should have let you know I was running late that night. And last but not least, I'm sorry if it seems like I've been trying to undermine your whole family-planning thing."

Joanna leaned forward. "You still don't get it, do you, Andrew? For someone as smart as you are, you are so incredibly stupid. It was never meant to be *my* family-planning thing. I don't give two shits about you going to Bakersfield or coming home late that night. What I care about is that my husband is an immature twit, who has no interest in becoming an actual adult and having a family."

"I never said I don't want to have a family."

"You also never said you do."

We were like a pair of battle-scarred warriors stalking one another, each looking for an opening.

"You're right. I never did say that. But I was okay with it because I knew how much you wanted to be a mother. I guess I just always thought of you as more of a feminist. Someone who didn't think having a kid was the only thing that mattered in life."

"I never said it was the only thing that mattered. If you knew anything about feminism, you'd know it's about having choices. Not being forced to live in a little box built by somebody else." Joanna looked past me for a moment and then refocused. "Look, Andrew, I know you think this is about me, and what I want. But it's not. It's about you, and what you want."

"Which is what?"

"More than anything else, to hold onto this perfect little world that you've built. Your guitars. Your books. Your records. Your runs along the Arroyo every day after school. All those things that you love and don't want to give up."

"Why should I have to give them up?"

"You shouldn't. Nobody said you had to give anything up, any more than I do. I don't plan to stop being a lawyer, or writing journal articles, or trying to make the front yard look like a garden instead of a botanical war zone. Having a kid means adding something to your life, not taking away from it."

I shifted in my seat. "It's not about that."

"So, what is it then?"

I knew what I wanted to say, but it took a while for the words to find their way out.

"You've seen me with my parents a million times. You've felt the tension, the distance. My relationship with them didn't used to be like this. Their relationship with each other didn't used to be like this."

"Okay."

"When my sister died, everything changed. It was like . . . somebody had dropped a bomb on our family. For the first six or seven weeks, I was almost catatonic. I didn't want to do anything. I couldn't eat. Couldn't sleep. Missed a ton of school. Didn't want to go anywhere or see anyone. Eventually—I'm talking like months later—the feelings of agony came a little less frequently. And they were a little less intense. But they never, ever went away." I looked down at the floor. "And I don't know if I can risk letting something like that happen again."

Joanna stood up and ambled toward me like a meandering river. She came to rest behind my chair and leaned down, her arms falling gently around my shoulders.

"What you lost, what your parents lost—I can't even imagine what that was like. And I don't blame you for wanting to protect yourself. But to not bring a new life into the world, someone you will love more than anything else, because you're afraid you might lose them some day—" She walked around in front of me, her eyes locked onto mine. "That would be the greatest loss of all."

Joanna could be tough at times, like a goddamn street fighter. But at other times, she could fuse the logic of a lawyer with the deft touch of a poet to craft an argument so elegant that it was impossible to refute. This was one of those times. I knew what she had said was true. And yet that didn't mean I could instantly bring down the walls it had taken most of a lifetime to put up. She cradled my head in her hands and stroked my face.

Neither of us said a word. When my phone rang at just the wrong moment, I was going to let the call go to voicemail. As usual, it fell to Joanna to be the responsible adult.

"You should talk to him," she said when Marty's name appeared on the display.

I hesitated a few seconds before picking up.

"You're actually returning my call?" I asked.

"Now that you're a doctor, I figured I had no choice. What's up?"

"We were just watching the news and saw the surgeon general doing a press conference."

"Talk about must-see TV."

"It seems the hospital overcrowding problem is not just happening in Bakersfield."

"Yeah, so I've heard."

"Interesting that the feds would trot out one of their heavy hitters so soon."

"I'm sure they want to get out in front of this before everybody freaks out."

I paused a moment. "She was talking about this CTE situation or whatever it's called. What does that stand for again?"

It was a sneaky little ploy that I never thought would work, but Marty actually started to answer. Unfortunately, I couldn't understand a word he was saying because Largo had gone into full barking mode again when Joanna opened a new bag of treats. I rushed through the living room and out the front door, apologizing along the way for the audio problems. When we finally got back to my CTE question, Marty gave me a very brief explanation. I wanted to hear more, but our phone call came to an abrupt end when he was called away to deal with the latest crisis in his ER.

I walked back to the kitchen, where Largo was happily munching on the last of his dessert.

"Everything okay with Dr. Olivo?" Joanna asked.

"Yeah, he's just busy, like always."

"When your phone rang, I thought at first it might be your little squeeze from Bakersfield."

"Sorry to disappoint you, and who says she's little?" Joanna allowed a tiny smile to escape. "So, according to Marty, CTE as it's being used here has nothing to do with brain damage."

"What does it stand for then?"

"Cessation of terminal events."

"What does *that* mean?"

"It means . . . a lot of people in these cities have basically stopped dying."

Joanna's head jerked back. "What do you mean they've stopped dying?"

"People are being brought into the ER or admitted to the hospital after they've had massive strokes, or they've been in bad accidents, or their organs have failed after a battle with cancer. All the usual things that cause people to die. Only they're not dying. For some reason, their hearts are continuing to beat."

"What?!"

"Or, in some cases, their heart might stop, but just briefly, and then it starts back up again."

"So, these people are okay after that?"

"No, they're not even conscious. But they are technically alive. There's so many of them, the hospitals can't keep up."

"That's the craziest thing I've ever heard."

CHAPTER 9

JOANNA AND I connected later that night in a way we hadn't for quite a while. No thoughts of babies, booming sounds, or the beating hearts of the undead. But while things might have improved in our house, by the next morning the rest of the world was even more jumbled than it had been the day before. It had only been twelve hours since the world first heard about the cessation-of-terminal-events phenomenon, but CTE—referring to something other than brain trauma—had already become part of the national lexicon. And two more cities—Meridian, Mississippi and Kingman, Arizona—had been added to the list of places that had experienced drastic increases in hospital admissions after having previously reported unexplained acoustic events. There *was* one minor bit of good news that day: The Air Force announced that recent test flights in the Ogden, Utah area were responsible for the booming sounds that local residents had reported there.

One mystery solved, dozens more still outstanding.

"I think it's fair to say that there is no rational explanation for why the hearts of CTE patients should continue to beat," I told my Integrated Science students that morning, "and yet that is exactly what they are doing. So, based on what you know about the human heart, what is the first thing that comes to mind?"

"Zombies!" Chad blurted out.

I was glad that at least some of us had kept our sense of humor, but that was not the answer I was looking for.

"Okay, and what would be the second?"

"That electricity is involved in some way," Charley said.

"And why is that?"

"Because electricity is what makes our hearts beat," Tanya answered.

"I didn't know that," said Krista.

"Yep, that's pretty much how it works," Tanya continued. "The average human heart is just slightly larger than a clenched fist and weighs less than a pound." She made a fist and rotated it slowly. "It beats about a hundred thousand times every day, which works out to almost three billion heartbeats over an eighty-year life span. All thanks to electricity."

That may have been a bit of an oversimplification, but the basic idea was correct. And by that point in the semester, no one was the least bit surprised when Tanya offered up a concise explanation of almost anything.

"So, I understand that our hearts beat because of electricity," Chad said. "What I don't get is how some super-sized electrical shock could reach so many people."

"What *I* don't get," I said, "is who comes up with all the acronyms everyone likes to toss around these days?"

"Wow, that was random," said Tanya.

"Wait, what's an acronym?" Chad asked.

"An abbreviation, like UAE or CTE," I said.

"Not to be a stickler, but technically those are initialisms, not acronyms," Tanya said, "because they're pronounced one letter a time. An acronym is pronounced as a whole word, like *radar* or *NASA*."

"Uh-oh, busted," Victor said.

I rolled my eyes. "Okay, technically, Tanya's right," I conceded, "but I'm still going to lump them all together and call them acronyms. Anyway, whatever we call them, they usually just confuse things. Sometimes I think there must be a secret cabal hidden away in some dingy basement where they come up with these little gems."

"You're really worked up over this, aren't you?" Victor asked.

"Yes, I am. At some point we're going to run out of combinations of letters, and then what will we do? I mean, it's already happening. We now know that CTE can mean more than one thing, and there are hundreds of examples like that. Look at PDA. It used to mean personal digital assistant. Now it means something very . . . different."

I might have continued to vent had there not been a knock at the door.

"Enter at your own risk," Victor called out, prompting gales of laughter from his classmates. Standing in the doorway was new student Amy Phan, an Asian-American girl with bright eyes and pigtails, whose family had just moved to South Pasadena from Washington, DC.

"Is this ISS 100?" she asked with hope in her voice.

"Uh-oh," Victor said, sparking more laughter.

"What?" Amy asked. "Did I say something funny?"

"No. I mean, kind of," I said. "But not really. Anyway, welcome. Good to have you with us."

A quick smile flashed across Amy's face. I introduced her to the class and directed her to the workstation that had been vacant the entire semester.

"So, is there anything I need to do to catch up?" she asked as she settled into her seat.

"I'll talk to you about that after class," I said. "Anybody have any suggestions for Amy before we move ahead?"

"Just one," said Victor. "Check your acronyms at the door."

✍

By the next day, Muncie, Indiana and Burlington, Vermont—two more cities that had reported unexplained acoustic events—were also now reporting CTEs. But even as the number of such cases around the country continued to grow, the media was only focusing minimal attention on the patients themselves. This may have been due, in part, to legitimate concerns about confidentiality, but there was more to it than that. For years, we had been transitioning from an analog to a digital world, seduced by the seeming clarity of numbers and data. There was little appetite for the messiness or nuance of personal stories. But CTE patients were more than just statistics. They were real human beings, living real lives. Until suddenly, and for no apparent reason, they weren't.

Most of these unfortunate individuals were middle-aged or older, but a handful of children had been afflicted as well. One of these was Tracey Wilkinson, a fifteen-year-old tenth-grader who lived with her family in Eau Claire, Wisconsin. Tracey had distinguished herself in and out of the classroom since the age of six, when she began visiting nursing home patients once a week after school. As a reward for her accomplishments—academic, athletic, and volunteer—she, along with three other girls from her school district, had been chosen to participate in a tour of Wisconsin state universities.

After visiting the final college on the tour, the girls were returning to Eau Claire late on a Friday afternoon. Less than a mile from their exit, a car in the next lane clipped their van, sending it careening across the highway into the center median. The van ricocheted back into traffic, where it was hit several times in a brief but brutal chain reaction. The right front portion of the vehicle, where Tracey was seated, took the brunt of the impact. The other girls sustained only minor bruises and contusions, but Tracey suffered massive internal injuries and lost a great deal of blood. Despite heroic measures by EMTs at the scene, she was close to death by the time she arrived at the hospital, and her heart stopped beating while doctors worked on her in the emergency room. The attending physician was about to call an end to resuscitation efforts when Tracey's heart flickered back to life. It resumed full function shortly thereafter, and as of a week later, continued to beat strongly. Sadly, it was the only part of Tracey's body that was still working.

When we talked about the CTE patients in class that day, I realized that many of my students were caught up in Tracey's story. But Tanya seemed to especially identify with the young girl from Wisconsin. "The way that accident happened—so totally random—it could have been any of us," she said. Everyone in the room agreed. Several students railed about the unfairness of a universe that could take the life of someone who had so much potential. I said very little during the discussion, not because I was uninterested, but because all I could think about was my sister—another extraordinary girl who was killed in a car crash at almost the same age.

Maybe that's why I was in somewhat of a dark mood toward the end of class when we resumed our work on the origins and development of life on Earth. One of the journal abstracts we were looking at suggested that comets might have brought the original ingredients for life to this planet; another examined the role of proteins in the growth and development of human life; and the final abstract we looked at proposed that today's birds may have been yesterday's dinosaurs, which—as I told the class— led us to the topic of evolution.

A hand went up the moment that word left my lips.

"Yes, Lawrence."

"Since you were talking about how dinosaurs might have evolved into birds, I was just kind of wondering about something."

I had a general idea what that something might be but didn't want to jump to any premature conclusions. "Okay, and what's that?"

"I wanted to know if we were also going to be, you know, reading or studying anything about creationism."

"To tell you the truth, Lawrence, I hadn't planned on including a religious perspective on this topic."

"I just meant that, you know, there's a lot of people who think that we should be looking at creationism and intelligent design when we talk about the beginnings of life."

I was, of course, well aware of that viewpoint and had no doubt that the Halloran family subscribed to it. Ordinarily, I would have found a way to nudge the discussion in another direction. But on that particular day, in my testy frame of mind, I felt compelled to be honest and tell my students what I really thought.

"Yes, and those are often the same people who ignore science and empirical evidence of any kind, think every word in the Bible should be taken literally, and believe that this planet is only six thousand years old and lies at the center of the solar system, if not the universe."

I think I even surprised myself with the surgical precision of the verbal takedown. Had I been too harsh toward a student who had no idea he was walking into a life science sucker punch? Possibly. Lawrence's face turned a deep shade of crimson; neither he nor anyone else in the room said a word. Even Victor, who was always good for a smartass comment or two, sat in silence.

❧

On my run along the Arroyo Seco trail later that afternoon, it occurred to me that we had already started to adjust to the cessation-of-terminal-events phenomenon. Not that we had the slightest idea what had caused it, but we were trying to cope, attempting to adapt. That's what all living things do when competitive factors and other circumstances demand it. In order to survive, we change; we evolve. Or at least, with all due respect to the Halloran family, most of us do. The ability to shrug off the old and embrace the new is so engrained in us that we have a well-worn cliché to describe it: we "turn the page." And the process is not limited to humans. Snakes and insects shed their skin, a salamander regenerates a damaged limb. Even oceanic trenches spew out new seafloor to cover the old.

On Thursday of that week, Charley, Tanya, and Victor unveiled a massive spreadsheet they had been working on until late the previous night. They explained that it would allow them to track and update information about the people and places touched by the booming sounds and CTEs. With Victor in his customary role as emcee, Charley and Tanya scrolled through the spreadsheet, explaining the various categories of data, which included the events themselves, the cities in which they'd occurred, and the individuals affected.

I thanked them for their work and asked the class if anyone had any questions. Amy raised her hand.

"Yes, Amy. You have a question?"

"Not a question exactly, but I was just thinking how we all worry and get upset about people dying whenever there's an accident or disaster of some kind. And now we're worried that people *aren't* dying. It's kind of ironic, don't you think?"

Not only did I share Amy's sense of irony, I was astonished that someone so young, who had hardly said a word since joining the class, could articulate something so insightful. And she was absolutely right. We spend most of our lives worrying about death—trying to deny, delay, or avoid it altogether. Yet when people stopped dying, we were terrified.

When the bell tone sounded that day, and everyone left the room, I leaned back on the demo table. Deserved or not, I allowed myself the briefest moment of satisfaction that my students could respond to the bizarre events of the past few weeks in a way that was not only mature but truly profound. I was convinced that, despite my father's carping to the contrary, my chosen profession was, in fact, worthwhile, and that I was contributing something of actual value to my students' lives. As it turned out, my father was not the only one who might have questioned that conclusion. I got a note from Janet Del Rio later that morning asking me to meet with her at the end of the day.

༄

Dr. Del Rio was seated at the circular conference table in her office when I walked in later that afternoon. To her right, as I would soon learn, was Margaret Halloran, the pale, plump mother of Lawrence. I had no idea why either of us was there but suspected it was not to discuss the latest breakthroughs in science education. We made it through perfunctory introductions, which included an unexpected statement from Mrs. Halloran about how much her son enjoyed my class. I focused on being as pleasantly innocuous as possible, knowing that Del Rio would get down to business soon enough—which is exactly what she did.

"Lawrence may find your class interesting, Andrew," Del Rio said, as if scolding an errant seven-year-old, "but Mr. and Mrs. Halloran are concerned that you appear to look down on those who don't share your personal views about the origins and development of life. Particularly those who believe that the Bible is a credible source of information and guidance on the subject."

I wouldn't say I was gobsmacked by the accusation, but I hadn't seen it coming.

"We did touch on the Bible very briefly in our class discussion. But I don't think I said anything that anyone would interpret as disrespectful or condescending."

Del Rio turned to Mrs. Halloran. "Mrs. Halloran, if you would, please."

Lawrence's mother pulled her phone from her handbag and tapped the screen. "I just meant that, you know, there's a lot of people who think that we should be looking at creationism and intelligent design when we talk about the beginnings of life."

I had a pretty good idea what was coming next.

"Yes, and those are generally the same people who ignore science and empirical evidence of any kind, think every word in the Bible should be taken literally, and believe that this planet is only six thousand years old and lies at the center of the solar system, if not the universe."

Mrs. Halloran tapped the screen again, and the playback stopped.

"I want you to know we had no intention of using what Lawrence recorded in your class for anything other than to help him study," she said. "He's always had a hard time remembering facts and information."

I was tempted to tell her that I didn't stress rote memorization in my classes, but this wasn't the time to delve into the subtleties of pedagogical theory.

"That's fine. I'm not upset about Lawrence recording the class. I probably should have used a different tone."

A grave look settled over Mrs. Halloran's face. "I know you must think my husband and I are nothing but religious fanatics with a lot of old-fashioned ideas. But the truth is, we're just church-going people trying to teach our son good values, so he can grow up the right way."

"And God bless you for that," Dr. Del Rio chimed in.

"You might not agree with us, Mr. Siegel, but there are a lot of others who believe the same as we do that the Bible is the word of God. Now, I'm sure you're a fine person and an excellent teacher. But it was very upsetting to hear the way you answered our son when all he asked was for you to include other ideas besides evolution to explain the miracle of life."

My initial inclination was to tell Mrs. Halloran exactly what I thought of her theories about miracles and whatever else. But I decided to avoid that impulse and take a more diplomatic approach. Talk about a miracle.

"You're absolutely right," I said. "Not about the Bible and its place in a science classroom. I couldn't disagree with you more about that. But the way I spoke to Lawrence was wrong. Hearing it played back, I did sound patronizing and sarcastic. I should have handled the situation differently. And for that I sincerely apologize."

Whether due to my sudden display of humility or something else, Mrs. Halloran's tone softened.

"I'm not trying to get anyone in trouble," she said, slipping her phone back in her bag. "I hope you understand that. I just want what's best for my son."

"And so do I."

"Well, thank you for that."

"No, thank *you*," Dr. Del Rio said with all the smarmy sincerity she could muster. "We try to do our best, but when we fall short, we depend on parents like you and your husband, who care enough to let us know that we've failed." Del Rio glanced in my direction, in case there was any doubt about who had failed in this instance. "I do hope you'll give us the chance to make things right. Lawrence means every bit as much to us as I know he does to you and Mr. Halloran."

I was on the verge of gagging.

"Thank you. We'll pray about it at home tonight."

Dr. Del Rio offered up a final overwrought apology to Mrs. Halloran and escorted her out of the office. When our esteemed interim principal returned a few minutes later, she walked behind me and clasped her fingers around the back of my chair like a raptorial bird. My gag reflex was nearly triggered a second time when she leaned down, and the thick scent of rose perfume flooded the air.

"I really don't know what to say to you, Andrew."

"I understand that what I said, or at least the way I said it, was wrong. But I did apologize, and I think she heard that."

"I'm not sure you do understand. Are you aware that Halloran Industries is one of the top construction firms in the state?"

"I'm well aware of that, but I'm not sure how it's relevant."

"It's relevant because the generosity of people like the Hallorans is what allows us to keep our doors open, provide financial assistance to those students who need it, and, oh, by the way, pay your salary."

"I get that. I'll try to do better in the future."

Dr. Del Rio walked to the window and stared out through the gleaming white mini blinds. "I don't know if it's because of your academic pedigree or your exaggerated sense of self-importance, but you clearly lack awareness about how the real world works. Whatever the reason, this is strike two for you, Andrew." She took a step back and turned to me with empty eyes. "I don't think I need to tell you what the consequences will be if there is a third strike."

⌇

The experience in Del Rio's office brought back childhood memories of having to sit through my father's blistering lectures, usually delivered after I'd committed some unpardonable sin, like forgetting to rake the leaves or put the trash cans out. How appropriate, then, that with Joanna out to dinner with her partners that night, I would be joining my parents at their house by myself.

I arrived a few minutes past the appointed hour with less than great expectations for the evening ahead. But after having been eviscerated by Dr. Del Rio just hours earlier, I found it unexpectedly comforting to sit with my mother and father on their back patio watching the sunlight drain from the sky. Unfortunately, that feeling was short-lived. Right on schedule, Mother began to slur her words after swilling down the first of several tumblers full of what she euphemistically referred to as "punch."

At times like this, it was almost impossible to remember that she once had more on her mind than strong cocktails and empty chatter. When I was nine years old, she ran a nonprofit that worked to bring parent-child counseling services to public schools in the Los Angeles area. Her days were spent giving speeches and attending conferences when she wasn't lobbying business people, government leaders, and anyone else who might be able to write a big check. Hard to believe that the tipsy woman seated next to me was the same person who once thought nothing of taking on the world and daring to make a difference.

We slogged through our usual exchange of idle claptrap until we got to the subject of work, and Mother asked how things were going at Bannister. That was what she usually called Banneker after knocking back a few drinks. But at least she made an effort to inquire about my job; my father never mentioned the subject. I didn't say anything about my experience in Del Rio's office that afternoon, offering instead a few tepid remarks about the school's expansion plans.

"By the way, have you heard about these strange sounds people say they're hearing all over the country?" Mother asked out of nowhere. As the queen of the jarring non-sequitur, she was always capable of hijacking any conversation with a whiplash-inducing segue.

"Yes, I have. It's been pretty hard to miss."

"Now they're saying people are having medical problems in a lot of these places. I tell you, if it's not one thing it's another. The ladies at my book club today couldn't talk about anything else."

I had no interest in hearing about Mother's literary adventures but did find it interesting that details about recent events had seeped into the privileged world of the shamelessly affluent. Perhaps that was to be expected, considering that more than six hundred lives had been mysteriously extended for no apparent reason. I thought about explaining that what she called "medical problems" were quite a bit more complicated than that. But even if she hadn't emptied most of a full bottle of vodka that night, Mother had never been one to appreciate the intricacies of science. And by the time she stumbled into the house for dinner, she was already on to other topics.

∽

We began our Integrated Science Studies class on Friday, as we had each day that week, by updating the list of locations reporting CTE cases. Since early Thursday morning, Utica, New York; Grand Junction, Colorado; and Amarillo, Texas had joined the growing number of cities reporting a shortage of beds in local hospitals. The total number of cities affected was still barely in double digits, so the problem remained somewhat manageable, at least for the time being. More disturbing was that no one in government, scientific, or medical circles had a plausible explanation for what might be causing the cessation of terminal events or the unexplained acoustic events that had preceded them. There was a growing consensus that some form of electrical energy was stimulating the hearts of the CTE patients, as my own students had suggested earlier that week. But beyond that, the so-called experts were drawing a collective blank.

My plan for the day, once we'd completed our review of the most-recent unexplained events, was to get back to our unit on the origins of life. I was well aware that Lawrence would be recording every word I said, which meant I needed to avoid saying anything even remotely controversial. There were four topics I thought about exploring that morning, two of which we had touched on previously. The first of these concerned ancient interplanetary dust particles and the pivotal role comets may have played in sparking the beginnings of life on Earth; the second involved ancient proteins and other possible genetic links between early, single-cell organisms and the much more complex, multi-cell organisms of today; the third topic focused on the discovery of more than seven hundred exoplanets in our galaxy, any of which might theoretically harbor life; and the fourth option was to investigate whether some form of methane-based life might be possible on or beneath the freezing surface of Saturn's moon Titan.

I was well aware that no matter which of these topics I selected, I risked offending the Hallorans of the world, who rejected any perspective that did not align with their personal religious views. With that in mind and strike three looming, I decided to put our origins of life unit on hold and instead explore large-scale threats to life—a topic I hoped would be far less likely to inflame or instigate. I brought up a series of images on the SMART Board to show my students that in about two and a half hours, an asteroid approximately three football fields in diameter would pass closer to Earth than the distance from this planet to the Moon.

"So, three football fields is like, what, about three hundred yards?" asked Victor.

"It's not *like* three hundred yards," said Chad, our resident jock, who was suddenly in his comfort zone. "It's exactly three hundred yards."

"A little more than a sixth of a mile," Tanya added.

"Fortunately," I reminded them, "NASA has located and is tracking most of the largest objects hurtling through space, especially those anywhere near this planet."

"The key word in that sentence is *most*," Tanya said. "NASA has identified about ninety-five percent of these so-called Near-Earth Objects, or NEOs, that are five-eighths of a mile or larger in diameter. If an asteroid that size hit this planet, it could put an end to civilization."

"So, I'm guessing the internet would be down, cell-phone reception would suck. . ." Victor said.

"Not to mention we'd all be dead," said Tanya to a thin ripple of laughter.

I clicked off the power on the SMART Board and walked around to the front of the demo table. "But, again," I said, "that is very, very unlikely. There are people working hard every day to detect asteroids that could pose a serious threat. Hopefully, before too long, we'll have a strategy in place for dealing with such objects, either by destroying them outright or by modifying their orbits, so they never get near us."

"Keep in mind though," Tanya countered, "asteroids like the one that's going to pass by in a couple hours are smaller than the ones that NASA has located ninety-five percent of."

"So that's good, right?" Krista asked. "Small is good."

"Yes," I said. "Small is good."

"Well, yes and no," Tanya said. "The ones that are smaller than five-eighths of a mile in diameter are still big enough to destroy an entire city. And they hit Earth about once every thousand years. There are around ten thousand of them out there, and NASA has only found about ten percent of those."

While everyone in the room mulled that unsettling piece of information, an office monitor walked in and handed me a note. I was almost relieved at the interruption, considering that Tanya had just reduced her fellow students to a collection of quivering blobs.

Then I read the note. Lawrence Halloran's mother was pulling her son from Integrated Science Studies.

So much for avoiding controversy.

CHAPTER 10

As of late Saturday morning, it had been more than thirty-six hours since any new cities had reported CTEs, but the number of cases in cities already affected continued to rise. To reassure an increasingly anxious public, several members of President Mike Martell's inner circle made appearances on Sunday morning news shows. Each of them stressed that the CTE problem was only temporary and that there were adequate resources in place to ensure that medical care would not be compromised. It all sounded fine, except for the fact that no one knew what was causing any of this, which meant no one could say with any certainty when it would end.

The United States might have been teetering on the edge of a medical abyss, but things in the Robbins-Siegel household had more or less stabilized. Joanna had submitted her journal manuscript, which immediately reduced her stress level. There were a number of unintended but positive consequences that resulted from that reduction, including an unspoken agreement between us that she would ease up on the subject of starting a family, while I would at least consider the idea. There were no guarantees that this pact would endure, but it was acceptable for the moment.

I spent part of Sunday preparing for Banneker's upcoming Family Night, the annual event at which parents of school-age children everywhere seek confirmation that their sons and daughters are geniuses. When I wasn't working on that, I was checking the news. As each hour passed and no new cities reported CTEs, media outlets began to project the faintest sliver of guarded optimism. If the CTE phenomenon did not spread beyond existing locations, and the medical outcome for patients currently afflicted returned to normal—meaning the usual sequence of life followed by death—perhaps we might once again get back to some semblance of normalcy in this country. And while it felt strange rooting for people to die, it was stranger still that an alarming number of them were no longer doing so.

A few minutes before the start of Integrated Science Studies on Monday, I entered the number 3 on the SMART Board, and beneath it, the number 775. Under normal circumstances, random numbers on the screen would have prompted at least a question or a snarky comment or two. But on that day at least, my students' thoughts were clearly elsewhere. The number of cities reporting CTEs might have been frozen since late the previous week, but almost everyone in class was still engrossed in the ongoing CTE mystery, in large part because of a teenage girl from Eau Claire, Wisconsin. Even Krista, who ordinarily displayed little interest in anything not related to herself, was following the story.

"I didn't hear anything over the weekend about that girl in Wisconsin," she said shortly after class began. "Does anybody know how she's doing?"

"Her name is Tracey Wilkinson," said Tanya," and you didn't hear anything because there's been no change in her condition."

The resignation in Tanya's voice echoed the darkening mood of the entire class. There was no credible reason to assume that any of the CTE patients would miraculously spring back to life, yet my students clung to the hope that Tracey might be the one to do just that. But as each day passed and that didn't happen, those hopes diminished.

"So, anybody know the significance of the numbers on the SMART Board?" I asked, hoping to shift the class's attention from the grim reality of Tracey's condition. "Let's start with the one on top—the number 3. Any ideas?"

Silence.

"Here's a clue: it has to do with something in the news."

"The number of days since any new cities have reported CTEs?" Charley said.

"Very good."

"I thought of that, but it seemed too obvious," Tanya said.

I highlighted the other number. "And what about the 775? Anybody?" Since Charley had figured out the first number, I expected the usually competitive Tanya would take a crack at the second. But she said nothing. "Here's another clue: it also has to do with the booming sounds and CTEs."

"The total number of CTE patients?" Krista asked.

"Good try, Krista, but that number has now gone beyond 775. Anybody else?"

No response. I entered *AD* following the number.

"Oh, it's a date. You didn't tell us that," Tanya said.

"Like it would have made a difference," said Chad.

"Actually, it would have," Tanya replied. "Scientists studying the rings of ancient cedar trees in Japan have discovered elevated levels of carbon-14 that date back to 775 AD, although some people think the correct date is 774 AD."

"Only you would know that, Tanya," Victor said.

"And high levels of beryllium-10 found in Antarctica have been traced back to that same time," Tanya continued.

I hit a pair of keys on my laptop, and additional details about the 775 AD event trickled down the SMART Board screen. "And these findings are significant because . . .?"

"At one point, scientists thought these elevated levels might have been caused by either a solar flare or an exploding supernova," Tanya replied. "But now, a couple guys with German names I can't pronounce are saying that it was—"

"Wait, there's actually something you can't do?" Victor interrupted. "I thought you knew everything."

Tanya shot him a look.

"What were you going to say, Tanya?" I asked.

"Just that these German scientists think it was probably a gamma-ray burst from two neutron stars that might have collided."

"And why do we care about this?" Krista asked.

"Because whatever it was that happened back in the eighth century, there was a lot of energy unleashed," Tanya replied. "And some people think that could be what's causing the booming sounds and the cessation of terminal events."

"So, you're telling me there's something out in space that could be blasting us with gamma rays?" Chad asked. "Like some kind of real-life video game?"

"There's no evidence of gamma-ray bursts anywhere close to our corner of the Milky Way," I said. "But there may be some form of electrical energy that's causing all this, just like there was in 770-whenever. If not a gamma-ray burst, what else could it be?"

"Well, like Tanya was saying about whatever happened back then, the sun could have something to do with it," Charley said.

"So, solar flares or storms or whatever they're called from

more than a thousand years ago could be responsible for everything that's going on?" Chad asked.

"Not the solar storms from then," Charley clarified, "the solar storms from now."

"They're called coronal mass ejections, or CMEs," Tanya said.

I advanced the image on-screen to a still photo of what looked like an eruption on the surface of the Sun. "Basically, the Sun blows out a huge gush of plasma," I said. "It happened twice just last week, which isn't unusual. During periods of extreme solar activity, there can be multiple coronal mass ejections in a single day." I clicked the remote, and the SMART Board dissolved to an old newspaper headline. "Anyone familiar with the Carrington Event of 1859?"

As with many questions that I posed in class, this one went unanswered until Tanya raised her hand after it became clear that no one else was going to respond.

"Maybe you should just stand up there and teach the class," Victor suggested, which brought scattered laughter from around the room.

"The Carrington Event was named for amateur British astronomer Richard Carrington," Tanya said with a trace of irritation in her voice. "He was the first to notice what he described as two patches of intensely bright white light erupting from a group of very large sunspots. This turned out to be the first sign of a major solar storm that knocked out telegraph lines over large areas of North America and Europe. The power of the storm was so great that it shocked telegraph operators when they touched their equipment."

"And in the years since then," I added, "there have been a number of other geomagnetic storms that have interfered with radio and GPS, as well as damaged power grids."

"Like in 1989," Tanya said, "when a solar storm fried the power grid across Canada, causing a blackout there and over most of the east coast of the U.S. Which is why I don't understand why people aren't looking at solar activity as a possible cause of the CTEs. There's obviously plenty of electrical energy coming from the Sun."

"That's true," I agreed. "But in all previous cases, solar activity has caused electrical *outages*. What we're seeing now is the opposite of that. Any other ideas?"

"I read the other day that there was some kind of magnetic field back when the universe was first forming," Chad said. "So maybe electricity from then is still hanging around and causing all this."

"Well, I read that there were electrical storms that nobody knew about in the upper atmosphere of one of the outer planets," said Krista. "Maybe that's where the electricity is coming from."

Neither Chad nor Krista had additional details to offer, but I was encouraged by their emerging curiosity.

"Thank you, Chad and Krista. Those are intriguing sidebars. But the issue isn't whether there's electrical energy in the universe. We know that there is. The question is: how could that energy cause the hearts of people who are basically dead to resume functioning?"

"What about dark energy?" Charley asked.

"What about it?"

"Supposedly, it makes up more than seventy percent of the universe. So, there's a lot of it. And some people think dark energy is what keeps the universe expanding instead of collapsing on itself, which is what gravity tries to make it do."

"Which would definitely suck, but I'm not seeing a connection with the CTEs."

"If there's enough dark energy to counteract gravity, why couldn't that same energy do something else, like make people's hearts beat?"

"Sounds kind of, somewhat reasonable. What do you guys think?" Amy raised her hand slowly, like she wasn't sure she wanted anyone to notice. "Yes, Amy."

"The thing about dark energy . . . I mean, it wasn't discovered until the late 1990s, and from everything I've read, it's still kind of sketchy."

"Sketchy?"

Amy smiled. "There's still a lot of questions about it."

"Like what?"

"Well, for one thing, not everyone agrees that it even exists."

"Okay."

"So, yeah, for something to be considered an actual discovery, there needs to be at least a five-sigma level of certainty. And I'm not sure we can say that about dark energy. At least not at this point."

"For those not familiar with the use of the Greek letter *sigma* in mathematics and statistics, can you explain what that means?"

"Can I use the SMART Board?"

"It's all yours."

Amy walked to the demo table. She took a quick look at the image on my laptop and entered a command. A string of numbers rippled down the SMART Board screen.

"So, say a team of scientists is doing experiments trying to confirm some theory, and they achieve three-sigma results. That means they have a 99.7 percent chance of being accurate, or just a 1 in 370 chance of being wrong. So that sounds pretty good."

"Excuse me, are you like channeling Tanya?" Victor asked.

Amy laughed. "No, but to make a true discovery you have

to hit 99.9999 percent." She entered another keystroke, bringing up more numbers on the SMART Board. "That means you'd only have a 1 in 1.7 *million* chance of being wrong. That's what's called five-sigma."

"Maybe that's what you call it," Victor said, "because you're the Asian math genius every science class is supposed to have."

Tanya exploded out of her seat, hurling herself at Victor like a heat-seeking missile. He instinctively raised both hands in front of his face. She grabbed his wrists and pulled them apart like she was snapping a wishbone. "Shut up, Victor, you racist little pig!" She clutched a handful of his hair in her left hand, then clenched her right fist and pulled it back into launch position. I forced myself between them and pulled Tanya off her terrified classmate just in time.

"What the hell is going on in here today?!" I shouted.

"Sorry, it was supposed to be a compliment," Victor said as the color slowly returned to his face. "Guess it came out wrong."

"Yeah, guess so," Tanya sneered on the way back to her seat.

"The point is," I said, trying to regain control over myself and everyone else in the room, "the threshold for making any kind of scientific discovery is extremely high." I tapped a key on my laptop, and the SMART Board display returned to the original two numbers we had started with at the beginning of class. "Who really knows what it all means? Maybe what's going on now is somehow related to dark energy, or solar storms, or some other kind of exotic electrical particles that are bombarding this planet for some reason nobody's figured out yet. There are labs full of sci-entists all over the world trying to answer the same questions we're grappling with here in this room. That's what science is all about; that's how it works. We learn, we struggle, we occasionally fight with one another." I made a point of looking at Victor and Tanya.

"We follow leads that lead nowhere. We progress, we regress, we make mistakes, we try again. And eventually, sometimes in increments so small they're almost imperceptible, we move forward."

It rarely happens this way, but the bell tone sounded right on cue, and my students filed out of the room with a slew of big ideas to think about. At least most of them did. I noticed Amy lagging behind the others on her way to the door.

"Amy—" She stopped midstride, her eyes fixed on the floor. "I'm sorry about what Victor said. I'm sure he didn't mean it the way it sounded."

"It's okay," she said quietly. "I'm used to it."

⌁

I made a quick trip home after school to get in a short run and feed Largo before returning to Banneker for Family Night. Tanya's mother and father were off exploring the Italian Riviera, but most of the other Integrated Science parents showed up and asked lots of good questions. When the session ended and everyone was leaving, I noticed a straggler lost in a maze of tubes and batteries that were piled up on a tabletop at the back of the room.

"Can I help you?"

"Yes, sorry. I'm David Phan, Amy's father," he said, walking toward me with a smile on his face and his right hand extended. It was immediately obvious where Amy had gotten her sunny disposition. "I was just looking through some of your equipment back there. It's been a while."

"Good to meet you. Amy's added a lot to the class."

"She's always been kind of a loner at school. I think this is the first time she's ever felt like she actually belonged. So, thank you for that."

He might not have thanked me had he known what happened

in class that morning. I almost said something but didn't want to dampen his enthusiasm.

"It's tough on kids when they arrive in the middle of a semester and don't know anybody," I said. "But Amy's done really well with that. Anyway, feel free to look around."

There were only a few minutes remaining before the next group was scheduled to arrive. I gathered up handouts that had gone unclaimed and began putting out materials for my AP Biology session. Mr. Phan walked alongside.

"We've moved a lot, so she's been the new kid in class way too many times."

"Are you in the military?"

He chuckled. "No, although I did get a job offer from the Defense Department when I finished school."

"What did you study?"

"I got my doctorate in computational mathematics and weapons engineering but decided to go in a different direction."

The door swung open, and the first few overeager parents walked into the room. "Oh, sorry!" a nervous mother said. "Are we early?"

"No, that's okay. Just sign in and find a seat."

"I should get going," Mr. Phan said. "I know you're busy."

"It's okay. I can walk and talk." I scrolled through the files on my laptop and brought up a PowerPoint summary of the bio syllabus. "So, what did you end up doing?"

"My wife and I spent the next twenty-one years working on sustainable development at the United Nations."

"That is definitely a different direction."

"The one downside was all the moving around we had to do. It wasn't easy for Amy. So, about six months ago we decided to make another big change and settle down."

"Back to math and science?"

"Different kind of science. We're growing California natives and non-native irises at the nursery we bought."

"You should meet my wife. She loves California natives."

He handed me his business card. "We've got plenty. You ought to bring her by sometime."

"I'll let her know." I scanned the card quickly. "Oh, wow, you're in Moorpark. That's quite a commute."

"Yeah, it is. But when we found out about Banneker, we knew this was the right school for our daughter."

At that point, I was *really* glad I hadn't said anything about that morning's little dustup.

"Well, I hope we can live up to your expectations."

"You already have."

We shook hands again, and Mr. Phan let himself out. If only my father could have been there to hear someone actually thank me for making a difference in his kid's life.

᠅

As of the following morning, it had been four days since any additional cities had reported CTEs, and the number of cases in cities already affected had begun to level off. I told my Integrated Science class that meant it was time for us to get back to our unit on the demise of the dinosaurs. Some of the students cheered; others groaned. Tanya reached into a cardboard box and pulled out a white sheet cake. It was decorated with balloons, swirls of colorful sprinkles, and a pair of thick candles that formed the number sixteen.

"Looks like somebody's going to have a happy birthday," I said.

"I'm not sure how happy it's going to be, but today is Tracey

Wilkinson's sixteenth birthday. I brought paper plates and forks for everybody, if that's okay."

"Hey, it's never too early for birthday cake. We'll save a few minutes at the end of the hour."

Back to the dinosaurs. Scientists had long agreed that the impact of an enormous asteroid had likely caused a blockage of light from the Sun that, in turn, led to drastic, worldwide climate disruption. But there had always been questions about why certain mammal species alive at that time were able to survive this catastrophic chain of events, while dinosaurs were not.

"Who knew that dinosaurs would turn out to be such wimps?" Victor said.

"They were hardly wimps, Victor," I responded. "Considering they had been roaming planet Earth for about 175 million years by that point, I'd say they had a pretty good run."

Like most of us, my students were fascinated by dinosaurs, even with the distraction of a waiting birthday cake. We had previously discussed some of the problems dinosaurs faced beyond the immediate effects of the asteroid collision. That day we talked about research that suggested the relatively small size of dinosaur babies as compared to the progeny of other species might have been a critical distinction. When food was plentiful, as it was before the impact of the asteroid, newborn dinosaurs were able to thrive. But post-impact, when food became scarce, the dinosaur young were forced to compete with their elders. It was a contest they had no chance of winning, one that may have led to the eventual extinction of the entire species. At least according to this theory.

"Speaking of food," I said, "anybody hungry?"

Fifteen hands shot up in the air, and we made the seamless transition from paleontology to birthday cake. Tanya lit the candles, and everyone sang "Happy Birthday" to the comatose young girl who hovered near death halfway across the country. That unspoken but unavoidable reality lent a somewhat somber aura to the proceedings. In hopes of lightening the mood a bit, I invited my students to talk about whatever they wanted to while they enjoyed their unexpected morning treat. Perhaps not surprisingly, most of them wanted to discuss the CTE halt or slowdown or whatever it turned out to be.

"Let's just say, no news is good news, right?" Chad asked.

"Unless you're Tracey Wilkinson or any of the others stuck in limbo," Tanya replied.

"That's true," Charley agreed. "But at least things don't seem to be getting any worse. That's kind of a victory in itself."

"Except I have this funny feeling that maybe we're missing something," Amy said.

I had just shoveled a large slab of cake in my mouth. "What do you think that could be?" I asked between bites.

"I don't know. Just that this whole thing might not be over yet."

"So, like, you think there might be more CTEs or booming sounds?" Chad asked.

"Yeah, maybe. I'm not sure. It's just a gut feeling."

"Well maybe you just need to feed your gut some more cake," Victor said, extending a second plate in her direction. "Truce?"

Amy's face lit up like the candles on the birthday cake.

"Okay!" she said, accepting Victor's peace offering without hesitation.

We might have had no idea what was causing the hearts of more than eight hundred moribund Americans to keep beating, but at least my Integrated Science students were learning to peacefully coexist.

CHAPTER 11

I WAS LISTENING to my usual classic country station on the way home that afternoon, lost in a reverie of twangy guitars and honky-tonk piano. DJ Donny Buchanan had just finished a pork-rind commercial and was beginning his introduction of a Patsy Cline song when he paused and announced that sixty-three-year-old CTE patient Alfredo Dominguez, a middle-school janitor from Bakersfield, California, had died at 2:37 p.m. local time. As Donny explained it, Dominguez's heart had briefly stopped two weeks earlier following a cerebral hemorrhage. Less than a minute later, it spontaneously resumed beating, which it continued to do until the end came that day at Doctors Hospital.

Joanna and I turned on the CBS Evening News during dinner, hoping to get more information about the death of Mr. Dominguez. Details about his passing were sparse, but we did learn that Edna Jane Willey, a seventy-four-year-old retired grandmother from Eau Claire, Wisconsin, had also expired that afternoon. The news anchor noted that it had been ten days since Mrs. Willey's heart had begun to beat again following renal failure and full cardiac arrest. The broadcast then took on a more upbeat tone with a story about the successful impregnation of a panda bear by her mate at the Washington, DC Zoo. But that report was interrupted by the news that a third CTE patient, sixty-two-year-old Judith Sonnenberg, who was a hair stylist in an assisted living facility in Greenwood, South Carolina, had passed away during the previous half hour. One week earlier, her heart had unexpectedly regained function after having previously stopped due to end-stage metastatic lung cancer.

The anchor then announced that the network would continue its coverage in "just a moment," meaning they were about to bludgeon viewers with commercials for the next several minutes. I changed the channel to ABC, which was reporting the death of Mitch Galenta, a fifty-eight-year-old heating and air conditioning contractor from Enid, Oklahoma. Galenta had sustained massive injuries in a fall from the roof of a four-story commercial building the previous week. According to the news story, his heart had regained normal rhythm after shutting down following the accident. But now he, too, had succumbed.

We began flipping back and forth between channels as it became clear that death's recent national holiday had ended. With CTE patients dying one after another, the networks rushed reporters and camera crews to as many hospitals and funeral homes as possible. Texts and phone calls from friends, family, and colleagues poured into the Robbins-Siegel residence until almost eleven o'clock that night, including four from mother, who sounded more tanked up with each successive call. Apparently, the fact that I was a science teacher meant I had some special insight into what was happening, like one of those Cal Tech spokespeople who dispense geological nuggets following earthquakes. Except there was no seismograph I could turn to for answers; I was just as clueless as everyone else.

As the week wore on and CTE patients continued to die,

those still alive—including Tracey Wilkinson—began to get more attention. My students had followed Tracey's story almost from the beginning, but now she had become America's child. Parents everywhere were asking themselves how they would feel if Tracey were their daughter. Would they want her to peacefully slip away into the folds of eternity, or would they pray for continued intervention, divine or otherwise, so that their precious baby might be granted more time? Tracey's parents, Doris and Earl Wilkinson, were deeply religious people, unaccustomed to the glare of national publicity. When she spoke to the media that week, Mrs. Wilkinson made a point to emphasize that she and her husband believed God had a plan for their daughter, who continued to hang on even as other CTE patients were losing their fights.

Over the course of the following weekend, the number of survivors dwindled further, until by Sunday morning only seven remained alive. After returning from church that afternoon, Mrs. Wilkinson talked with reporters who had congregated outside her family's home in Eau Claire. In her words, Tracey was "holding her own under the good Lord's watchful eye and protection." By Monday morning, four more CTE patients had died, leaving Tracey and two others as the lone remaining members of this rapidly shrinking community.

I tried to put things in perspective for my Integrated Science students that day, reminding them that life's impermanence had always been an unavoidable reality, not just for humans but for all living things. As an example, I brought up the Great Dying, a protracted mass extinction event that scientists believe killed ninety-seven percent of life on Earth about two hundred and fifty million years ago. Conventional explanations for this episode, which took place over tens of thousands of years and marked the end of the Permian period, have focused on massive volcanic eruptions that filled the atmosphere with carbon dioxide. This may have accelerated ocean acidification, leading to the subsequent death of marine life and pushing global temperatures to unprecedented levels. But according to the latest research, the primary instigator might have been a microbe whose activities led to an increase in methane. According to this theory, the rising methane level led to a disruption of the carbon cycle, which ultimately resulted in the death of nearly everything on Earth, with the exception of terrestrial plants. Even insects, which had made it through two previous mass extinctions, were unable to survive.

"Of course, since all this took place a quarter of a billion years ago," I said, "there's no way to really know how or why things happened the way they did. Many scientists believe that for an extinction event on that scale to have taken place, there would—" The sound of an incoming text stopped me in midsentence. When Tanya looked down at her phone, I was fairly sure who the culprit was. "Hey, turn that thing off, Tanya. I was just getting to the good part." Tanya sat motionless, staring at her phone. I expected her to chime in at any moment with a flood of information about mass extinctions. "So, getting back to the insects—"

"Tracey Wilkinson is dead," Tanya said. "She passed away at 10:27 a.m. Wisconsin time."

Tanya was more invested in Tracey's story than anyone else in class, but everyone had been touched by it. I didn't say anything at first, knowing my students would need a few moments to process what they'd just heard.

"There is a great deal of uncertainty in life," I finally said, "but there are certain immutable realities that have always been true. One of these is that the time will come when each of us will die. For reasons that no one understands, we have recently had cause to question whether that particular reality still holds. And today we've learned that it does."

In an unsteady voice scarcely above a whisper, Tanya asked if we could turn on the TV, which I did. A wide shot of the hospital corridor framed the Wilkinson family and their many friends. Nearly everyone was crying, many while embracing loved ones who were similarly overcome. An elderly man, later identified as Tracey's grandfather, leaned against a wall and sobbed. Tracey's aunt, a small woman with deep circles beneath her eyes, stepped forward to address reporters and others who had gathered around her. "Tracey is with the Lord now. We know He will guide and protect her for all eternity. For those of us in the Wilkinson family, we thank God for sharing His daughter with us over these past sixteen years. We also want to thank all of the doctors and nurses who took care of our beautiful angel like she was their own. Our special thanks to everyone around the country for keeping Tracey in their hearts and prayers. We will never forget your love and generosity."

Many of my students wept as Tracey's aunt spoke. These fifteen- and sixteen-year-olds, trapped between childhood and young adulthood, so often tried to project an image of steely toughness and indifference. But they were unabashedly emotional that day as they struggled to understand how Tracey Wilkinson's life could have ended the way it did. After listening to several of her classmates express their thoughts and feelings, Amy raised her hand.

"Go ahead, Amy."

"I know everyone is sad," she said. "This is hard for all of us. Especially you, Tanya. But I think we need to do more than just feel bad. I think we should do something."

"Maybe she could have some kind of a statue," Chad said. "Like when football players make it into the Hall of Fame."

However well-intended it may have been, Chad's sports analogy drew groans from around the room.

"I don't know," Amy said. "It just seems like there should be something that we or somebody could do to make Tracey's life kind of continue in a way."

"What do you mean, 'make her life continue'?" Krista asked. "She's dead."

"She might not be alive physically, but that doesn't mean her life can't still mean something."

"Did you have something specific in mind?" I asked.

"Well, I was thinking, since she was on a trip to see different colleges when this happened, maybe there could be a scholarship in her name for people who don't have enough money to go to college. I don't know how that would work exactly, but if somebody set that up, maybe we could contribute to it."

Tanya, who had been silent up to that point, finally found her voice. "Why do we have to wait for somebody else to do it? Why don't we do it ourselves?"

"You mean like go door-to-door and try to collect money like charities do?" asked Krista.

"It would take a long time to knock on all those doors," Chad said.

"I know some people who are in different bands," said Tanya. "I could talk to them about maybe doing a benefit. But if we want to reach the most people possible, we should start a crowd-funding campaign and try to raise the money that way."

I told the class that if they wanted to go that route, they'd have to get moving on it quickly, while Tracey Wilkinson was still part of the national conversation.

"I'd be up for it," said Tanya.

"Yeah, me too," Amy and several others said.

Within seconds they began dividing up the work and laying out a rough timeline. They were about to embark on something unlike anything they'd ever undertaken. I had no idea if they'd be successful, but I had never been so proud of them.

≈

By the end of that day, the two remaining CTE patients had died. The last to expire was Francesca Rinaldi, a fifty-two-year-old optometrist from Grand Junction, Colorado. Her heart had stopped and then restarted eight days earlier after she'd suffered a massive stroke. She passed away at Grand Junction Community Hospital at 4:42 p.m. Her husband and son were with her at the end.

Perhaps it was fitting that the last surviving CTE patient had lived in Colorado. That was the home state of President Mike Martell, who was expected to make a statement from the White House that night at nine o'clock eastern time. This would be the first time the president had weighed in on the subject of either the unexplained acoustic events or the CTEs. The forty-six-year-old former governor and moderate Democrat had been elected the previous November after promising to bring the nation together following four tumultuous years under the leadership of a self-serving and divisive president, who often employed bullying tactics that pitted one group against another.

In his speech that night, President Martell—whose face was lined from years spent enjoying the great Colorado outdoors—offered condolences to "all who have suffered personal loss" and noted that recent events had "touched every American regardless of where they live." The president announced that he had appointed Vice President Lee Tewksbury to head a commission of medical, scientific, and military experts that would conduct what he called "a thorough and transparent investigation" into the mysterious events that had tormented the nation over the past several weeks. President Martell made a point of mentioning that the commission would be given a full six months to complete its work. "Enough time to do a complicated, difficult job," he said, "but not so long that the American people are left wondering if their government has forgotten about them."

When the speech ended, about fourteen minutes after it began, network pundits offered the usual blend of analysis and commentary that follows most presidential addresses. Citing the six-month timetable, one analyst praised the president for not rushing things. "I thought he might promise to wrap everything up in three or four weeks," she said. "That might be politically popular," another panel member added, "but it wouldn't be enough time to come up with any real answers."

I couldn't help but think how little these people understood about the glacial pace at which scientists generally work. Teams of researchers around the world could spend years, if not decades, trying to figure out if an unimaginably small speck of matter even exists. But now the president of the United States was pledging to determine in six short months what had precipitated arguably the most baffling chain of events in human history.

Over the next few weeks, life for the vast majority of Americans began returning to normal. Mother enjoyed her day-and-night regimen of bottled deliverance, Joanna and I continued to dance around the topic of procreation, and my Integrated Science students balanced their regular classroom studies with work on the Tracey Wilkinson Memorial Scholarship Fund.

Even my old friend Marty Olivo eased off the professional

throttle long enough to spend a weekend with Joanna and me in Altadena and collect his long-delayed lemon-meringue birthday pie. Between late Friday night and Sunday morning, as summer's last gasp teased us with a hint of fall, Marty and I managed to squeeze in two lengthy runs along the Arroyo; refinish an aging redwood fence in the backyard; visit a new country-music bar that had received more positive reviews than it probably deserved; and pull off one very late Saturday night jam session in our garage, facilitated by a six-pack of craft beer, a couple of sweet-sounding Telecasters, and some very patient neighbors. Even Joanna joined in the musical revelry that night after learning that her manuscript had been accepted with only minor editorial changes requested. When Marty pulled his Audi SUV out of our driveway shortly after nine o'clock Sunday morning, I wasn't sure which one of us was more in need of a nap. Considering that he had a two-hour ride ahead of him, I hoped it wasn't Marty, who was leaving early to get back to work because of multiple auto accidents that had taken place in Bakersfield overnight.

∾

With our weekend houseguest heading out earlier than expected, the rest of the day was now unexpectedly open. Joanna suggested that we call Kim Adler to see if she and Brian might like to get together. Joanna had hung out with them a few times since Danny's funeral, but I hadn't seen them since the night we brought over takeout from Osteria Vecchia. As it turned out, they were free that afternoon, so we made plans to meet up for a picnic at a park that Kim said she, Danny, and Brian liked to go to in South Pasadena.

When we pulled into the parking lot, I thought it looked familiar. Then I saw the sign in front, which removed any doubt.

I hadn't been to Garfield Park since my Olympics-themed tenth birthday party, but as soon as we got out of the car, everything came flooding back, including memories of pouring salt on a family of unsuspecting snails.

I spread out our picnic blanket on a grassy area near the children's swings, and Joanna handed out the deli sandwiches, chips, and fruit we'd picked up. After lunch, Brian proudly showed off the baseball glove and bat his father had surprised him with on his sixth birthday. It took me back to the time in my life when I was around the same age, and my father introduced me to America's pastime. For the next couple of years, he and I spent countless Sunday afternoons at the park—Dad hitting me fly balls, pitching batting practice, and demonstrating how to lay down a perfect drag bunt.

And then Katie died, and everything stopped.

Brian and I took a walk to check out the baseball field, which looked like it hadn't seen a pair of cleats in twenty years. The infield was apparently home to every gopher in South Pasadena; the shriveled pitching mound was almost invisible, concealed beneath a clump of weeds and rock-hard dirt. And yet, turf conditions aside, it felt good to be standing on a baseball diamond again. I did my best to impart to my young friend what little wisdom I had retained about the fine points of hitting, fielding, and throwing. To my surprise, he patrolled the area around shortstop like it was his second home, scooping up ground balls as if he'd been doing it his entire life. But even more important, he was having fun—putting aside, if only for a few minutes, the terrible sadness that had consumed him since his father died.

As I stood at home plate hitting grounders out to Brian, I started thinking about what it might be like to bring a child of my own to a park like that someday—to share what I'd learned about baseball or anything else. And then I reminded myself that every time I'd had the chance to start down that road, I'd laced up my track shoes and run in the other direction. I had told Joanna that my fears about becoming a father stemmed from watching my parents' lives implode after my sister died. I was well aware that most couples don't lose a young child, but in light of what had happened in my family, it was hard for me to ignore the possibility altogether. The question was, would I allow that possibility, however remote, to stop me from becoming a parent myself? That was something I still needed to figure out. Danny, on the other hand, had had no such qualms. He was all-in on fatherhood right from the beginning, which made it seem especially unfair that I was the one playing baseball with his son that day. I could only hope that, wherever he was, Danny could see that his little boy was growing up and would do just fine. And that maybe before too long, Danny's best friend would do some growing up of his own.

CHAPTER 12

I wasn't convinced that the president's commission would get to the bottom of the CTE mystery, but at least that bizarre national nightmare was over, which meant, among other things, that my Integrated Science class could continue to follow the course syllabus and further explore the origins of life. We'd previously looked at the possibility that comets traveling from somewhere in outer space may have brought the chemical ingredients necessary for life to this planet. On that Monday morning, I planned to focus on a related theory that suggested the so-called building blocks of life may have initially formed on Mars and later traveled to Earth via a meteorite after an asteroid slammed into the Martian surface.

While I found that possibility fascinating, my students were more interested in working on their crowdfunding project. At one time in my teaching career, I might have stuck to my lesson plan and force-fed them what I thought they needed to learn. But with everything we had all been through recently, I decided to back off and give them a voice, at least temporarily, in curriculum decisions. There would be plenty of time in the weeks and months ahead to explore the role that comets, asteroids, and Martian meteorites may have played in bringing life to planet Earth.

At the end of that afternoon, I stopped at our neighborhood dry cleaner for the first time in years to pick up a few things for Joanna, who was swamped at work and couldn't get there before they closed. My wardrobe at that point was very simple; almost nothing required ironing, let alone dry cleaning. But judging by the line that stretched nearly out the door, there were plenty of people who, like my wife, still relied on the cleaning process I'd always believed must involve some form of magic. The basic customer-service protocol was just as I remembered: the person at the front desk pushing buttons on a little metal box suspended from the ceiling; the mechanical rack delivering pristine garments, each wrapped in a clear plastic bag; and a uniquely disgusting chemical smell permeating the premises—an odor difficult to describe, but once experienced, impossible to forget.

But there was something different since the last time I'd been to the dry cleaner. There was now a flat-screen TV monitor on the wall behind the front counter, just as there had been at Osteria Vecchia, our favorite Italian restaurant and, like the dry cleaner, an old-world, family-owned business. While pondering that coincidence, I noticed there were five split-screen images on the TV, each containing footage of a deadly accident that had taken place that day: a rollover crash that had killed four in Oklahoma; a train derailment in Massachusetts that had left thirteen dead; a bus crash in Alabama that had claimed the lives of a recently married youth pastor and his new wife; a single-engine private plane that had crashed shortly after takeoff from a Utah airport, killing all seven aboard; and the crash of an air tanker that had been dropping fire retardant on a remote wildfire in Colorado, killing both passengers.

I reached the front of the line just as the news anchor was concluding her report: "And so, if anyone still doubts that death has resumed its seat at the national table, this grisly string of accidents around the country should serve as ample proof that the mortality siesta many Americans have enjoyed over the past several weeks has ended."

I might have quibbled with her use of the word "enjoyed," considering that not a single CTE patient had actually recovered. In fact, one could argue that the pain and suffering of those patients and their families had simply been prolonged. But that was a minor rhetorical complaint; the news report was otherwise factually correct. A slew of fatal accidents had occurred across multiple states over the previous twenty-four hours, marking a clear departure from what we had been seeing in recent weeks.

Although I didn't know it at the time, that series of horrific crashes was just a prelude to what would unfold that evening. In upstate New York, a top-heavy beverage truck broadsided a car, killing the driver and his wife, who was eight months pregnant and on the way to the hospital to have her baby. (The premature baby boy was delivered successfully and, per the obstetrician, would likely survive, albeit as an orphan.) Two of the other accidents that night involved buses: in the first of these, twelve parishioners were killed on a chartered bus returning to Tennessee from a weekend event in North Carolina, when the power steering in an oncoming SUV malfunctioned, causing the vehicle to cross the center median and slam into the bus; the second was a double-decker casino bus that overturned while traveling from Texas to Oklahoma, killing seven and injuring a dozen more. In Florida, six people were killed when a rotor malfunction caused their helicopter to crash in a heavily wooded area. Finally, an Indiana commuter train crash, a chain-reaction highway collision in Texas, and the crash of a small plane in Illinois claimed an additional twenty-seven lives that night.

Driving to school the next morning, I thought about this sudden uptick in deadly accidents around the country and debated whether to broach the subject in my Integrated Science class. The tragedies themselves had nothing to do with the origins of life, but I wondered if talking about them might help my students purge any lingering residue left by the CTEs, when death had seemed to be on hiatus.

Before I could say a word about any of this in class, Amy announced that she and her classmates had made a decision about the crowdfunding site they wanted to use for their scholarship project.

"It's called 'Make It Happen,'" she said. "They've only been around a few years, but they've done a great job."

Tanya then rattled off some of the site's successful fundraising efforts, including multiple memorial scholarships, as well as a campaign to raise money for a high school in Indiana that had been devastated by flooding the previous winter.

"What's your financial goal going to be?" I asked, sounding more like a certified financial planner than a high-school science teacher.

"A hundred and twenty-five thousand dollars," Victor said like he was considering a new pair of sneakers.

"Wow! You guys aren't messing around. I thought most of these things were memorial funds that raise five hundred or a thousand bucks for funeral expenses."

"Yeah, there are quite a few like that," Amy said, "but there are also scholarship funds that have raised as much as a hundred thousand dollars or more."

I walked out from behind the demo table. "Look, don't take

this the wrong way. I'm all for setting your goals high, but that's a lot of money. Considering your age, some people are going to question whether you know what you're doing."

"Thanks for the vote of no-confidence," Tanya said.

"Hey, I know that you guys are brilliant and amazing. I'm just telling you what people who don't know you might say."

"Maybe they'd feel better if they knew we've worked out the annual financial requirements and investment projections for the next fifteen years," Amy said.

"Based on state university tuition and conservative investment of the initial principal," Charley added. "Factoring in inflation, of course. Basically, like an annuity. I can walk you through the calculations if you'd like."

I had no doubt that Charley could have sliced, diced, and spit-shined those numbers until they were positively gleaming. But no matter how capable and committed my students were, they were still just kids. I didn't want to dilute their enthusiasm, but at the same time, they needed to temper that with a dose of reality. And they needed to do it in a hurry.

"Why don't you shoot me an email tonight with your business plan, and we can talk about it tomorrow. We don't want to let too much time go by and run the risk that people might lose interest in Tracey's story. Especially with all these accidents the past couple of days that seem to have moved CTEs out of the headlines."

I knew it was a funky transition, but it was the best I could come up with at the moment. Nearly everyone in class had heard about the rash of recent accidents. Tanya, to no one's surprise, had memorized all the pertinent facts. She had also spotted something that no one else, including her science teacher, had noticed.

"I'm not saying there's any connection," she said, "but with the exception of four states, every state where these accidents have taken place has also previously reported booming sounds and CTEs."

I had brought up the surge in fatal accidents to help my students get past any possible lingering effects of the CTE phenomenon. It never occurred to me that there could be some sort of link between them. "How many states have reported these sorts of accidents?" I asked. "Do we know that?"

"Eleven," Tanya replied.

"Okay, so out of eleven states reporting unusual numbers of fatalities, four have not previously reported booming sounds or CTEs. Meaning seven have. Is that what you're saying?"

"That's what I'm saying."

"Sounds like basic arithmetic to me," said Charley.

"It's not the math I'm questioning," I said. "I'm just trying to figure out what it means, if anything."

"Maybe it means we should all think about moving out of the country," Victor suggested. "I've heard Denmark is nice."

"I don't think anyone needs to start packing just yet," I said.

But there were more accidents still to come. By the time I got home at the end of that day, five people had died in Arizona when a driver lost control of a van that had flipped several times and burst into flames. Nine were killed in Vermont when a freight train collided with a transit bus that had stalled while attempting to cross the tracks. A South Carolina helicopter crash claimed the lives of eight when it lost power suddenly. And a twelve-year-old Mississippi girl died when her hair was caught in the engine of her family's ATV, which had unexpectedly turned back on after having been shut off.

✍

The following morning, I informed my Integrated Science students that I had read through their crowdfunding materials and wasn't sure I understood what they were looking for in potential scholarship winners.

"We're still working on that," Tanya said, "but we're thinking the winner should be someone who has the same qualities that made Tracey Wilkinson the person she was."

"And who's going to make that decision each year? You guys are going to be graduating in a couple of years, so it's not going to be you."

"We want to set up some kind of local board from Tracey's community," said Amy. "That would be their job."

"Okay, so here's another question: How do you plan to touch people with her story? You're gonna need to get them emotionally involved if they're going to contribute."

"The best way is probably through Tracey herself," Tanya said.

"And how are you going to do that?"

"Actually, we were thinking you could do it."

"*I* could do it?"

"So, we were hoping you could contact her family and ask them to send us some photos and videos," Amy said with her usual disarming smile.

"And why have I been selected for this assignment?"

"Because you're the adult, which means you have credibility," Amy said.

I laughed out loud. "You should ask my wife how adult I am."

There was a sharp knock at the door, and Janet Del Rio burst in like she was leading an invasion. After a momentary brain freeze, I did my best to appear delighted.

"Dr. Del Rio! What a nice surprise!"

"Hello, everyone."

"I didn't know you were stopping by."

"I've been making unannounced visits all over campus this morning, hoping to get a closer look at all the great work our students are doing."

"Well, we're certainly glad you could join us."

Del Rio strutted across the room and positioned herself beneath the wall clock. "Please don't let me interrupt," she said. "I'm just here to observe."

"Would you like to sit down?" I asked, pointing to the chair that had been vacant since Lawrence's departure.

"No, I'm fine. You all just carry on."

Victor popped out of his seat like a jack-in-the-box and made a grand sweeping motion toward the open chair.

"Please, I insist."

Del Rio's smile morphed into a chilly glare.

"I said I was fine, young man. You can take your seat."

"Yes, ma'am."

Dr. Del Rio had not only smacked down the class clown, she had drained the room of all signs of life. As tone deaf as the interim principal was, even she knew she had brought things to a screeching halt.

"Don't worry about me," she said. "Just go back to whatever you were talking about."

I retreated to the area behind the demo table. "We were just beginning our discussion about the origins of carbon and hydrogen," I said.

"We were?" Chad asked.

"Well, we were about to."

"I thought we were talking about the memorial scholarship

fund." Chad clearly did not understand that the goal here was not full disclosure. It was only when he noticed his classmates giving him the death stare that he realized something was amiss. "What's everybody looking at me for? Isn't that what we were talking about?" he asked.

"Excuse me, I'm confused," Del Rio said. "What memorial scholarship are you referring to?"

Chad looked at me like a drowning man grasping for a rope.

"I think I can explain," I said. "Several of the students decided that they wanted to honor the memory of one of the young CTE patients who recently died. They're setting up a memorial scholarship in her name to help needy high school students pay for college."

"I see," Del Rio said, her eyebrows arching upward. "And you felt this was something you should use classroom time to work on?"

Suddenly, I was the one who needed rescuing.

"Actually, we've been mostly working on it outside of school," Tanya said.

Del Rio pointed to Chad. "But according to this student, you were discussing it in class."

"We were just giving Mr. Siegel a very quick update," Amy clarified.

Del Rio walked to the demo table. She gave me a sideways look.

"I think it's admirable that your students are interested in doing something positive to promote education."

"Thank you. I feel the same way."

"But I don't think I have to remind you that these youngsters will be taking standardized tests soon. The results will have an impact not only on them but on the reputation of this school."

"I couldn't agree more. And I know they're going to do great on those tests." I walked out from behind the demo table. "But I also know that when Dr. Marshall created this school, he wanted to provide a rich and balanced experience for its students. Sometimes that means exposing them to things that aren't found in books."

The corners of Del Rio's mouth sagged for a moment before her imperious smile snapped back into place.

"Well, thank you all for the opportunity to spend a few minutes here this morning. It's been most . . . enlightening. I do hope you'll find time to have that discussion about—what was it again?"

"Carbon and hydrogen."

"Ah, yes. Carbon and hydrogen. Two very important subjects. Nice to know your students will be learning something about actual science in their science class."

And with that, Banneker's most unexpected chemistry enthusiast marched out the door. There were no shouts of joy, no applause. Just a palpable sense of relief.

"Well, that was awkward," Victor said.

It had to be the understatement of the century.

CHAPTER 13

THE NEXT DAY, we finally got around to talking about carbon and hydrogen in class. I'm sure Dr. Del Rio would have been thrilled. She might have been less excited to learn that we also spent time discussing the recent string of accidents around the country, which had continued overnight. Only a couple of days earlier, the idea that there could be a connection between those tragedies and the unexplained booming sounds and CTEs hadn't even been considered, other than by Tanya. But in the intervening forty-eight hours, that notion had begun to gain traction both in and out of my Integrated Science Studies class, where Charley fired up the SMART Board, and a series of red dots appeared on a digital map of the United States.

"Okay, so these are the locations of the original booming sounds and the cessation-of-terminal-events cases," Charley said. A group of green dots popped on next, most in close proximity to the red ones. "And here we have the locations of the states, now up to fifteen, where there have been multiple deadly accidents over the past few days. As Tanya said the other day, and as you can see on the map, many of these have occurred in the same states where there were unexplained acoustic events and CTEs."

"With the exception of four states," I said, walking around the demo desk and pointing to the SMART Board, "where there were lives lost in various accidents but no unexplained booming sounds or CTEs. Is that number still the same?"

"Yes, it is," said Tanya. "Massachusetts, Tennessee, Florida, and Utah being the states."

"What's interesting," Charley continued, "is that other than in those four states, the cities where the accidents have taken place are on average only about eighty miles from the unexplained acoustic events and CTEs." Charley let that information sink in around the room. "I'm not suggesting that there is a causal relationship between these events. I don't think we have the data to establish that at this point. Still, though, eleven out of fifteen states—"

"73.3 percent," Tanya noted.

"—is, at the very least, quite a coincidence."

"An even bigger coincidence," Tanya added, "is that all of the original states where there were booming sounds and CTEs have also seen a spike in deadly accidents. With the exception of a single state."

"Which is?" I asked.

Charley zoomed in on the map.

"Wisconsin," Tanya said. "Home state of Tracey Wilkinson."

"Ooh, I just got goose bumps," Krista said.

I think we all had. Amy raised her hand.

"Yes, Amy."

"I did some research into these accidents last night to see if there might be other connections besides geography."

"Okay."

Amy joined Charley at the demo table and entered a quick command on the laptop. The SMART Board image dissolved from a map of Wisconsin to a chart that broke down recent accidents by type.

"So, we know that every one of the accidents so far has involved a car or some other form of transportation," she said. "A train, helicopter, bus, plane, et cetera. In every case where a cause has been established, there was an electrical malfunction of some kind that directly contributed to the accident."

"Holy shit!" Chad said.

Holy shit indeed. And to think the first person to figure this out was a fifteen-year-old student still catching up on missed assignments.

"Wait, you're saying electrical problems caused all these accidents?" Krista asked.

"We don't know that yet," Amy said. "There are still accidents where the cause hasn't been determined. But for the ones where it has been, there is definitely an electrical connection."

"No pun intended," said Victor.

I ducked into the teachers' lounge at lunch to catch a few minutes of the news and find out if anyone outside my Integrated Science class had discovered the correlations that Charley, Tanya, and Amy had picked up on. Two instructors I didn't know were talking quietly on the other side of the room, hunched over a stack of open books. I turned on the TV and lowered the volume to a point where it was barely audible.

When my colleagues finally left the room, I turned up the sound. The anchor was talking about the recent spate of fatal accidents, noting that some of them had taken place close to the locations of previous booming sounds and CTEs. He quickly added that many other accidents had occurred in areas that were nowhere near the sites of those earlier events.

I wasn't sure why he felt the need to make that point. No one had ever said there wouldn't be random accidents around the country, just as there had always been. But to ignore the fact that so many had happened in the same areas as earlier unexplained events made no sense.

Just then, the door opened and quickly closed. I turned to the sound of the lock clicking shut.

The midday news was about to lose a viewer.

"Dr. Del Rio! Hello."

"Andrew."

"Another unexpected meeting. What a coincidence!"

"There's nothing coincidental about it. I waited until the others left, so I could speak with you privately."

"Oh, okay. Did you want to sit down? I always seem to be asking you that these days," I said with a chuckle.

"No, actually I'd prefer to stand."

She walked toward me like a hungry predator considering dinner options.

"I wanted to let you know that I did not appreciate your attempt to embarrass me in front of your students yesterday."

I knew from day one that Del Rio would never be an ally, but I had not expected a direct frontal assault.

"I . . . I'm sorry. I don't know what you mean."

I knew very well what she meant, but I was stalling like a woozy boxer after a knockdown.

"Your little speech about what Dr. Marshall wanted for his students. How education is more than just books, or however you put that. Remember now?"

"Oh, that. I am so sorry if it came across like I was trying to make you look bad. Is that what you thought? That was the farthest thing from my mind."

"Spare me the false apology, Andrew. Just know that every instructor will be reviewed at the end of the school year, including you. There is no tenure track here at Banneker."

"Okay. I mean, I never thought there was, but—"

"And just to let you know, it is highly unlikely that Simeon Marshall will be back next year or ever. The board has already informed me that I will be retained beyond this school year and that the word *interim* will be removed from my title."

"Congratulations. I'm sure your appointment is well-deserved."

"Thank you." Del Rio glared at me for several very uncomfortable seconds, after which she turned on her designer stilettos and click-clacked her way out of the room.

❧

On the drive home from school that day, I listened to radio coverage of President Martell's visit to Deauville, the seaside resort in northwestern France where the latest round of G-7 meetings was being held. After the day's final session, the president made a brief statement to reporters about the climate-change initiative that had been the main focus of the conference. In the scrum that followed, many of them shouted questions, not about global warming, but about the recent string of accidents.

President Martell appeared somewhat flustered at first, but he recovered quickly, noting that "tragedies like these, while unfortunate, do take place on almost a daily basis." As for the apparent geographic overlap between some of the accidents and earlier acoustic events and CTEs—well, that was pure coincidence, according to the president.

Mike Martell had been celebrated on the campaign trail for

his can-do approach to chronic domestic challenges, like jobs, tax policy, and healthcare. Dealing with something out of the ordinary, especially something that could potentially pose a threat to national security, was not necessarily his strong suit. But the reporters at Deauville were persistent.

"Mr. President," one of them asked, "we've learned today that many of these accidents appear to have been caused by electrical malfunctions of one kind or another. Considering that a number of prominent cardiologists have suggested that some form of electrical stimulation may have also caused the hearts of the CTE patients to continue beating, do you still think this is all just a coincidence?"

"Well, this is the first time I've heard that about the accidents," the president replied. "As you know, I've been in closed-session meetings all day and have not yet had the chance to meet with staff about anything other than what's on our agenda here in Deauville. But that said, to the best of my knowledge, there is nothing to suggest a credible link between these accidents and the so-called CTE cases. And so, while we all wish that tragedies of this nature happened less frequently, the fact is—as I said a moment ago—they are a part of life, although certainly a regrettable one. Thank you all very much."

There was another flurry of questions, but aides were already whisking the president away. Whatever else the impromptu press conference may have accomplished, it established that Amy Phan was not the only one to notice that electricity may have played a role in both the CTE cases and the recent string of accidents. Still, I did take solace in the fact that one of my tenth-grade students, on at least this occasion, had been better informed about a matter of public health and safety than the president of the United States.

∽

On Friday of that week, I informed my Integrated Science students that Doris Wilkinson had given us written permission to move forward with the crowdfunding project and promised to provide visual materials as soon as possible. While that was good news, I was concerned that it may have come too late. CTEs seemed like ancient history by that point.

Over the next several weeks, the wave of fatal accidents around the United States also began getting less attention after the number of fatalities dropped to well within the normal range. Administration sources pointed out during this period that even when that number had been rising, the national total amounted to less than the typical death toll from two or three commercial airline crashes. In light of that, they argued, this entire matter had probably gotten more attention than it deserved. Accidents were simply a normal part of life, just as the president had said. And, as the president had also stated, the geographic overlap of booming sounds, CTEs, and fatal accidents was likely nothing more than coincidence.

Coincidence or not, that didn't stop the cable news networks and academic community from pumping out an endless stream of theories, hypotheses, and other acronym-rich, pseudo-scientific blather. Among the more bizarre examples was an article written by a well-respected statistician about something he called the Deadly Events and Tragic Happenings, or DEATH, index. Like a twisted form of redlining—which was twisted enough on its own—this statistical construct utilized a complex mathematical formula to assign risk ratings to cities around the country for what it termed the Likelihood of Accidental Death, or LOAD, factor. This rating was derived by dividing the number of deaths within a given period by the number of incidents that had caused the fatalities, then multiplying the result by a variable based on total population, geographic area, and several other factors. I wasn't convinced there was an overwhelming need for the DEATH index, but our collective inclination to reduce everything to its quantifiable constituent parts trumped common sense and perspective. Not to mention the investment caveat that past results are no guarantee of future performance.

❧

With the surge in accidents now behind us, our national obsession with unexplained events subsided, and life slowly returned to normal—just as it had when the CTE episodes concluded. People complained about their jobs, argued with their spouses, struggled to understand their children, and frittered away countless hours on social media, sharing photos of kids, pets, and drinks with umbrellas.

In my Integrated Science class, we shifted our focus once again from mysterious phenomena to the far less captivating standard curriculum. But even as most Americans returned to business as usual, there were some notable changes taking place. After going live in early October, the Tracey Wilkinson crowdfunding project tapped into a wellspring of public compassion and surpassed its financial target before the end of the month. Perhaps even more surprising, in the Robbins-Siegel household, Joanna and I finally found common ground on the baby-making front. Or, to put it more accurately, I finally decided that fear was not going to control my life.

At long last, it was all systems go.

CHAPTER 14

As OCTOBER DRIFTED into November, my Integrated Science students' interest in our regular curriculum began to wane. I wasn't happy about that, but I also wasn't surprised. There was no way the humdrum reality of everyday schoolwork could compete with the lure of unexplained phenomena. I was forced to rely on academic sleight-of-hand to engage the class, with middling results at best. One welcome exception came on the fifth of November, when I announced that it was not only Guy Fawkes Day in the United Kingdom—which went over the head of everyone but Tanya, who traced her lineage to England—but also the birthday of another Englishman, our old friend J.B.S. Haldane. As I said on the first day of the school year, it was Haldane who observed a century earlier that the universe is "not only queerer than we suppose, but queerer than we can suppose." With that in mind, I invited my students to untether themselves from the curriculum and ask me anything at all about the universe.

Chad, who to that point had shown no particular interest in cosmology, wanted to know what came before the Big Bang.

"You couldn't have started things off with something a little easier?" I joked.

"Hey, you said we could ask you anything."

I smiled back at him. "It's okay. I once asked my cosmology professor the same thing."

"So, what was the answer?"

"He reminded me that I wasn't in a physics-for-poets class and said I should leave those kinds of questions to the philosophers and theologians."

Unfortunately, I didn't have that luxury with my Integrated Science students. Victor asked if there could have been another universe before ours with its own Big Bang. Krista wondered if there could be other universes in existence right now. And Tanya brought up the possibility that there might even be a parallel universe.

"You never know," I said, leaning back against the demo table. "As we've talked about, our universe might be part of a multiverse. And if it is, maybe there are other universes exactly like this one."

"I kind of get that there could be other universes," Chad said. "But another one that's the same as ours? That's a little out there."

"It's definitely a pretty strange concept," I acknowledged. "But if there are other universes besides this one—not just one or two but, theoretically, an infinite number—maybe there really is one that's just like ours."

"Does that mean there's another me living there?" Chad asked.

"God, let's hope not," Victor said, prompting a burst of laughter from around the room.

"Maybe I'll get to meet him someday," Chad persisted.

"Don't get your hopes up," said Tanya. "This universe is about ninety billion light years across. So even if there are others, it's pretty unlikely we'll ever reach any of them."

"Actually," Amy said, "my dad and I were talking about string theory the other day, and he was saying—"

"Wait, there's a theory about strings?" Chad asked.

"These are different kinds of strings," Amy said, trying not to laugh. "So, yeah, my dad was saying that other universes could be very close by, like maybe even all around us, but they'd still be undetectable because they occupy a different dimension."

"And your dad might be right," I said. "If there's one piece of advice we can take from J.B.S. Haldane, it's that we shouldn't limit ourselves to what we already know, or think we do, in trying to understand this or any other universe. The truth, if there even is such a thing, could be something we haven't even thought about."

∽

One truth I had done an excellent job of not thinking about was the impending arrival of my thirty-seventh birthday the following Sunday. It wasn't so much the event itself that bothered me. I was more concerned that Joanna and I would have to spend the day with my parents, who had invited us to join them for a birthday barbecue at their house. When the big day arrived, my father called first thing that morning to inform me that we would have to postpone our celebration because a migraine (code for nasty hangover) had sent Mother to bed for the day. I was sorry to hear that she wasn't feeling well, but my parents couldn't have given me a better birthday present.

Joanna and I thought about making last-minute plans with friends but decided instead to do a quiet barbecue ourselves at home. After spending some time in the garage adjusting the temperamental truss rod on my latest Fender Telecaster, I headed out to Whole Foods to pick up a pair of rib eyes for Joanna and me, and a meaty bone for Largo. Good thing I didn't overlook the canine member of the family. When I got back home, he and Joanna were sitting at attention sporting goofy birthday hats. There were also four numbered gifts lined up in the living room, three of which were wrapped, and one that was stuffed in a lawn bag. Joanna arranged them in their preferred order and signaled that it was time for the festivities to begin.

"Socks!" I proclaimed, ripping open box number one, which contained a dozen colorful pairs of socks in a box that resembled a shipping container.

"Just so you know, socks are the new necktie," Joanna informed me. "Use them to liberate your inner fashionista."

"I can hardly wait." I moved on to present number two and tore off the wrapping paper. "Now this is a gift that needs no explanation." It was a hardcover book about the star clusters, nebulae, and galaxies that French astronomer Charles Messier catalogued in the eighteenth century. I often complained about not having a decent roadmap for my astronomical explorations, and now that problem had been solved.

Next up was the lawn bag. If nothing else, it got the award for most inventive wrap job. I undid the twist tie at the top and pulled out . . . a blue carry-on suitcase so bright it was almost glowing.

"Don't worry," Joanna said. "I got you the whole set."

"I wasn't actually worried but thanks. It's very . . . blue."

"That ratty, old luggage you've had since high school needed to be retired. Plus, this will be much easier for you to spot at the airport."

"My inner fashionista is thrilled." I gave the carry-on a light tap, and it rolled across the hardwood floor. "This is quite a haul. Did you get an early bonus at work?"

"You've got one more."

The final item was a tiny silver box with a white bow on top. My initial thought was that it might be a ring or a watch or some other unnecessary indulgence. I was about to protest that my lovely wife had gone overboard. Then I lifted the cover off the box and saw a small, cream-colored plastic tile floating on a swab of cotton.

"Isn't this supposed to have a letter on it and come with a Scrabble board?" I asked. A closer look revealed a very faint plus-sign barely visible on the tile. Still thinking Scrabble, I was perplexed. Why would Joanna give me a random piece from a board game as a birthday gift? I stalled for a moment, hoping for more information.

"Congratulations, papa," she said softly.

I heard the words, but my brain was not cooperating. Thirty-seven years old and already losing my faculties.

Then it hit me in a rushing blur of joy and disbelief.

"Oh, my God! You're serious!"

She nodded her head. "Yep."

Joanna was doing her best not to cry, but it was a futile effort. I jumped to my feet and pulled her up from her chair. We collapsed into each other, spinning around like a pair of drunken ice skaters.

"I love you so much," I said.

"I love you too."

Even Largo looked excited. I sat Joanna down on the sofa like she was a piece of fine china.

"Are you sure? Did you repeat the test?"

"Yes, my skeptical science nerd. You're going to be a father. God help us all."

It hadn't been easy getting to that point. We had thought

about it, talked about it, and fought over it. I dealt with the anatomical details of life every day as a biology teacher, but this went way beyond looking at cells under a microscope. Suddenly, everything seemed different. I almost couldn't remember what it felt like not to want this.

"Do you need anything?" I asked.

"Like what?"

"I don't know. Crackers, maybe?"

"Why would I want crackers?"

"I thought all pregnant women eat crackers."

"Crackers sound terrible. I would like some water though."

She started to get up. I put my hands on her shoulders and pushed her back down. "You need to rest. I'll get it."

"It's okay," she said, pushing back. "I haven't lost the use of my legs."

I stepped aside, and Joanna headed off to the kitchen. While she was gone, my brain jumped from one scary thought to another.

"I do have a few questions," I said when she returned.

"Okay."

"What about childcare?"

"I'm in favor of it."

"But I mean, should we have someone come in during the day? Or do we drop the baby off at some daycare place? God, I can't believe we're actually talking about this."

"I don't know. We'll figure it out."

I got up and began pacing around the room. "You think maybe we should move someplace with an extra bedroom?"

"Probably at some point, if we still want to have a study. The baby's going to need a place to sleep and hang out and play with mobiles."

"It's going to play with mobiles?"

"I guess we'll find out."

"Wow, there's a lot to think about. We'll have to get it books and toys and music. And clothes."

"I agree. Our kid should definitely wear clothes. Any other questions?"

"Well . . . oh, never mind. It can wait."

"What can wait?"

I knew what I wanted to say but didn't know quite how to put it.

"Is it okay if I still, y'know . . ."

"No, I don't know. What are you trying to work up the courage to ask me?"

"Is it okay if I still . . . touch you?"

"I'm going to have a baby, Andrew. I'm not moving to a convent."

CHAPTER 15

JOANNA AND I spent the rest of that day and the first part of the following week in a cocoon of expectant euphoria. Separately and together, at all hours of the day and night, we pondered what our child would look like, talk like, and do for a living. There was a steady stream of congratulations from friends and family; even my parents seemed genuinely happy for us. And Joanna's parents, who wouldn't leave their island paradise for anything short of an act of God—which I guess this was—promised to fly over in time for the birth in late July of the following year.

The wave of elation that grew out of our baby news diminished somewhat on Tuesday night and early Wednesday when we learned that the recent slowdown in deadly accidents had merely been a temporary respite. A new cluster of tragedies had occurred that were not only linked geographically but by causation. In Texas, thirty-three members of a farming community lost their lives in a fertilizer-plant explosion. Twelve people perished in Colorado when a powerful gas explosion ripped through an office building. A string of explosions aboard a fuel barge on the Mobile River in Alabama killed eight, while a gas-tanker explosion in Oklahoma left twenty dead. Three more explosions in Oregon, South Carolina, and Utah snuffed out an additional nineteen lives.

Speculation about other possible linkages among these tragedies was rife on social media and online news sites. Administration officials, however, stayed relentlessly on message, insisting that these were random events with no connection to one another or to the booming sounds and CTEs that had preceded them. The president had said all along that tragic accidents were simply an unfortunate but unavoidable part of life. His spokespeople reinforced that perspective at every opportunity, pointing out that the actual body count remained relatively low.

On Wednesday, when my Integrated Science students talked about the recent series of explosions, there was sharp disagreement over the significance of their geographic distribution. Charley, in contrast to the president's team, argued that the locations did not appear to be random, noting that five of the seven fatal events had taken place in states where there had previously been unexplained acoustic events and CTEs.

"But still, it's not like explosions don't happen from time to time," said Krista, channeling her inner President Martell.

"That many happening within less than twenty-four hours is not what I'd call time to time," Tanya countered.

The torrent of deadly accidents continued around the country that afternoon and evening, with most occurring in states where there had been reports of mysterious sounds and CTEs in late August and September. As with the cluster of explosions, these incidents were all linked by a common cause: collapses of various kinds. In Syracuse, New York, an eight-story apartment complex caved in, killing thirty-one residents. There were similar accidents involving buildings or balconies that collapsed in New Mexico, Indiana, and Arizona.

But there were also collapses that did not involve structures, including two in which cranes malfunctioned. In the first of these, a crane doing bridge repair work gave way about an hour north of Bakersfield, killing three workers. A second crane failed at a construction site in Biloxi, Mississippi, fatally injuring an employee who was just weeks away from retirement. Two additional collapses were notable, not only for the loss of life but for the freakish nature of the incidents. A seven-year old Illinois boy was killed when a flight-display sign fell on him at an airport outside of Joliet. About an hour later, an Alabama dental hygiene student had just gotten in her car when a silver maple tree in the front yard ripped out of the ground and crushed the vehicle, killing the young woman instantly. Investigators later determined that the car's ignition system had malfunctioned seconds before the massive tree came crashing down.

⬥

When seventy-two-year-old Illinois Senator Lee Tewksbury had agreed to run on the Democratic ticket, he did so in the belief that the vice-presidency would be a well-earned victory lap at the end of a distinguished forty-five-year career in government. For Mike Martell, the decision to name Senator Tewksbury as his running mate had been more about garnering support among aging baby boomers than bestowing a lifetime achievement award. Whatever the political calculus that had put him on the ticket, Vice President Tewksbury now found himself heading up the panel tasked to investigate several hundred CTE cases around the country. Tewksbury had accomplished many things during his four and a half decades of public service, but mastery of medical science was not among them. So perhaps it should have come as no surprise that others in the administration were effectively running the investigation, with the vice president functioning as little more than a befuddled figurehead.

Initially, no one in the president's inner circle had made any official comment about the latest slew of accidents. But in the face of mounting public concern, the administration again dispatched high-ranking officials to appear on Sunday morning political shows to calm the nerves of an increasingly frazzled nation. Each of these surrogates did their job as instructed, hewing to the party line that there was no evidence of any connection between the recent accidents and the cessation-of-terminal-events cases the vice president and his team were investigating. It was hard to know if they actually believed that or were simply trying to head off a stampede of public anxiety. But they were unwavering in making their case.

The guests on that morning's TV programs may not have broken any new ground with their answers, but the panelists began using a new abbreviation, *ATE*, which stood for "accelerated terminal event." So, we had gone from CTEs—when the gravely ill would not die—to ATEs, when the perfectly healthy were doing so at staggering rates. And the vice president, the man charged with untangling the CTE portion of this acronym-laden mess, was still trying to figure out how to message his fourteen-year-old granddaughter on Instagram.

The next day at school, several of my Integrated Science students argued that there had to be a link between the latest group of calamities and earlier, unexplained events. A smaller group, led by unlikely activist Krista, insisted that this conclusion was unfounded, given that a number of the most recent explosions and collapses had taken place in locations where there had been no booming sounds or CTEs.

"But even if the geographic overlap isn't consistent in every case," Amy countered, "the way these things are happening in bunches—first crashes, then explosions, now collapses—can't just be coincidental."

Amy's observation was not only on point but prescient, as the chain of tragic episodes resumed the very next day with a series of drowning incidents. The first of these involved cousins, ages five and three, who were found dead in a suburban New York swimming pool. Preliminary evidence from a nearby security camera indicated that the children had slipped through a gap in a neighbor's fence and run onto the pool's cover, which then apparently opened on its own. Two more individuals also died in separate drowning accidents that same afternoon along the South Carolina coast. Local authorities did not release details, citing privacy concerns.

Two days later, a series of avalanches and slides took more lives. The first of these occurred in Colorado's Clear Creek Mountains, which had been hit by a massive snow storm just prior to an avalanche that killed seven snowboarders. A family of four in Utah was also killed that day when a rockslide destroyed their home. Meteorologists blamed the slide on unprecedented snowfall and temperatures in the area that were lower than at any time in the previous hundred years. But the single deadliest event in this group of tragedies was an Indiana mudslide in which twenty-one people were confirmed dead and another twelve listed as missing. A sheriff's department spokesperson noted that heavy rainfall had turned the affected area into quicksand, with mud up to twenty feet deep.

By Friday of that week, even Krista acknowledged that the way these episodes were occurring in clusters was "a little creepy." And despite the best efforts of administration officials to assuage the public's fears, hoarding was becoming commonplace around the country. This was true even in cities that were well beyond the eighty-mile average distance between recent accident locations and sites of earlier booming sounds and CTEs.

On my monthly trek to Costco that Saturday, people who normally would have been filling their carts with frozen turkeys and pumpkin pies were grabbing fistfuls of batteries, bottled water, and any first-aid kits still on the shelves. Standing in the checkout line, I overheard a man on the phone desperately trying to track down a generator, a task made more difficult by the near total depletion of local inventory. Frayed nerves even seeped into the Robbins-Siegel residence, where the domestic bliss of recent weeks gave way to minor but frequent bickering. Instead of musing about which Ivy League college our future offspring would attend, we were questioning the wisdom of bringing a baby into this suddenly unhinged world.

The national mood didn't improve late Saturday night or Sunday when a series of fires devastated multiple locations around the country. A family of five and their teenage houseguest died in a central Pennsylvania fire that started after frozen fish sticks were left cooking overnight in the oven. Four people in an Oklahoma logging community lost their lives when an over-loaded extension cord shorted out, sparking a rush of flames in a thatched-roof cabin. In a Vermont apartment, a candle toppled over, igniting the nearby draperies in floor-to-ceiling flames that quickly engulfed one of the bedrooms. Three young children, who had been huddled together to keep warm before the fire broke out, were pronounced dead at the scene. Their mother reportedly made repeated attempts to pull them to safety but was overcome by smoke and collapsed just outside their bedroom. Neighbors said the family had been using candles for light after the utility company had turned off their electricity because the unemployed single mom had been consistently late with her monthly payments. There were also deadly fires in Texas and Indiana, as well as one in Alabama that claimed fourteen lives when an early morning blaze roared through a Montgomery trailer park. With the exception of the Pennsylvania fire, every one of the others took place in states where there had previously been CTEs and unexplained sounds.

On Monday morning, Charley powered up the SMART Board and updated the spreadsheet and map he and his group had been using to track unexplained events. He reminded the class that most of the recent tragedies had occurred within the eighty-mile average distance from previous booming sounds and CTEs.

Krista was quick to note, however, that some of the incidents had actually taken place hundreds of miles away from those earlier events.

Charley grudgingly conceded the point, admitting that he couldn't explain these "outliers," as he called them. "It's a little like the SAT," he complained, "where the first three numbers are two, four, and six, and the next number is forty-one, and they ask you to figure out what comes after that."

That night I called Marty Olivo and got the reassuring news that everything had returned to normal in the Bakersfield area following the recent crane collapse. When he asked about how Joanna was doing, I droned on about the perils of pregnancy, especially those of an intestinal nature. I requested his professional advice even though I knew he hadn't had to deal with ob-gyn questions since medical school.

All he could manage was a rather unprofessional, "Ooh, yuck."

While we were riffing on the general subject of women,

Marty mentioned that he had been seeing someone for the past month or so and hoped Joanna and I could meet her "one of these days." For a guy who was notoriously private about such matters, this was tantamount to a wedding announcement. Realizing that he had perhaps revealed too much, Marty changed the subject, giving me a brief update about several of our MIT buddies, including our former roommate, Rich Esposito. Rich was now part of a team of scientists in Minnesota doing what Marty described as groundbreaking research into electromagnetic fields and dark matter. I thanked Marty for the alumni news and wished him well with his new romantic adventure. I also asked for his girlfriend's contact information so that I could warn her to get out while there was still time. Perhaps not surprisingly, he declined my request.

News about Marty's personal life and the professional accomplishments of old MIT friends would soon be eclipsed by much more pressing developments. Within the next thirty-six hours, a barrage of gruesome tragedies roiled the nation, including deadly fires in New York, Illinois and Alabama, explosions in Utah and Texas, multiple drowning incidents off the coast of Florida, and major crashes on land and in the air in Mississippi, Vermont, Arizona, Oklahoma, and California. The good news for Marty and the residents of Bakersfield was that their city had been spared in the California carnage. The bad news was that fourteen people had lost their lives in California's Santa Clarita Valley, best known as the home of Six Flags Magic Mountain. I'm not sure what prompted me to do this, but for some reason I checked the distance between the city of Santa Clarita and Bakersfield: it was exactly eighty miles. Even more disturbing, Santa Clarita was only a half-hour drive from Altadena.

Suddenly, this had become much more personal.

CHAPTER 16

THE RISING DEATH toll didn't put anyone in the mood to celebrate, but Joanna and I had already accepted an invitation to join my parents on Thanksgiving for what I expected would be our typical train wreck of a family dinner. Much to my surprise, the afternoon and evening turned out to be quite pleasant. For the first time in years, Mother was clear-headed throughout the entire event, consuming nothing stronger than iced tea spiked with lemonade. Apparently, her doctor had told her if she didn't cut out the booze she wouldn't live to see her grandchild's first birthday. I wasn't convinced she could navigate the journey to sobriety entirely on her own, but at least she was making the effort.

Having survived the Thanksgiving holiday, Joanna and I looked forward to a quiet weekend at home. She had recently begun to develop a number of interesting dietary quirks, including a craving for Spanish omelettes with fresh salsa, which we had run out of earlier in the week. So, first thing Saturday morning, I headed out to Ray's Ranch Market, our go-to local grocery store, to replenish our supply. Ray's was not only close to home—it had the area's best selection of Asian, Middle Eastern, and Mexican foods, including salsa.

On the way there, I drove past a few of the neighborhood landmarks that I'd always found somewhat comforting, especially at times when the ordered flow of everyday life goes off the rails. With its white picket fence and perfectly tended red and yellow roses poking through the slats, Mrs. Benson's cottage on Olive Street looked like something out of a children's story. A couple of blocks down from there, I passed the old Atwood place on Glenrose Avenue. Martha Atwood had converted the pre-war residence to a daycare center and nursery school after her children had grown up and moved away. A chain-link fence enclosed the front yard, which was overflowing as usual with kids' toys, bikes, and scooters. It was almost impossible to drive by that house and not get a whiff of youthful optimism.

But my favorite neighborhood sight was not a house but a person: Hank Jackson, an African-American gentleman in his late eighties, whom everyone in the area called "The Colonel," was a daily fixture on Palm Street. The world could be boiling over around him, but there he'd be, walking up and down the street—once in the morning and then again in the late afternoon—with the regularity of an atomic clock. The Colonel was right on schedule that day, leaning forward on the cane that I never saw him without. I waved when he crossed in front of me, and he replied, as he always did, with a nod of his head.

There were many things I appreciated about Altadena, but what I liked most was that we lived in an actual neighborhood instead of a cookie-cutter subdivision—a place where diversity was celebrated rather than feared. There might have been a random break-in or two over the years, but for the most part it was a safe, friendly, and welcoming community.

Or at least it always had been. The last thing I expected to see at the end of my drive to Ray's that morning was the mob scene I encountered at the back of the store. Grim-faced security officers with walkie-talkies were letting shoppers in one at a time, while a line of cars circled the jammed parking lot like a kettle of scavenging vultures. Every minute or two, a shopper with cart stacked high would emerge from the store and trudge through the lot. The car at the front of the line would slowly follow, poised to pounce on the prized chunk of asphalt about to become available.

I had just about given up hope after driving up and down the packed rows of cars for several minutes. Then I spotted an empty space one aisle over. Spooling up from zero to insanity in a nanosecond, I raced around to grab it. But I was not alone; another driver had seen the same vacancy. We roared up from opposite directions, arriving grill-to-grill on the brink of auto-motive Armageddon. Both of us wanted that parking space and were more than willing to act like jerks to get it. Horns were honked and profanities exchanged. The other driver gunned his engine multiple times to underscore his seriousness. I returned fire, but in the end, I was the one who blinked. The world might have been going nuts, but I wasn't ready to get into a fistfight over a jar of salsa.

On my way out of the parking lot, I realized that the throng of overeager shoppers I'd seen the previous weekend at Costco had been a precursor to what was unfolding that Saturday morning at Ray's Ranch Market and probably lots of other places. The fine line between rising anxiety and naked panic was beginning to blur.

Driving south on Fair Oaks Avenue in search of other grocery-store options, I passed by the familiar lineup of aging storefronts that had occupied that street for years. On the left, the old auto-repair shop (now offering free tire rotation with any service), followed by the retirement home, the burger joint, and the check-cashing place. A block further down on the other side of the street, I drove by the ancient liquor store with its rusted sign that read "_im's." I had always wondered if the full name was Jim's, Tim's, Kim's, or something else altogether. I had thought about going in on any number of occasions to inquire about the missing letter but never quite got around to it. And on this particular day, there were much more important things on my mind.

Actually, there was only one thing: My life had been reduced to a quest for fresh salsa.

I hit a total of five markets over the next half hour, extending my search to Pasadena and South Pasadena. Along the way I encountered a succession of parking lots that were full or grocery stores that were empty. Or, if not empty, picked over. I did manage to find a solitary jar of salsa at one of them, but it was the thick processed kind that my wife the salsa snob would have mocked me for buying.

I finally admitted defeat and started back toward the house. Heading up Fair Oaks, I spotted a road sign with an arrow pointing toward the 210 Freeway East. Ordinarily, I wouldn't have even noticed. But in that moment, the wisp of an idea was born, and I sped onto the freeway, propelled by a combination of fear and bravado. Everyone else on the road must have inhaled that same potent blend. All of us were blasting down the interstate like our engines were on fire. Drivers cut each other off, laid on their horns, and raised their middle fingers in the greatest display of collective road rage I had ever witnessed.

I had no idea where any of those other desperate souls were headed, but this obsessed fool was bound for a *carniceria* in Rosemead, a mostly Asian and Hispanic community where I had once bought carne asada for a neighborhood block party. For whatever reason, that Mexican meat market with a name I'd long ago forgotten had surfaced from somewhere deep in the cluttered folds of my memory and become my last, best hope for salsa salvation.

I knew I needed to head south for quite a while when I got off the freeway at San Gabriel Boulevard, but that was all I could remember. I also knew I needed to call Joanna to inform her that I had encountered some minor obstacles during my grocery-store run. Whether I got my salsa or not, I didn't want to repeat the Bakersfield fiasco when I went off the communications grid for an entire day and returned home to an exceedingly chilly reception.

Joanna and I had just finished talking when I crossed under the Highway 10 overpass. Spanish signs and billboards were beginning to appear more frequently, which meant I was getting close. Most of the businesses in the area were mom-and-pop stores slammed together in strip malls like the one I had just passed that was home to a beauty-supply shop, florist, laundry, and massage parlor. About six or seven blocks further south, I spotted a vaguely familiar monument sign that featured the neon outline of a smiling man wearing a sombrero. I slowed down to get a better look at the stores lined up behind the sign—and there it was: Lupe's Carniceria, a humble little meat market that welcomed me like an answered prayer.

I had my pick of more than a dozen empty spaces in the parking lot. A kid who looked about ten, with enough energy to light up a city, had turned the lot into his personal hand-ball court. His playmate was a short-haired little dog he called Sammy. There was no hoarding. No endless line of cars or guards with walkie-talkies. Just a boy, his dog, and a ball.

Maybe the whole world hadn't gone crazy after all.

◈

Joanna's eyes brightened the moment she saw I'd hit the salsa mother lode. But she looked like she'd reached culinary nirvana when she realized that I had also brought home a dozen tamales, a small vat of ceviche, two pounds of pork carnitas, and a full complement of rice, beans, and tortillas.

"I only wish you could have been with me, just to get away for a while," I said during the feeding frenzy that followed.

"A combat zone at Ray's and a stock-car race on the freeway. Sounds delightful."

"I meant after that, at the carniceria. It was like going from total lunacy to a little oasis of sanity."

"Your idea of getting away is finding a Mexican meat market. Mine is spending the day with my hands in the dirt. So, how about instead of gorging ourselves to the point of explosion"— she grabbed my plate and took it into the kitchen—"we run down to that new nursery on Orange Grove?"

"If I tried to run anywhere right now, bad things would happen." I followed her to the kitchen and began washing dishes. "What's so special about the nursery on Orange Grove anyway?"

"They've got some great deals on succulents and natives. I'd love to pick some up and work in the garden the rest of the day."

That idea from Joanna sparked one of my own.

"Yeah, we could do that. Or what would you think about taking a little ride and getting all the way out of cuckoo-land for a few hours?"

Joanna picked up a towel and started drying. "A little ride where?"

"Someplace with the best selection of California natives and succulents you've ever seen."

"Excuse me, when did you become an expert on drought-tolerant plants?"

"Well, we are in the middle of a historic water shortage."

She wiped off the counter with her towel. "Not sure I'm buying that explanation, but I'm not going to argue with a trip to a nursery."

✍

Within the hour we were driving down twisty country roads with names like Spring Lane and Walnut Canyon. There were groves of fruit trees that stretched out for miles in every direction. I got so caught up trying to take it all in that I almost missed the cardboard sign—taped to a mailbox on the side of the road—with the words "Pacific Coast Nursery" scribbled on it. We turned left onto a winding gravel driveway that took us past a shack with rotted wood siding and a broken-down cube truck missing its cab. The road curved around to the right, eventually leading to an RV trailer that was sunk into the ground under a sagging tree. We parked just beyond that, next to a tower of plastic pots that had been stacked up one inside another.

A chorus of chirping birds greeted us when we got out of the car, and a light breeze whistled through the pepper trees that rimmed the property. We walked over to a covered area where dozens of potted plants were lined up in rows like drummers in a marching band.

"Is this some kind of greenhouse or something?" I asked Joanna.

"Yeah, greenhouse, shade house. Same thing."

"Where's the actual nursery?"

"You're standing in it."

I was expecting a building of some sort, maybe even a gift

shop, but there was no sign of retail activity. Not that it really mattered. For Joanna, this was paradise, and that's why we were there.

"Hey, you made it!" a voice called out from behind us. David Phan came bounding down the steps of the trailer and headed our way. Before I could get the words *Family Night* out of my mouth to explain how we'd met, he and Joanna were deep in conversation about bearded irises and other exotic plant life. It didn't take long for David to figure out that only one of us knew the first thing about horticulture.

"You know, Andrew," he said, "unless you would be fascinated by a discussion of climate requirements and soil drainage—"

"Let me stop you right there."

"You're welcome to join us, of course. But Joanna and I have a lot to see. And there's someone back in the propagation area who would love to say hello."

"Someone in the what?"

"The propagation area," he said, pointing behind us. "Where all these plants get their start."

"There's someone there who wants to talk with me?"

"Actually, there are a couple of people. Why don't you walk over, and we'll meet you there when we're done."

They took off on their rounds, and I headed toward an open work space that had a corrugated metal roof. When I peeked inside, I saw Amy and Tanya sloshing their hands through a wet potting mixture and giggling like a pair of toddlers playing with finger paints. Once I got over my initial shock at seeing them and we'd said our hellos, I asked the girls if they were just having fun or doing something productive. Amy replied that they were doing both and offered a lengthy explanation of the propagation process, telling me more than I ever wanted to know about the tiny white pebbles called perlite that she said play a role in fostering root growth. Meanwhile, Tanya was happily running her fingers through the muck with no concern for its chemical composition or any other details she normally would have already committed to memory.

"I had no idea you two were such avid gardeners," I said.

"I've been coming out almost every weekend with my dad," said Amy. "Just trying to help out with the planting."

"What about you, Tanya? What brings you out here?"

"So, Amy asked me a while back if I wanted to hang out. And I thought, sure, why not? It's not like I had anything better to do. Anyway, I've been coming back ever since."

"Looks like you're enjoying yourself."

"Yeah, I like it here. It's kind of nice to give my brain a rest every once in a while."

Joanna and David showed up a few minutes later, laughing like the teenagers I'd just been talking to. They were pushing a metal cart stacked with more plants than my car could probably hold.

"What are you two so happy about?" I asked.

"Duh," Joanna said. "Obviously the *Arctostaphylos* and *Epilobium canum* we're going to be taking home with us."

"Oh, I thought maybe you were just excited about the perlite in the propagation area."

"Whoa, listen to you!" she said.

"I see the girls taught you something," David added.

"Yep, I just got a crash course in gardening 101. But the most important thing I learned was that two of my best students are best friends."

"Tanya's like a member of the family," David said. "We love having her here."

The joy on Tanya's face when she heard those words was unmistakable. This remarkable girl, who spent most of her time hiding behind a blizzard of facts, really just wanted to be part of a family that wanted her. And now, it seemed, she was.

❧

It was getting late. The dimming sunlight filtered through the trees, sketching shadows in the dirt. A day that had begun on the verge of chaos outside our neighborhood market had turned into something very different. From a carniceria in Rosemead to a nursery in Moorpark, it had been a journey of small discoveries and quiet reassurance. The sanctuary offered may have only been temporary, but it was very much appreciated just the same.

CHAPTER 17

THE PRESIDENT'S TEAM hit the airwaves again on Sunday morning amid widespread reports that the administration was preparing contingency plans for so-called hot zones, where looting and other civil disturbances had taken place. According to the rumors, FEMA was gearing up to deliver food and emergency supplies to these areas, and the National Guard was standing by, ready to move in if local law enforcement couldn't maintain order. The president's surrogates were vague about all this, trying to avoid what one of them called "counter-productive speculation about hypotheticals." But they did not deny the rumors, which only intensified in the face of this ambiguity.

At school the next day, a sense of dread hung in the air like a mid-summer inversion layer. My Integrated Science students were uncharacteristically subdued for the first few minutes before launching into a lively discussion.

Charley got things started when he speculated that something we were all missing would connect recent tragedies and previous unexplained events.

Amy reiterated her belief that electricity was likely the common thread.

Krista disagreed, arguing that electrical malfunctions couldn't be responsible for nonelectrical events like explosions, fires, collapses, drownings, and slides.

Tanya cautioned that it might be premature to minimize the role of electricity, citing as an example the two small children in New York who drowned when their neighbor's electric pool cover opened on its own.

Charley brought up the falling tree in Alabama that killed a young woman in her car after an electrical failure disabled the vehicle's ignition system.

Victor made the case that the Vermont apartment fire that killed three children would have never happened had the local utility company not cut off the family's electricity.

And Amy noted that the massive mudslide in Indiana had been triggered by an unexpected electrical storm.

I found these examples collectively intriguing but still wasn't sure we could make the jump from a few scattered electrical problems to an overarching explanation for everything.

✍

Joanna and her partners were out for their weekly meeting that night, which meant Largo and I were on our own for dinner. He probably would have been happy with his usual dried kibble, but in the spirit of roommate equality, I made the executive decision to bump him up to premium class for the evening. The refrigerator pickings were sparse, but we feasted nonetheless on leftover salmon, bowtie pasta, and a medley of pooch-friendly raw veggies hiding at the back of the produce drawer.

Ordinarily, I might have jumped online after dinner and combed through news accounts of the latest deadly accidents around the country. But on this particular night, I had no interest in further immersing myself in the national turmoil that was deepening by the day. Instead, I headed out to the garage to spend some quality time with my Fender Telecasters, including my latest addition: a 1957 model with the classic Telecaster blonde finish and maple neck, packed in its original tweed, hardshell case. I always felt a sense of peace in the presence of these magnificent instruments, many of which were older than I was. Each had its own story, which I always tried to untangle—mostly without success. I was like a frustrated historian, haunted by questions about these guitars and those who had played them over the course of the journey that eventually led to the Robbins-Siegel garage.

Lost in my Telecaster reverie, I almost forgot about unexplained events and associated phenomena. But two somewhat related thoughts still managed to sneak up on me. First, I realized that I was always on the trail of some elusive piece of information, be it the history of an aging musical instrument or the truth behind a chain of mysterious occurrences. It also struck me that, while I was surrounded by a throng of electric guitars that night, the rest of the country, too, was in the grips of electrical energy, although in a very different form. My brain leaped from that pair of realizations to something Marty had mentioned about our former college roommate and the work he was doing in Minnesota. I had no reason to think there was any connection between dark matter and recent events, but since nothing else held much promise at that point, I figured I might as well turn that stone over and make sure there was nothing lurking beneath it.

❧

I hadn't had any contact with Rich Esposito for years, so I decided to break the email ice with a slightly off-the-wall appeal to his ego. I told him that the version of spaghetti carbonara he used to make at school was far superior to the runny abomination they offer at most Italian restaurants and asked if he could send the recipe. I also asked if we might schedule a videoconference so that he could talk with my Integrated Science class about his dark-matter research. I knew he was probably swamped at work but hoped he'd find time to respond, if for no other reason than because I had given him props for his cooking skills.

With the schmooze fest at Harrison, Kearns & McMillan running late that night, Largo and I ventured out to explore the neighborhood. We were less than a block into our walk when a call came in from an area code that I didn't recognize. Out-of-the-area calls were usually scripted appeals from people I didn't know trying to sell me things I didn't want, which is why I rarely answered them. But for some reason my guard was down that night.

"Hello?"

"Yo, paisan, what's happening?"

I hadn't spoken to Rich since college, but his stock greeting was instantly recognizable. He assured me that carbonara relief would soon be on the way and said he'd be happy to talk with my Integrated Science class. But he went beyond that, offering to meet with them in person at his research lab in Minnesota. He said it was called the Soudan Mine Underground Physics Lab, situated a half-mile below the surface in an abandoned iron-ore mine that U.S. Steel had donated to the state of Minnesota in the early 1960s. As an added enticement, he mentioned that there was an excellent public tour of the lab that would be perfect for my students.

While I was grateful for the offer, I had to explain that field trips were off the table for the remainder of the semester, thanks to our interim principal. Rich reiterated his offer to do a videoconference with the class but said that I was also welcome to fly up on my own. That was an interesting idea, one that I might have ordinarily jumped at, but there was an additional complication to consider: the little Siegel in the oven, as Mother liked to call our future family member. When he heard the baby news, Rich offered a quick congrats, followed by a good-natured lament that all of his MIT buddies seemed to be getting married and having kids. I laughingly reminded him that we were all headed for the wrong side of forty and said I'd let him know in the next couple of days if I could make the trip.

On the way back home, I thought about what I could realistically expect to gain by flying halfway across the country and whether that justified leaving my wife at home by herself. Dark matter had been the subject of intense fascination among physicists for decades, but no one had proved with absolute certainty that it even existed. To assume that it did, and that it might be linked in some way with the unexplained events of the past few months, seemed like quite a stretch. So, I decided to mention the Minnesota travel idea to Joanna very casually. If she objected, that would be the end of it.

When Largo and I walked in the house, Joanna was curled up on the living room sofa, sipping hot tea from her favorite mug.

"Hi," I said.

"Hey."

Her clipped response suggested fatigue coupled with mild annoyance. And I hadn't even mentioned Minnesota.

"How was your day?" I asked.

"You mean apart from the fact that Harrison senior referred to me as 'little lady' at the partners' meeting and asked me not once but twice to refresh his coffee?"

If timing is everything, mine couldn't have been much worse. Joanna had just been through a day from hell at the old boys' club otherwise known as Harrison, Kearns & McMillan, and I was about to broach the subject of a solo trip to the land of ten thousand lakes two weeks before Christmas.

She listened without saying anything when I presented the idea, which suggested the decision could go either way.

"I think you should do it," she finally said.

"You do?"

"Yes. You have to go."

"Why do I have to go?"

"Because if you don't, you'll regret it. And then you'll be a bitter and depressed pain in the ass, and our kid will grow up guilty and neurotic and need therapy. Which will cost a fortune and deplete our college fund. That's why."

As usual, Joanna's logic was impeccable.

∽

The next morning, Tanya told our Integrated Science class about an article she had read concerning the male Y chromosome and whether it was or was not in long-term decline. After several minutes of spirited debate, which not surprisingly broke down along gender lines, we moved on to a quick update about the Tracey Wilkinson project. My students had designed a small plexiglass obelisk in Tracey's memory, which we planned to ship to her parents once it was finished. I informed the class that I had placed the fabrication order that morning, and we then discussed shipping options.

There were updates of another kind that day as well. Tanya, Charley, Victor, and Amy—who by that point was a full partner on their investigative team—presented a summary of geographic and other data related to the unexplained acoustic events, CTEs, and fatal accidents through the middle of the previous week. Their presentation was clear and informative, as always, but it didn't include anything we hadn't heard before. Charley was noticeably quiet throughout, contributing little more than a series of loud yawns.

"Sorry if this is boring you, Charley," I said.

As we soon learned, Charley wasn't bored but exhausted. He explained that he'd been up until three in the morning writing computer code for what he described as a "sociometric search engine designed to uncover and/or establish otherwise unrecognized linkages among data points."

"Wait, what?"

"I don't understand."

"What are you talking about?"

Charley's description, while technically correct, was somewhat vague, so it wasn't surprising that most of his classmates were confused.

"Maybe this will make more sense," Charley said. He brought up a map of the United States on the SMART Board. "Tanya, if you wouldn't mind . . ."

With photos of people's faces fading on and off in pairs around the map, Tanya recited first and last names and other information that established unmistakable connections between the individuals who comprised each pair.

"Expired CTE patient James Kilgore, resident of Enid, Oklahoma, co-worker of Eugene Garson, killed in rollover automobile crash in Ardmore, Oklahoma. Distance between Enid and Ardmore: 159 miles."

"Expired CTE patient Maryanne De Leone, resident of Muncie, Indiana, sister-in-law of Constance Abreu-De Leone, killed in building collapse in Fort Wayne, Indiana. Distance between Muncie and Fort Wayne: 66 miles."

"Expired CTE patient David Alan Jennings, resident of Greenwood, South Carolina, former neighbor of Marcus Wilhite, killed in avalanche in Clear Creek County, Colorado. Distance between Greenwood and Clear Creek: 1,595 miles."

"Expired CTE patient Marsha Tomasini, resident of Kingman, Arizona, former elementary school teacher of Charles F. Milberg, killed in train collision in Chandler, Arizona. Distance between Kingman and Chandler: 182 miles."

"Expired CTE patient Harley Comstock, resident of Utica, New York, captain of community bowling team that included John J. Hastings, killed in motel fire in Binghamton, New York. Distance between Utica and Binghamton: 78 miles."

On and on it went, with Tanya citing linkages that no one other than Charley had recognized. In every case, the personal connection was there, even if the geographic link was not. I finally asked Tanya to halt the recitation, not because everyone in the room wasn't transfixed by the litany of deadly connections, but because Charley's search engine had already made its point.

"If it's okay," said Tanya, "I did want to mention one more name that came up in Charley's search. It's a little different from the others."

"Sure, go ahead."

"The name is Gerald Lester." A photo of Mr. Lester appeared on the map. "He doesn't fit into either of the two groups—CTE patients or accident victims—but his name came up multiple times in connection with several people in both groups."

"What do we know about him?"

"Well, we know he's still living, unlike the other people we've been talking about. We also know that he's a sixty-two-year-old physicist, but that's about it. There's very little information about him other than some old addresses. There might have been something employment related in one of the databases Charley pulled from, but it had been redacted."

"Like we don't have enough mysteries," I said with a laugh. "Thanks for adding one more to the list."

I often invited students to join me in my classroom at noon for a quick lunch and informal discussion about whatever was on their minds. But that day I closed and locked the door at lunchtime, so I could have some quiet time to digest the information that Charley had uncovered. I thought about the mammoth global footprint of social media, made possible by a vast web of personal connections among billions of people. According to one study, only 3.5 people stand between any two Facebook users anywhere in the world. So, it probably shouldn't have come as a surprise that there might be connections between some CTE patients and ATE victims.

But Charley's search engine didn't just offer up a few scattered names; it uncovered linkages among dozens of people. Was it possible that those connections were nothing more than random coincidences? Yes, but it was also possible that they weren't random at all, but rather one more wrinkle in the baffling series of mysteries that had been churning for months. Maybe that was why I couldn't shake the feeling that I had to go to Minnesota. I knew it was the longest of long shots, but I needed to know what exactly had caught the attention of Rich Esposito and his team of dark-matter detectives a half mile beneath the surface.

Driving home that afternoon, I found myself making connections of a different kind. The distance between Ely, Minnesota—the site of the Soudan Mine Underground Physics Lab—and Eau Claire, Wisconsin, where Tracey Wilkinson's family lived, was only about two hundred and fifty miles. That was close enough to deliver Tracey's obelisk myself, instead of relying on some impersonal delivery service to drop it off. Joanna had already given her blessing to my Minnesota trip, but adding Wisconsin would extend things by a full day. Fortunately, when I presented the idea that night, she was all for it. I could take a red eye to Duluth, Minnesota on Friday night, then drive up to Ely the next morning. After meeting with Rich in the afternoon, I'd drive to Eau Claire, spend the night at a hotel, and visit with the Wilkinson family on Sunday before flying back to L.A. that evening. I sent emails confirming the details to Doris Wilkinson and to Rich, and everything was set.

∽

An actual field trip might not have been possible, but I still wanted my students to feel involved in my upcoming journey. So, I talked them through my itinerary the next day. "Any questions, comments, or travel tips?" I asked after I'd finished.

"I have a suggestion," Victor said.

"Okay."

"I think some of us should go with you."

"Yeah," Tanya agreed. "Think of it as a substitute for the field trip to Bakersfield we didn't get to take." I had never explained the real reason that trip had been cancelled, or that Dr. Del Rio had grounded the class for the remainder of the semester. But now I felt like I had no choice but to tell them the whole story—minus the part about the growing tension between Del Rio and myself.

By the following Monday, most of my students had accepted the fact that they wouldn't be going with me to Minnesota and Wisconsin, but several still had reservations about the trip.

"If this really is all about electricity," Charley wondered, "wouldn't something with energy in its name—like, say, dark energy—make more sense?"

I conceded that might seem logical but reminded the class that the existence of dark energy was even more questionable than dark matter, which would make it an even more elusive target. Not to mention that my Rich Esposito dark-matter connection gave me access to test results and other data that I wouldn't have if I tried to chase down other kinds of exotic particles.

That answer seemed to quell their primary objection, but they had others as well. A few of my students questioned whether it was even safe for me to fly, given that there had been so many more plane crashes than normal during recent months.

"Not that we're actually worried about you," Victor explained, "but it would kind of suck to have to break in a substitute this far into the semester."

As it turned out, my students weren't the only ones who had misgivings about my upcoming trip. My father, too, thought it was a bad idea. He called the next night and demanded that I cancel my plans in light of Joanna's "condition." I reminded him that it was Joanna who had convinced me to go in the first place, but he sidestepped that inconvenient fact and lashed out at me for being a "selfish husband who quite clearly lacks the maturity to be a father." I had to hand it to him—impugning my abilities as both a spouse and a future parent, all in the space of a single sentence, was quite the rhetorical achievement, even for my father. But I really shouldn't have been surprised. Going into attack mode was something he had done with great success for as long as I could remember. Only this time, instead of caving in to his demands, I did something I had never done before—something that proved remarkably cathartic.

I hung up on him.

CHAPTER 18

LATE FRIDAY AFTERNOON, I wrapped the obelisk in a towel and stuffed it in my carry-on, along with my laptop, power cords, shaving kit, extra shoes, three books, some physics journals, and whatever clothing I could squeeze into the space remaining. The weather in Minnesota had risen to a balmy forty-nine degrees that day, but I jammed in a scarf and gloves just in case and coaxed the zipper shut.

"Is there anything you're not taking with you?" Joanna asked when she walked into the bedroom and saw my bloated carry-on.

"Nope, I think that's just about everything."

"I hope you're taking a heavy coat."

"Yeah, I'm going to carry it on."

"Do you have a scarf?"

"Yes."

"Gloves?"

"Yep."

"Hat?"

Pause.

"Hat?"

"No."

"You're flying to Minnesota in the middle of December, and you don't have a hat?"

"I have one, but I forgot to pack it. And I'm not going to open that thing. Anyway, they're having a heat wave up there."

"You do know that weather sometimes changes."

"I've heard that, yes."

"And you are going to have to open that once you get there, if not before, when you go through security."

"Yes, I know."

"Where's your hat?"

"I'm not opening the bag."

"Can you just get the hat, please?" I rummaged through a bag of old ski clothes in the closet and pulled out a wool hat. Joanna stuffed it in the side pocket of my parka. "Problem solved."

"That's why you made it through law school and I didn't."

Joanna dropped me at LAX for the LA to Chicago leg of my trip just before ten o'clock that night. I allowed myself a moment of smug satisfaction when I saw the line of passengers waiting to check their luggage. Then I noticed that TSA agents in the security area were randomly asking people in front of me to open their carry-on bags. Fortunately, I was waved through, thus averting a potential carry-on catastrophe.

I began to perspire shortly after boarding, which was normal for me whenever I placed my life in the hands of strangers while strapped inside a metal tube at an altitude of seven miles. Making matters worse, I hadn't been able to get an aisle or window seat, so I ended up stuck between two well-fed gentlemen, one of whom spent the entire flight slumped over what was, in theory, our shared armrest. Fortunately, the remainder of my journey— flying from Chicago to Duluth and driving from there up to Ely—was pleasant and uneventful.

❧

"Welcome to Soudan: Home of Minnesota's Oldest, Richest, Deepest Underground Mine." With some minor changes in wording, the peeling wood sign would have looked perfect in front of the local bait and tackle shop. But this was the site of the Cryogenic Dark Matter Search, or CDMS, one of the most advanced scientific research projects in the world. The Soudan Mine Underground Physics Lab may have lacked the cachet of the world-renowned research installations in Europe, but the work going on in Minnesota a half mile underground was every bit as important.

For most of the thirty or so people who had signed up for the 1:00 p.m. public tour, the next hour would be an informative diversion, like visiting a planetarium or going to a museum. For me, it would be an exercise in killing time while waiting to pick Rich Esposito's brain about the work he and his colleagues had been doing. Normally, that might not have warranted a two-thousand-mile trip right before Christmas. But on the off chance that there could be some sort of connection between what Rich and his team were working on and the bizarre events of the last several months, I thought it was worth a shot. And fortunately, so did my wife.

Tour guide Nick Swenson, a recent University of Minnesota physics graduate with thick glasses and spiky, bleached-blond hair, welcomed us to Ely, which he said rhymes with "feely"— as in "touchy-feely." He informed us that we'd be making our descent in a pair of eighty-year-old electric hoists made of steel, "just like the ones the miners used to travel up and down in." Nick explained that the lab was located more than two thousand feet beneath the surface in order to shield the experiments from possible contamination by the sun's cosmic rays. He then issued each of us a hardhat; and away we went, following behind him in single file like a flock of well-trained ducks.

After a three-minute journey down through the darkness, the door to cage number one clanked open, and we walked out onto level twenty-seven, the lowest point in the mine. Nick corralled us into the no-frills underground physics lab, which was set in a cavern four stories high and nearly as long as a football field. He said the rock that comprised the cavern walls—appropriately known as Ely Greenstone—dated back some 2.7 billion years, making it one of the oldest rocks on Earth. The lab furnishings were basic but functional—standard-issue tables, chairs, and benches—no different from those found in public schools and government offices everywhere. Scientific charts, photos, drawings, and posters—depicting everything from the Oort Cloud beyond the solar system to the chemical composition of recently discovered elements—had been tacked or taped on display stands scattered around the area. But the centerpiece of the cavern was a towering orange mural that paid homage to those who years earlier had paved the way in the nascent field of particle physics.

Like the guy who warms up the audience before a TV taping, Nick asked where everyone was from. Most were Minnesota natives from places like Rochester, Duluth, and Hibbing, which Nick said was best known as the hometown of Bob Dylan, who, he noted, had not signed up for the tour that day. If physics was Nick's major, standup comedy must have been his minor. He followed his basic description of dark matter with a joke about turf wars between the WIMPs (Weakly Interacting Massive Particles) and the MACHOs (Massive Astrophysical Compact Halo Objects) thought to comprise it. It occurred to me as Nick prattled on that I might have been standing in the world's only underground comedy club. All in all, though, it was a well-done presentation—ideal for those with a bit of curiosity about science, but not bad for anyone looking to kill an hour or two on their way to someplace else.

Nick told us that although there has never been visual confirmation of dark matter, scientists believe it must exist because the total visible matter in the universe doesn't exert enough gravity to keep stars spinning around the cores of their galaxies. There has to be another source of gravity that we can't see. And that other gravitational source, he explained, is dark matter.

"So, let me throw some numbers at you," he continued. "Dark matter is thought to make up about eighty percent of all matter in the universe. But since the universe is not comprised solely of matter, that translates to about twenty-five percent of everything. Ordinary matter, on the other hand—what scientists call 'baryonic' matter, like you, me, the cars and buses you drove up here in, and the annoying sweater your aunt wears every Christmas—accounts for only about five percent of the universe."

The only thing missing from Nick's comedy routine was the rim shot.

"So, five plus twenty-five equals thirty. What about the other seventy percent?" a young male voice called out from the rear of the group. "What's it made of?"

Before Nick could answer, the voice of a young female rang out from the back. "And why are these particles called WIMPs and MACHOs?"

"Yeah, what's the deal with all the acronyms?" a third youthful voice blurted out from the same area. I swung my head around to see who was asking all these questions. Had I eaten lunch that day, I no doubt would have lost it at that moment. Standing at the back of the Soudan Mine Underground Physics

Lab, with hardhats on their heads and crazy grins on their faces, were my students—Victor, Charley, Tanya and Amy—who had apparently travelled to the bottom of the Soudan mine in steel cage number two.

"Oh my God!" I said, pushing my way toward them. "What are you doing here?"

"Shhh!" Victor said, putting his index finger up to his lips.

"We'll explain later," Tanya whispered.

I turned back around to Nick. "Sorry, I know these people."

"You never know who you'll run into at the bottom of a mine," he said. I certainly hadn't expected to run into four of my students there but knew I'd need to wait until the tour was over to get the whole story. "Alright, so let me take those questions in order," Nick continued. "The seventy percent of the universe that's not comprised of matter is something we call dark energy. As for WIMPs and MACHOs, we use acronyms for the sake of brevity and because they are so incredibly catchy. Any other questions before we move on?"

"If this matter stuff is dark, how can we see it?" asked a freckle-faced boy wearing a Minnesota Twins baseball cap.

"Excellent question! And in fact, we can't see it, which is why we call it dark matter, because it doesn't absorb or emit light. But we do have ways of detecting it through research projects like this one."

"Are dark energy and dark matter related?" a preteen girl with pigtails asked.

"Yes, they're third cousins twice removed." There were a few chuckles and several groans from the audience. "Just kidding, although they are related in a way because both of them appear to have some connection to gravity. In the case of dark matter, it's gravitational attraction that keeps things together. With dark energy, it's gravitational repulsion that pushes them apart."

And so it went for the rest of the hour, with our physicist-slash-comedian doing his best to provide a peek behind the curtain of the universe without overwhelming anyone with unnecessary details.

"I want to thank all of you for being such an attentive group here today," Nick said, wrapping things up at the end. "Some very good questions, especially from our young physicists-in-training. Now before we all scatter like so many particles of baryonic matter, I want to make sure you know that you are standing just a few feet from one of the coldest spots in the universe. Glad at least some of you brought your winter parkas with you today." Nick asked us to follow him into an adjacent area that housed multiple tanks of liquid nitrogen used in the actual dark-matter experiments. "We've cooled the detector used for hunting dark matter to just a fraction of a degree above absolute zero. Does anyone here happen to know what absolute zero is?"

"Absolute zero is the theoretical coldest temperature anywhere in the universe," Tanya answered.

"Very good, young lady," Nick said with just the slightest hint of condescension. "Bet you don't know what that temperature is?"

For Nick's sake, I was glad he hadn't attached a dollar amount to the wager.

"That would be minus 459.67 degrees Fahrenheit," Tanya answered, as if someone had asked her to add two plus two.

"Somebody did some studying before coming out here today. Now folks, just remember: if anyone asks about your tour of the Soudan Mine Underground Physics Lab, you can tell them it was really cool!" Another groan rippled through the crowd. "Thank you very much, I'll be here all week. Hope you all enjoyed the tour today."

Everyone gave Nick a nice round of applause, and all but the California contingent followed him to the waiting lifts for the trip back to the surface. Once they'd left the area, I turned to my students.

"Are your parents here?"

"No, unfortunately they couldn't make it," Victor answered, just before a door opened at the rear of the lab area.

"Yo, paisan, I see you survived the tour," Rich said, walking in with a big, loopy smile on his face.

"It was touch and go there for a while, but yes we did."

We shared a slightly awkward hug and stepped back to size each other up. It had been almost fifteen years since I'd seen him, but other than perhaps indulging in a bit too much spaghetti carbonara, Rich hadn't changed much. And his rumpled hoodie and cargo pants looked like they could have come straight from his dorm-room closet.

"So, did Nick tell you the one about the proton, neutron, and electron who walk into a bar?" he asked.

"That might have been the only joke he left out."

Rich's eyes widened, and a sound came out of his mouth that I hadn't heard since college—something between a wheeze and a screech that was his version of laughter. It kept going (and going) until Rich mercifully ran out of air. Once he'd started breathing again, he noticed my students.

"Are they with you?" he asked.

"Yes, it seems they are."

"I thought you said no field trip."

"Last minute change of plans," Victor said.

I took care of introductions, and Rich walked us into a

narrow room he called mission control. It looked nothing like any of the NASA installations I'd ever seen, with its bank of mismatched computers shoved together like leftovers at a yard sale. Rich explained that employees at the lab used this equipment to monitor the machinery on-site, while most of the scientists did their work at another location nearby. He took us up a flight of stairs to the employee break room and invited us to play a game of ping pong or enjoy some snacks from the vending machines.

"Wow," said Victor, perusing the available options. "I've never had a bag of chips in an underground mine before."

"Have you had them in a mine that's not underground?" Tanya asked.

"Come to think of it, I have not," Victor admitted.

Rich informed us that the lab director had scheduled a last-minute meeting for three thirty that afternoon, which meant our time with him would be extremely limited unless we wanted to come back that night or the next day.

Since that wasn't possible, I suggested we skip the snacks and ping pong and use the time remaining to talk about the work Rich and his colleagues had been doing.

He agreed, with one minor caveat: He'd been "down in the hole" most of the day, he said, and wanted to get some fresh air before his meeting.

It was much warmer outside than it had been down below, which was a welcome surprise. Another surprise was that Rich sounded more like a shill for the military-industrial complex than someone doing trailblazing work in the field of particle physics. He told us in very general terms about his team's research, as well as their ongoing struggle to secure funding from the government and other sources.

I wasn't sure if he was keeping things vague because my

students were there or for other reasons, but I hadn't flown to Minnesota just to find out that Rich's lab was planning to add a new particle detector sometime the following year.

"So, Rich—and I apologize in advance for being forward— we'd kind of like to know what you guys are doing here that we can't read about on your website."

A little grin snuck across his face. "Oh, so you want to know about the *crazy* shit. Is it okay to say bad words in front of the kids?"

"We won't tell if you won't," Victor said.

"We want to know about the *really* crazy shit," I said. "Like what's going on with electromagnetic fields that Marty said was potentially groundbreaking?"

"Marty said *that*?"

"In those exact words."

Rich broke into another laugh-wheeze combo. This one passed more quickly than the first.

"Well, nothing official."

"Anything unofficial?" I asked.

"Possibly."

"What does that mean?"

"It means everybody's paranoid about making a mistake that could put our funding at risk. That's why we don't want to make any official announcements just yet."

"What is it you don't want to officially announce?" Tanya asked.

Most of the people who had been milling around the area had left, but there were still three or four within earshot. "Anybody up for a walk?" Rich asked.

"As long as you've got time," I said.

"Why don't we head over to the lake. We can talk on the way."

I could see Lake Vermillion poking out between the boulders on our way down the hiking trail. Rich led us to a rocky escarpment jutting out over the water. He stopped walking and admired the view for a few moments, then turned to Tanya. "Sorry, what was your question again?"

"You said there was something you didn't want to announce officially. Are you able to talk about it?"

"Let's just say the WIMPs aren't what we were expecting. You guys know what WIMPs are, right?"

"Weakly Interacting Massive Particles," Victor answered. "It was part of the tour."

"But we already knew anyway," Amy clarified.

"So how are they different?" Charley asked.

"They're a lot bigger than we thought. About five times the gigavolts."

Rich started walking again. The rest of us followed close behind.

"So, instead of seven or eight, you saw, what, thirty-five or forty?" Tanya asked.

"You've trained them well," Rich said, looking at me.

"Trust me, it's a work in progress."

"What do you think it means?" asked Charley.

"We don't know yet. Could be something going on with the particles themselves, or it's possible we're picking up different particles than any we've detected in the past."

"Would that really qualify as groundbreaking?" Victor asked.

Rich smiled. "Now I know why I never went into teaching. These kids are tough."

"Anything else different besides the size of the particles?" Tanya persisted.

Rich paused a moment. "Possibly."

We crossed over to another trail and found ourselves walking alongside a woman and two kids. After a minute or so, Rich brought us to a halt; the trio next to us kept going.

"There's a pine forest near here that's kind of cool," he said, pointing to a remote area off to the right. "There probably won't be anyone else there." At that point, we would have agreed to anything; we just wanted Rich to keep talking—which he did as we headed toward the forest. "Most models of dark matter are based on particles that are different from what we see around us in everyday life. They're not only invisible—they don't interact with ordinary matter. And they don't carry any sort of electric charge. At least that's what we've always thought."

"So, you might be thinking something else?" Charley asked.

"It's still very early."

The forest was nearly dark except for scattered sunbeams that flashed through the trees. "I love it in here," Rich said. "Such a great place to come and get away from everything. Birdlife is incredible." My students nodded their heads enthusiastically, as if they were all seasoned ornithologists. "So . . ." Rich continued, letting the word hang in the air, "we've detected something the past few months that we've never seen before with these particles."

We waited patiently for him to tell us what that something might be, but he kept us in suspense.

"What is it?" Tanya finally asked. "What have you seen?"

"The particles have doughnut-shaped electromagnetic fields around them."

"Electromagnetic as in electricity?" asked Victor.

"Right. The kind of thing you'd normally only expect to see with everyday matter."

Amy looked at me. "So that's what your friend Marty was talking about."

I nodded quickly, not wanting to say or do anything that might spook Rich.

"Although, like I said," he continued, "it's still way too early to know what, if anything, that might mean."

"You said you started seeing this during the past few months. So, like, sometime in August or September?" Tanya asked.

"Middle of August. The fifteenth to be exact."

"Any chance this could have something to do with every-thing that's been happening around the country since right about that time?" asked Victor.

There was a warbling sound overhead. I looked up and caught a glimpse of a yellow blur darting through the branches.

"What are you referring to exactly?"

"The UAEs, CTEs, and ATEs," Tanya answered.

Rich had a blank look on his face.

"You know, the whole alphabet-soup thing," Victor said. "The really, *really* crazy shit."

"You're talking about the beating hearts and all the accidents?"

"Yeah, and the booming sounds before that," said Charley.

"A lot of those things seem to have some link to electricity," Tanya said. "Maybe it's just a coincidence, but that all started right after you began seeing those particles with electromagnetic fields around them."

Rich folded his arms. "That's quite a leap," he said.

"That's what people told Alfred Wegener in the 1920s," Tanya replied, "when he said continental drift broke apart the supercontinent Pangaea three hundred million years ago."

"Until plate tectonics proved that Wegener was right," Amy added.

Rich reached up and grabbed a fistful of pine needles. He rolled them between his hands. "I'm impressed with your knowledge of geology," he said, "but you folks need to slow this train down. As I'm sure Mr. Wegener would tell you if he were still with us, two things can happen at the same time without there being any causal connection between them. Just because there's nice weather on the day of an earthquake doesn't mean sunshine causes earthquakes. I don't care how big the WIMPs are or what kind of electromagnetic fields we're detecting around them. Do you seriously think a bunch of dark matter particles all got together one day and decided to wreak havoc on the United States of America? What kind of Southern California Kool-Aid have these kids been drinking, Andrew?"

I wasn't sure about my students' drinking habits, but I did know they were asking questions and gathering information exactly as I'd taught them to do. Sometimes that process can bruise a few egos along the way. To their credit, they didn't get defensive in the face of Rich's criticism. But quite clearly, a sudden chill had crept into the otherwise temperate Minnesota air. We left the forest without another word and began the trek back. A woman wearing a hardhat broke the silence when she walked by. She seemed to be in a hurry.

"You heading back down?" she asked Rich.

"Yeah, I'll be right there."

"I think G.L. wants to get started a little early."

"Okay, tell him I'm on my way."

"Will do," she called back over her shoulder.

"Sorry, I'm going to have to cut things short," Rich said. "Our director is not known for his patience."

It was probably just as well. Our host had obviously divulged as much as he wanted to and didn't appear interested in further discussion. He led us the rest of the way to the mine entrance and offered a somewhat curt good-bye before heading back down to the physics lab.

❧

"Well that was kind of rude," said Tanya.

"We'll get to that in a minute," I said. "What are you guys doing here?" No response. My four students, who just minutes earlier were bombarding Rich with questions, had now apparently lost the ability to speak. "I'm waiting."

They stared at the ground and said nothing.

Victor finally looked up. "Basically, we just decided we missed one field trip—we weren't going to miss another."

He made it sound so reasonable that it took me a few seconds to respond. "That's fine, except there is no field trip."

"Our parents don't know that," Charley said.

"Your parents think you're on a field trip?"

"My parents are cruising the Greek islands at the moment," Tanya said, tracing an arc in the dirt with the tip of her boot. "So, they have no idea where I am. But my aunt is staying at the house, and she thinks I'm on a field trip."

My brain was flooded with questions.

"How did you convince your parents, or your aunts, or whoever, that you were going to be taking a field trip?"

"Can we get something to eat?" Victor asked. "I'm starving."

"We'll eat after I get some answers."

"Well then, can we at least sit down for this little Q and A?"

We headed over to a nearby picnic table and settled in.

"So, what made them think you were going on a field trip?" I asked again.

"We showed them the paperwork from school," Victor replied.

"What paperwork from school? There isn't any."

"Actually, there is," Tanya said.

"Since when?"

"Since I created it," Charley said.

Considering that Charley had recently created his own search engine, there was no reason to doubt that he could dummy up a school form.

"So, you faked some permission forms, and then what? You forged signatures and basically lied to your families?"

"Yep, that's pretty much what we did," Victor said.

It occurred to me at that point that one member of the foursome hadn't said a word.

"Anything you'd like to add, Amy?"

"I just told my parents the truth about what was going on. How the school wouldn't let you do any field trips, but that this was a really good learning opportunity. And since my father had met you at Family Night—"

"And at the nursery," Tanya chimed in.

"—yeah, at the nursery too. So, anyway, they said I could go."

"And how did the rest of you convince your families there was a field trip when there was no one from school meeting you at the airport?"

"That's where things got a little more challenging," Victor said.

"My older brother is a freshman at Cal State Northridge," said Charley. "He sort of helped us."

"Helped you how?"

"He told my parents that he would take me to the airport and make sure I got on the plane okay."

"That was very generous of him. I imagine he could get into some trouble if your parents found out."

"It wasn't generosity exactly. He's not the greatest student in the world. I offered to help him with one of his term papers and tutor him in his algebra class."

"And I told my aunt that Charley's brother was going to pick us up," Tanya said.

"Yeah, I told my mom the same thing," said Victor. "She was relieved because she had to work and probably couldn't have gotten time off."

"And your father couldn't have taken you?"

"My stepfather," he corrected me. "And no, we haven't seen him recently."

"What about the cost? How did you convince your parents to pay for a trip like this?"

"I told them the trip wasn't required, but that if I didn't go, it might hurt my grade," Charley said.

"My mom said she didn't have the money to send me," said Victor. "I told her not to worry. The school would cover it."

"The school that doesn't know about the field trip? That school?"

"Turns out, I had another source of funding."

"Okay, and that was . . .?"

"My parents have a petty cash fund at the house," Tanya answered. "It's for emergencies when they're gone. So, yeah, I decided fronting Victor the money qualified."

"Even though you were ready to beat his brains in not long ago."

Tanya and Victor exchanged a quick glance.

"It took a little time, but we got past that," Tanya said.

Victor nodded. "Yeah, Tanya told me she'd finish what she started in class if I ever messed with Amy again."

"But we're all great friends now," Amy said with a triumphant smile. "And here we are."

I felt like a chess player running out of moves. "What about a hotel last night? Don't you need someone over twenty-one to even check in? Or did you take a red-eye and skip all that?"

"No, there was only one red-eye, and we knew you'd be on it," Victor said. "So, we flew out earlier and found a youth hostel in Duluth. We were a little under the minimum age, but I talked them into it."

That didn't surprise me; Victor could sell rain gutters in the Sahara. "How did you know I was taking the red-eye?"

"You told us in class," Amy answered.

"I did?"

"Yeah, you told us a lot about your trip," Charley said. "Not everything, but we were able to fill in the blanks."

I thought back to the day when I'd walked them through my itinerary to make them feel like they were part of it. It never occurred to me that they would take that as an opportunity.

"It's not like I wrote it all down and handed it out," I said.

"I remembered what you told us," Tanya replied.

"Of course you did."

Between Charley's computer skills and Tanya, the human tape recorder, this had been pretty easy for them. There was still one more question, but it was for me to answer, not them. "I hope you realize you've put me in a difficult position."

"What do you mean?" Amy asked.

"I mean, what do I do with you? I should probably just call your parents and tell them that you concocted this nonexistent field trip and lied to them. Everyone other than Amy. But if I did that, you'd most likely get suspended, if not expelled. All because you were curious and wanted to learn something. So, that's my little dilemma to work through."

They'd had an answer for everything to that point, but suddenly everyone got quiet again.

"Well, I guess you just have to do what you think is right," Amy said.

"I'm not even sure what that is. If you want to ride along with me to Eau Claire, I guess that would be okay. I'll figure out what to do once we get there."

I started toward the car but realized after a few steps that I was walking by myself. The four of them were still standing right where I'd left them.

"You're not coming with me?" I asked.

"We took a bus up here this morning," Victor said. "We need to get our stuff from the office."

"Oh. I didn't think of that."

"Good thing you've got us here to help you think of things," Tanya said with a sly smile.

CHAPTER 19

I EXPECTED MY students to start taking random shots at Rich the second they got in the car. But they were quiet and seemed a bit preoccupied, perhaps due to the realization that their little stunt could get them into serious trouble. Whatever the reason, their energy was down, and they said very little during the first few minutes of our ride south.

"So, what did you think about what Rich said?" I asked once they began flickering back to life.

"You mean apart from the fact that he was totally condescending and treated us like brats?" asked Tanya.

"Yes, apart from that."

"I thought what he said about the electromagnetic fields was pretty interesting," Charley said.

"Although it did seem strange that he wouldn't even consider the possibility that there could be a connection between that and everything that's been happening the past few months," said Victor.

"Yeah, he was really closed about that," Amy agreed. "J.B.S. Haldane would not have been amused."

After graduating from MIT, Rich had gone on to graduate

school at UC Berkeley, where he earned both his doctorate and the respect of every heavy-hitter in the field of particle physics. I, on the other hand, had a cup of coffee at law school before becoming a high-school science teacher and impressing almost no one, least of all my father. Rich's raw intellect, his ability to crunch numbers and gallop from one equation to another, dwarfed mine. But if you were looking for someone to connect the dots in an unexpected way, Rich was not that guy.

As we got closer to Duluth, thoughts about dark matter and Rich Esposito's shortcomings gave way to other, more immediate concerns. None of us had eaten more than a bag of airline pretzels since leaving Los Angeles. Charley did a quick online search of restaurant options, and we settled on Ramona's Saloon and Grill, which had gotten raves on Yelp and was located just off the highway.

The bubbly hostess with the bouffant hairdo and easy smile greeted us like we were old friends. She was earnest and cheerful, like nearly everyone we had encountered to that point. Even the ads and announcements on the walls were upbeat, like the notice about a church fundraiser for a local family that had fallen on hard times, or the ad for a car battery that included a 200% lifetime guarantee not to leak. I wasn't sure how that improved on a 100% guarantee, but I admired the optimism.

Our hostess led the way to a corner booth that formed a semicircle around a butcher-block table. She handed us menus in which words like fried, creamy, butter, and thick were used like terms of endearment. In my case, that meant hearty meatloaf served with buttery mashed potatoes and golden gravy, a wedge salad drowning in blue-cheese dressing, and a chocolate milkshake thick enough to stand up a straw. Ramona's might not have qualified as gourmet cuisine, but it was the perfect choice on a day when we were teetering on the brink of starvation and primed to worship at the altar of unambiguous comfort food.

Once we'd placed our orders, the conversation turned to Rich Esposito and what we had learned at the Soudan Mine Underground Physics Lab. All of us agreed with Rich that dark-matter particles had likely not banded together in a conspiracy to terrorize America. But when Amy suggested it was equally illogical to attribute the rash of unexplained events to random acts of nature, the consensus around the table evaporated.

"Who really knows?" Victor asked. "I mean, maybe this *has* just been some sort of wacked-out series of wild coincidences."

"I don't see anything coincidental about people's hearts continuing to beat after they've basically died," Tanya countered.

"And even if you forget that the cardiac episodes and crazy number of accidents happened in a lot of the same places," Amy added, "do you really think the connections Charley uncovered between the CTE patients and the accident victims were coincidental?"

"Maybe not coincidental," I said, "but what if they're just a part of life these days? Kind of a variation on the Baconian degrees of separation principle, where everyone is connected to everyone else."

"Baconian? Is that even a word?" Tanya asked as our waitress arrived with several precariously balanced plates of hot deliciousness.

"It is now," I said. "Derived from Bacon, as in Kevin. Not to be confused with the edible variety, whose glorious smell is wafting through the air at this very moment." I inhaled deeply. "Maybe I should have ordered a BLT."

"You can always get one to go," said Amy.

"And by the way," Victor said, "congratulations on being the first teacher to work Kevin Bacon into a discussion of dark matter."

The table erupted in laughter that stopped abruptly when Tanya slammed her glass of lemonade down with a loud crack.

"That lady said 'G.L.,'" she announced to no one in particular.

"What lady?" Victor asked.

"The lady at the mine. The one who came up to Rich right before we left. She said G.L. wanted to start the meeting early."

"Who's G.L.?" asked Charley.

"Rich said he's the director of the lab."

"Okay, so?"

"Remember the guy on your search engine list who was still alive—the one we didn't know anything about other than his name and occupation?"

"Yeah, kind of."

"His name was Gerald Lester. He's a physicist."

Amy's mouth fell open. We had just had another holy shit moment.

⁓

My students had been talking nonstop about the Gerald Lester revelation, but once we pulled back onto Highway 53, the predictable food coma set in, and all four of them conked out. With no prospect of stimulating conversation to keep myself alert, I lowered the window just enough to let the bracing late afternoon air wash over me. I thought about turning on the radio but didn't want to wake anyone. Then I decided that being awakened from a nap was preferable to being wrapped around a tree.

As it turned out, the radio was AM/FM only, and the presets

offered nothing of interest. I worked my way past the rock-and-roll oldies, local news, and lame talk-radio shows until I finally hit audio pay dirt: traditional country music. Not the big-echo, pop-flavored pablum contemporary country stations played, but the genuine article. Everything around us might have been spinning out of control, but inside our cramped subcompact, a measure of much-needed musical sanity had been restored—and my energy along with it.

∿

Compared to the charmingly indigenous Ramona's Saloon and Grill, Eau Claire's Hometown Inn was unabashedly derivative. There was nothing really wrong with it, other than the fact that it was indistinguishable from every other antiseptic lodging option on the American motel landscape. Once we'd navigated our way through the registration process, I was less interested in being a motel critic than getting a good night's sleep, assuming that would even be possible on the rollaway cot the pimply-faced kid from housekeeping brought up to the room I'd be sharing with Charley and Victor.

I called Joanna to let her know I'd arrived in Wisconsin with some unexpected guests. She declined to offer any specific advice but did say I would probably get blamed as an accessory if the real story ever came out. That had occurred to me also, but I still couldn't bring myself to turn my students in and subject them to the shit show that would almost certainly follow.

What the four of them had done was wrong, but there was at least an element of truth in the way they had represented the weekend getaway to their families. They had said they would be visiting the site of an advanced scientific study in Minnesota, as well as the home of a former CTE patient in Wisconsin, and that they would do both under the supervision of their science teacher—all of which was true. And even if I drove them to the airport and put them on the next flight to LA, that would still mean a next-day departure, which would get them home just a few hours earlier than if they flew back with me Sunday night. I shot a quick email to Doris Wilkinson letting her know that I wouldn't be visiting alone—and informed my four very relieved stowaways that I wouldn't be turning them in after all.

⌘

As someone who had spent most of my adult professional life in the company of teenagers, I probably should have been familiar with their dietary habits. But I was surprised when my students informed me—less than three hours after our late-afternoon feast at Ramona's—that they were hungry again. They also let me know that, while they had appreciated the novelty of Ramona's menu, they were leaning toward something more "normal" for dinner—which was code for salt, grease, and heat lamps. We ended up at the closest fast-food place within walking distance. Which is not to say we walked there—just that we could have had everyone not pleaded exhaustion and badgered me into driving.

My ravenous travel companions replenished themselves with nearly every item on the menu that didn't include the word *salad*. I half expected them to pass out after that, but they had enough energy left to hunker down with their assorted mobile devices. At some point, Charley looked up from his screen and pointed to a spot on the floor.

"What is that?"

"What is what?" Amy asked.

"That thing. It looks like it's moving."

"Warning—advanced sleep deprivation may cause hallucinations," Tanya cautioned.

Victor walked over to take a closer look.

"It's probably just dirt or something stuck to the floor," said Amy.

"I swear it just moved," Charley said.

By that point, all of us were looking.

"Charley's right," Victor announced. "It's one of those bugs that rolls itself into a little ball. What are they called again?"

"I believe the technical term is roly-poly," Tanya said.

The sole of Victor's shoe came down on our rotund visitor with the swift finality of a judge's gavel.

"Actually, I believe the technical term is floorkill," he said.

"Why did you do that?" I asked.

"Do what?"

"Kill that whatever-it-is."

"Because I felt like it. Since when do you need a reason to step on a bug?"

"It's not like he ever did anything to you."

All eyes were suddenly on me.

"Looks like Charley's not the only one who needs some sleep," Amy said.

"Sorry, Victor. I didn't mean to snap at you like that. I just felt kind of bad for the poor little guy."

"Whatever."

I felt the sudden need to change the subject. "Anybody want dessert? My treat."

"Ice cream, ice cream, ice cream," everyone chanted in gluttonous unison.

Nothing like a little sugar fix to mend fences after a very long day.

∽

I had spent nearly every night of the previous fifteen years in the company of my wife, mostly at home in Altadena. So, it felt more than a little odd to be sharing a room with a pair of teenagers in a Wisconsin motel. But any awkwardness I might have felt was brief because sleep arrived quickly. Sometime during the night, the fog of slumber transported me back to my tenth birthday party at Garfield Park. The Olympics-inspired athletic events and closing ceremonies were exactly as I remembered them. So, too, was the family of snails grouped together on the grass. Under Danny Adler's direction, my birthday guests showered the tiny creatures with salt, just as they'd done years earlier at my party. But unlike that day at Garfield Park, this time I refused to join them. Instead, I grabbed Danny by the shoulders and shook him hard.

"Why did you do that?!" I screamed.

"Because I felt like it!" He joined the other kids in a chorus of "ice cream, ice cream, ice cream," which morphed into "Andrew, Andrew, Andrew."

They desperately wanted me to dump salt on that snail, and I was just as determined not to do it. The salt packet ripped open on its own, its tiny crystalline granules spilling out in slow motion and falling harmlessly to the ground. When I looked around, my friends had vanished. A pair of new and seemingly healthy snails flanked the original survivor. Moments later, there were dozens more, then hundreds, and then thousands, splayed out in all directions as far as I could see. I reached down to pick one up and felt nothing but air. I tried again, with the same result. After several more failed attempts, I realized I wasn't looking at actual snails but at projections of some kind.

I woke up just before three o'clock, unsure at first where I was. There was little hope of getting back to sleep if I simply lay there, but there weren't a lot of good alternatives at that hour. Phone in hand, I felt my way through the darkness into the bathroom, where I slumped down on the floor. The acrylic bathtub felt smooth and cool as I leaned back against it and raised my phone up to eye level. My fingers raced across the glass keyboard, scrambling to outrun sleep's impending ambush and transcribe what I had just dreamt.

⤙

The banging on the door was loud and rapid-fire, like an early morning drug bust.

"Open up!" Victor said.

I pulled myself up from the bathroom floor and stumbled out, then shuffled over to my cot and slouched down on the mattress.

"Is this yours?" Victor asked a few minutes later, standing in front of me with my phone in his hand. I glanced up and nodded, struggling to jumpstart my brain after four hours of fitful sleep wedged between the bathtub and the toilet.

The five of us met up in the hall about an hour later. Charley, who had become our unofficial restaurant concierge, pulled out his phone and found a local foodie blog. After scanning the available options, he suggested a breakfast place called The Nuance, located just across the Chippewa River.

There was a line of people that extended out onto the sidewalk when we got there, but it moved quickly, and we were seated in just a few minutes. The décor was minimalist and uncluttered, with polished concrete floors and natural light streaming in through a pair of skylights. The menu offered a range of eclectic options, including chorizo breakfast burritos, which all four of my students ordered, and lemon-ricotta hotcakes, which was my choice. We might have been in the heart of flyover country, but this could just as easily have been a trendy eatery in Old Town Pasadena.

We talked while we ate, mostly about what to expect at the Wilkinson house. This was a family in the throes of a devastating loss, which meant my four travel partners would need to modulate their usual exuberance. With that topic covered, I moved on to a detailed description of my Garfield Park birthday dream. None of the kids had the slightest interest in any of it until I got to the part about the snails.

"I knew you were upset when I stepped on that thing at dinner last night," Victor said, "but I didn't think you'd turn it into a full-blown nightmare."

"When I was a kid, I actually had an Olympics-theme birthday party where a bunch of snails ended up just like the ones in my dream."

"No disrespect to your childhood memories, but can we possibly wait until after breakfast to talk about snail guts?" Tanya requested.

"How about if we forget about their guts but talk about something else snail related?" Amy suggested.

"What is up with this snail obsession?" asked Tanya.

"Sorry," Amy said, "but that snail dream reminded me of something my dad said a few weeks ago."

"You and your father talk about snails?" Victor asked. "You are so weird."

"No," Amy laughed. "We were talking about all the electrical stuff that's been going on."

"So, what did he say?" I asked.

"He was talking about how everything has kind of a signature. Like a chemical or electrical fingerprint."

"How did my snail dream remind you of that?"

"I was just thinking that maybe the snail in your dream duplicated his signature and made virtual copies of himself."

"Which confused his attackers and allowed him to survive."

"Exactly."

"Did somebody here spike the food?" Victor asked. "You guys are *both* weird."

❧

For the residents of Eau Claire, Wisconsin, the death of Tracey Wilkinson was more than somebody else's sad story to be viewed from a distance. It was a deeply felt, personal loss for everyone who lived in that city. When we drove past Tracey's high school, the first thing we saw was the massive digital billboard that loomed over the front lawn. Under normal circumstances, its LED clusters would have displayed all the latest details about upcoming events, like football games, SAT exams, and the holiday recess. But the towering sign had recently come to serve a very different purpose. It was now a rallying point for the entire Eau Claire community, spelling out a message that was heartbreaking in its simplicity: "For Tracey . . . We Believe."

Turning onto Laurel Street, we drove past rows of leafless elm trees and neatly trimmed shrubs. The mostly single-story, wood-frame houses were unpretentious and welcoming. Walls and fences were almost nonexistent. Once we parked the car, Tanya led us up the curving brick path to the Wilkinsons' front door and rang the doorbell, which triggered a cascade of chimes. The doormat was dirty and worn, but the words "Home Sweet Home" were still visible, framed by a pattern of faded roses.

When Doris opened the door, I was struck by how much smaller and hunched over she looked in person. Her cheekbones rose slightly to reveal a weary smile that could not hide the pain of the past several weeks.

"It's so good to have you all here," she said. "Please come in." She took our coats and sweaters and hung them on a rack by the door. "I'm glad the weather has been so mild. For you to come all this way . . . well, it's just such a blessing."

"We wouldn't have missed it for anything," Tanya said. She pulled the obelisk from the towel I'd packed it in and handed it to Doris. "This is for you."

"Oh, my Lord," Doris said, her eyes glistening behind a veil of tears. "It looks like it's reaching up to my baby in heaven." Her fingers traced the contour of the plexiglass structure as it narrowed toward the top. "I will treasure this forever. I can't tell you what it means that you would start a scholarship in Tracey's name. Thank you so much. For everything."

"It was the least we could do," Victor said, revealing a sensitivity I never knew existed.

Doris placed the obelisk on a small table beside the coat rack. "I do hope you brought your appetites," she said. "I made us some lunch."

"If you've ever been around teenagers," I said, "you know they bring their appetites wherever they go."

Even if all four of my students hadn't glared at me, I should have known that was the wrong thing to say. The last thing I'd meant to do was question whether Doris had had experience with teenagers, considering she had just buried one of her own. If she was hurt by my unintended gaffe, she didn't let on. All she said was that she hoped we could wait a few minutes to eat because she wanted to show us around the house.

As we followed Doris from room to room, I felt the presence of God everywhere: in the crucifixes above the doors, the framed religious homilies on the walls—even the pictures of Jesus on the refrigerator magnets. This was a home in which God was not a visitor but a member of the family. I might have felt uncomfortable in a place like that at one time in my life. But on that day, at least, I could respect and appreciate the Wilkinsons' beliefs even if I didn't share them.

Doris walked us through the narrow hallway leading to the bedrooms, confiding along the way that she sometimes felt like she'd lost both her children. She told us that her son, Bobby, had recently dropped out of community college to join the army and was stationed at a base in Georgia awaiting deployment to the Middle East. When we walked past the closed door of what I presumed was the master bedroom, Doris apologized that her husband, Earl, would not be joining us. She explained that he had taken a leave of absence from his job as an electrical lineman and had been sleeping a lot.

When we reached Tracey's room, my first thought was that we had wandered into a child's dollhouse. Pink throw pillows piled up on a ruffled comforter covered the top half of the bed. A watercolor painting that read "God Loves You" was pinned to a corkboard just above Tracey's desk, which was adorned with small plastic boxes for jewelry and other keepsakes. Doris told us with a mix of pride and terrible sadness that Tracey made sure her room was absolutely perfect every morning before she left for school, including the day she left for the last time.

We ended our tour of the house in the kitchen, sliding into the built-in booth that Doris said had always been the family's main gathering place. She set out a platter of sandwiches and asked each of the kids about themselves and their goals in life.

This was not the idle chitchat of someone trying to be polite. Doris wanted to get to know each of them as well as she could in the short time we had together that day. Somehow, they knew this was not the time for their usual brand of snarky teenage humor. They answered every one of her questions with the utmost sincerity and respect. Maybe it was the unmistakable presence of God in that house, but they were as close to angels as I'd ever seen them.

When all of us had finished our sandwiches, Doris began clearing the table. She stopped suddenly and apologized for not asking me about *my* life. I felt almost guilty telling her that Joanna and I were expecting our first child, but she couldn't have been more gracious. "You'll be a wonderful father," she said as she opened the oven and the welcoming aroma of chocolate chip cookies flooded the room. She suggested that we move to the den to watch a home movie while they cooled.

We walked down a single step onto the magenta shag carpet, but it felt like we had walked into another world. The walls were covered with dark vinyl paneling, and a mounted deer's head looked down from above the fireplace, whose bricks had been painted white. Doris fumbled with the multiple remotes lined up on the massive coffee table and apologized for not fully under-standing how to use them. "That's always been Earl's job," she explained. She finally managed to turn on the old Magnavox console and inserted a video cassette.

For the next twenty minutes, we watched Tracey Wilkinson's life unfold before us. Had she still been alive, this would have been just another home movie about a kid growing up—no different from the millions of others that parents everywhere inflict on family and friends. But Tracey Wilkinson was not alive and would not be growing up. And that changed everything.

If that video just kept playing, I thought to myself, maybe the little girl on the screen might somehow keep smiling, talking, and running—and never stop. That was my hope, at least, until the inevitable moment when the video ended, and that fleeting possibility ended with it.

When we said our goodbyes that day, my students and I knew that we would probably never see Doris again, would never meet Earl or Bobby, and would never again come that close to feeling like we had known Tracey. But we also knew that none of us would ever forget that day on Laurel Street.

Nobody said much during the drive to the Minneapolis-St. Paul Airport. I think we all understood that the usual clichés people lean on to make sense of things that make no sense were plainly inadequate, and I was glad no one had felt the need to invoke them. It wasn't until we got to the car-rental lot at the airport that Tanya found a simple way to sum up what those last two days had meant. "So long, Minnesota and Wisconsin," she said, clutching the bag of chocolate chip cookies that Mrs. Wilkinson had given us on our way out the door. "It wasn't exactly easy to get here. But I'm really glad we came."

CHAPTER 20

MY FELLOW TRAVELERS and I were so exhausted by the time we boarded the plane that we did little more than gaze out our windows and fiddle with our phones for the next three and a half hours. Actually, they did the bulk of the fiddling. I shut my phone off and slept most of the way home, unaware that massive quantities of shit were about to hit the proverbial fan. Once we landed, Charley informed me that his brother had texted a heads-up during the flight. Apparently, he had let something slip to his parents that afternoon, which led to the complete unravelling of the story Charley and his classmates had so meticulously crafted about their weekend field trip.

I spotted Joanna the moment we walked through the security doors. She was standing with David Phan amid the usual airport assortment of limo drivers, luggage carts, and lovestruck teens clutching bouquets—as well as a small contingent of Banneker parents awaiting the return of their children. I was working my way toward her, trying to keep an eye on my students, when I spotted a blurred figure closing in from the side. A split second later, Janet Del Rio pushed past Joanna and stepped in front of me.

"What in the name of God were you thinking? Do you have

any idea what you did?" I ignored the questions and attempted to walk around her, but she blocked me a second time. "Child endangerment, gross negligence. And that's just for starters. You should pray you're not charged with kidnapping."

Based on my conversation with Charley, I knew there might be blowback from parents or school officials at some point; I had no idea it would start the minute we got off the plane.

"It's not his fault," Charley said as he tapped Del Rio on the shoulder. "He had nothing to do with it."

Del Rio spun around. "Don't you touch me, young man!"

"Go stand outside with your father, now!" Charley's mother said. She pulled her son aside sharply and walked out with him.

Tanya's aunt and Victor's mother led their youngsters away without a word.

Amy, who had been standing beside her father, bolted in front of Del Rio. "You don't understand!" she pleaded.

"No, you don't understand!" Del Rio shot back.

David Phan draped a protective arm around his sobbing daughter and walked her toward the exit.

With children and family members out of the combat zone, Del Rio and I locked eyes and circled each other like fighters in a cage match.

Joanna inserted herself between us and extended her right hand to Dr. Del Rio. "Excuse me, I don't think we've met. I'm Joanna Robbins, Andrew's wife."

Del Rio stepped around her like she was invisible.

"You are on administrative leave effective immediately!" she barked, thrusting her index finger in my face. "You are not to communicate with your students, nor are you to set foot on school grounds until further notice. Is that clear?"

"Very."

I was about to tack on something more colorful to my response but restrained myself and walked off with Joanna. Only moments earlier my wife had tried to play peacemaker; now she was spewing out seething threats about lawsuits. By the time we got home, an email had arrived from Del Rio informing me that the board of directors would take the matter up at their Thursday night meeting, which I would be permitted to attend. Until then I was not to return to school.

"That bitch has been out to get you from day one," Joanna fumed.

"Unfortunately, Banneker is a private school. They can pretty much do whatever they want."

"Bullshit! No, they can't!"

I had withstood the initial onslaught from Dr. Del Rio. Whether I would be able to avoid the scourge of friendly fire was still to be determined.

I woke up the next morning feeling like I'd been sentenced to house arrest; the only thing missing was the ankle bracelet. I spent most of the morning doing research into the arcane legal details of nonprofit boards, reminding myself in the process why I had dropped out of law school. I knew I wanted to walk into the board room Thursday night with something solid to hold onto—if not a fully scripted speech, at least some talking points. What complicated things was that I didn't know how the board would come at me. Would they limit their inquiry to events that had taken place the previous weekend, or would they broaden their fishing expedition to include everything I had said or done over the entire semester? Either way, I knew that I would likely be the guest of honor at a public execution Thursday night.

Joanna had left the house that morning only slightly less enraged than she was the night before. I'd hoped that a day at work might temper her fury somewhat but wasn't sure what to expect when she walked in the door, just after six.

"Hi!" I said from the kitchen, where I was making dinner.

"So, I was talking to one of my partners this morning—"

"Glad to hear you're on speaking terms." I offered a quick kiss, which she grudgingly accepted.

"—Who informed me that, according to California law, the board-meeting agenda can't be altered this close to the meeting date."

"Okay, and why is that significant?"

"Because the board can only take action on items that are on the agenda, which your employment status is not. They can discuss whatever they want to, but they can't do anything about it if it's not on the agenda."

"So, in other words, they can trash me verbally, but they can't actually terminate me until later."

"Correct. Next week at the earliest."

I wasn't sure that delay was necessarily a good thing, but I wasn't about to get into a debate with my wife at that point.

"How was your day otherwise?" I asked.

"Terrific. Just great," she said without a hint of conviction.

"I made us some pasta and a spinach salad."

"I really don't have much of an appetite."

"You need to eat though, don't you?" I pointed to her stomach, which was still impressively flat.

"We'll be fine, Andrew."

When Joanna stitched my name onto the end of a sentence, especially with a side of extra sarcasm, it was best to smile and move on. In this case she was the one who moved on, heading off to the bedroom to change out of her work clothes.

With our dinner no longer a priority, I filled Largo's bowl with his. I was watching him tear through that when a text arrived from Tanya.

"Have you heard what happened?"

That could have meant almost anything. "At school?" I texted back.

"No, in the real world. Seriously crazy shit."

I had no idea what she was referring to, but the "seriously" got my attention. I opened the browser on my phone and spotted the news story that had obviously prompted her text. Joanna walked in from the bedroom just as I finished reading it; she ambled over to the counter and helped herself to a leaf of spinach salad.

"I thought you weren't hungry."

"I'm not. Just being polite." She grabbed a pair of tongs and politely helped herself to some bowtie pasta. "So, how was your first day on hiatus?"

"Pretty uneventful. I spent most of it thinking about what I want to say to the board Thursday night."

"I hope what you'll say is that the real problem at Banneker is Janet Del Rio."

"That may be true, but there's more going on here than a self-serving principal trying to take down a rebellious science teacher."

"Well, yeah, there is the little matter of your students sneaking off to the middle of the country last weekend."

"I was thinking more about what happened after they got home."

"You mean the airport greeting from Del Rio?"

"No. I just found out that forty-one people were killed in

Eau Claire, Wisconsin today." The color drained from Joanna's face. "There was a chain-reaction highway crash, an electrical storm that triggered a mudslide, and an explosion in a meat-packing plant."

"Oh my God."

"Things like that have been happening all over the country for months, but until now, Eau Claire had been spared. Then, the day after we get back, all hell breaks loose. Almost like tit for tat."

"You just lost me. What's like tit for tat?"

"I mean, think about it. Once we figured out that military testing or other human activity wasn't causing all this stuff, everyone assumed that some sort of natural force must be responsible."

"Natural force, meaning . . ."

"Like solar activity, geomagnetic shifts. Some natural source of energy run amok. Except the things that happened today in Wisconsin were not natural."

"And you know this because . . .?"

"We were just there . . . and the very next day forty-one people are dead. Just like that. I'm sorry—that can't just be a coincidence."

"Coincidences do happen, you know."

"As our president likes to remind us."

"But even if you're right—if it's not something natural, and it's not caused by people, what else is there?"

"I don't know. I don't have an explanation. Not yet, anyway. But I'm starting to think it happened on purpose." Joanna looked at me like I'd just lost my mind. "I don't know what that purpose is, but whatever it is, the so-called accidents that happened back there today happened for a reason. There was nothing accidental about any of it."

CHAPTER 21

THE BOARDROOM AT the Benjamin Banneker School was little more than a dusty shell when I first saw it taking shape amid a chorus of circular saws and clanking hammers early that summer. But once finished, it had become the jewel of the campus, with a hand-carved conference table the length of a small aircraft carrier, walls of imported cherry wood, and a massive chandelier that cast shards of light in every direction. The only thing missing was the man who had made it all possible. I couldn't help but wonder how things might have turned out if Simeon Marshall had been at the helm of Banneker that semester.

When I looked around the room that night, I was surprised at how few people I recognized in the visitors' gallery, where Joanna and I were seated. There were a couple of parents I recalled from Family Night, including David Phan, who gave me an earnest thumbs-up when we made eye contact. Janet Del Rio and Margaret Halloran were, not surprisingly, seated front and center in the first row. One person I knew exceedingly well was the beguiling individual to my immediate left, who also happened to be my wife. Joanna had been my staunchest supporter and legal advisor throughout this entire sordid episode, although at that moment she seemed more focused on her phone settings than anything else.

At exactly seven o'clock, Joanna pointed to a last-second straggler who had entered the chamber just as portly and patrician board chairman C. Richard Davidoff was about to call the meeting to order. This wasn't just any late arrival—it was my father, primed to witness the vultures of community decency pick away at the carcass formerly known as his son. I knew he was capable of almost anything, but his decision to come and watch the carnage in person was a new low.

Once the meeting started, everything went strictly by the numbers. Over the course of the next two hours, we endured a mind-numbing onslaught of reports, analysis, and discussion covering everything from state-accreditation issues to the environmental impact of a proposed new parking structure. The last remaining item on the agenda, tucked in just before "Adjournment," was "Other." That sounded harmless enough; I was beginning to wonder if they'd forgotten about me. Shortly after 9:00 p.m., the chair asked if there was any other business that needed to be discussed. Vice-Chair Harold McDuff, a spindly man with thinning gray hair and a dyspeptic disposition, replied that there was one additional matter for the board to consider. He then requested that Dr. Del Rio step forward.

Apparently, they hadn't forgotten me after all.

Del Rio lumbered up to the lectern and slipped on a pair of bifocals. There were no introductory remarks, no attempts at diplomacy. The interim principal turned to a bookmarked page in her black leather binder and launched into a summary of what she called my "semester-long series of errors, lapses, and oversights." These included my decision made "without appropriate consultation" to de-emphasize state testing preparation, my "callous unwillingness" to provide students with reasonable opportunities to explore viewpoints and perspectives different from my own, and, finally, the sequence of "staggeringly bad decisions" I had made prior to and during the previous weekend in Minnesota and Wisconsin, which she described as my "ultimate wrongdoing."

I knew going into the meeting that I would be skewered for not alerting authorities and parents when my students showed up in Minnesota; I wasn't expecting anyone to blame me for the fact that they went there in the first place. But that's exactly what Del Rio was doing, and she was just getting started.

"Within the first few weeks of the school year, Mr. Siegel distributed permission slips to his Integrated Science students for a class field trip to Bakersfield—one that I canceled because it was ill-advised and would have been counterproductive. Instead of disposing of the forms, as he should have done, he kept them in his classroom in full view of his students. With just the slightest modification, those forms could be altered to say just about anything, almost like blank checks. And lo and behold, that's exactly what happened. One of his more industrious students was able to revise the original dates and locations and substitute new details about a fictitious field trip to Minnesota and Wisconsin."

"I'm surprised she doesn't blame you for world hunger," Joanna whispered.

"Give her time."

"But that was just the first of Mr. Siegel's poor decisions," Del Rio continued. "He also set the stage for what took place this past weekend by laying out his full itinerary for the entire class. Several of the youngsters had already expressed interest in going with him, and yet, Mr. Siegel thought nothing of whetting their appetites still further by giving them all the details they would need to make that possible. And with the forged permission slips looking every bit as legitimate as real ones, there was no reason for parents to suspect that there was anything improper going on."

"Unbelievable," Joanna muttered.

"Now, you may be thinking that what happened last weekend was not solely the fault of Mr. Siegel, and you would be correct. The students themselves bear some responsibility as well, and they will face appropriate disciplinary action in the very near future. But the person who is primarily to blame is the man who has shown a disturbing pattern of arrogance and insubordination throughout his time at this school. I am, of course, referring to Andrew Siegel. And while it gives me no pleasure to do so, I must recommend that the board remove Mr. Siegel from his position on the Benjamin Banneker School faculty, bar him from entering the school grounds, and not permit any further contact between Mr. Siegel and the students who attend this school. Thank you."

Del Rio stepped away from the lectern and conferred briefly with Mrs. Halloran before returning to the microphone. "Mr. Chairman, one of our parents had intended to make a statement in support of this recommendation but, in light of the late hour, has decided not to do so."

The board chair covered his microphone and whispered something to the vice-chair, who nodded.

"Thank you, Dr. Del Rio," Chairman Davidoff said, leaning in toward the mic. "As you know, the board is unable to formally consider your request during tonight's proceedings. We will, however, reconvene telephonically next week and revisit this matter at that time. In the interest of fairness, however, we would like to offer Mr. Siegel or anyone else who wishes to speak on his behalf the opportunity to do so before we adjourn."

I was not expecting a show of support from anyone that

night, so I was surprised when David Phan stood up at his seat in the row behind us.

"Excuse me, Mr. Chairman. My daughter is a student in Mr. Siegel's Integrated Science Studies class. Can I say something?"

"Yes, of course," the chair said, motioning to the podium. David made his way across the aisle and walked to the speaker's stand. "What is your name, sir?"

"David Phan. P-H-A-N. I'm Amy Phan's father."

"Alright, Mr. Phan, the floor is yours."

David took a sip from the bottle of water he had brought up with him. "Thank you, Mr. Chairman. My wife and I moved to the United States when we were both quite young. We knew that we wanted to have a family someday and wanted to raise our children in a place where freedom is guaranteed. Not just political freedom, but the freedom of opportunity that comes from education. From my own experience, a good education depends on many things, but nothing more important than teachers who can inspire their students. We have been fortunate to find a teacher like that here at Banneker. His name is Andrew Siegel."

I peeked over at Joanna; her eyes were riveted on David.

"Since our daughter, Amy, joined Mr. Siegel's Integrated Science class, she has been more inquisitive and motivated than I can ever remember. It would be a terrible loss, not only for Amy but for all of our children, if Mr. Siegel was not allowed to continue teaching here. Thank you."

"Wow," Joanna said. "I knew I liked him."

David's statement might not have changed any minds on the board of directors, but it prompted Janet Del Rio to confer a second time with Margaret Halloran, before addressing the chair.

"Mr. Chairman, I said earlier that one of our parents who had planned to speak tonight would not be doing so. But with the chair's permission, she has decided that she would like to address the board, if that might be possible."

"Alright, that's fine."

Mrs. Halloran approached the speaker's stand. She leaned in to the microphone and tapped it twice, then recoiled when it made a high-pitched screeching sound.

"What is your name, please?" the chair asked.

"I'm Margaret—Mrs. Frederick—Halloran." She grabbed onto the sides of the lectern. "My son, Lawrence, Lawrence Halloran, was previously a student in Mr. Siegel's class, which he no longer is. He's still a student. But he's no longer a student in that same class. The one that Mr. Siegel teaches. Sorry. I'm not used to talking in front of people."

"That's alright, ma'am. You just take your time."

Mrs. Halloran took a deep breath and cleared her throat. "What I wanted to say was that, first of all, I appreciated what the last gentleman who talked before me was saying about how—when they came here to this country—it was because they wanted to be somewhere that has freedom. I think that's why all of us are here. Or, in the case of our ancestors, why they came here in the first place. But I think that being free also means that you should be able to practice what your religious beliefs are and be able to say something in class that you might have learned at home or at church. In my opinion, if a teacher does not allow you to do that, then he is not allowing you to have the freedom to have your own beliefs. Even if those beliefs are not the same ones that he has." She looked up at Chairman Davidoff. "That's really all I wanted to say. Thank you very much."

Mrs. Halloran returned to her seat and an effusive welcome from Dr. Del Rio. She would never win a public speaking contest, but she got her point across, and I actually agreed with it.

Regardless of what I thought about Lawrence's suggestion that we include creationism in our discussion of the origins of life, he had every right to voice his opinion. And he deserved an answer that wasn't laced with sarcasm.

The chair looked down at his watch. "Thank you to both of the parents who have shared their views here tonight," he said. "The board always appreciates hearing from the families of our students and other members of the community. We are, however, mindful of the time. So, if there are no further comments, we invite Mr. Siegel to come up and offer any thoughts that he may have about this matter, if he would like to do so."

I was about to walk to the podium when I noticed that my father was standing at his seat near the back of the visitors' gallery.

"Excuse me, Mr. Chairman," he said. "I'm probably not the Mr. Siegel you were referring to. I am Arthur Siegel, Andrew's father. If the board might allow me to, I'd like to say something."

"Alright, but we would request that you keep your comments as brief as possible."

"Yes, of course."

Mr. Siegel, Sr. walked past Joanna and me without making eye contact with either of us. When he reached the lectern, he surveyed the room as if preparing to address a jury like the trial lawyer he once was.

"Thank you, Mr. Chairman. I'm sure most of you are thinking that, as Andrew's father, I will naturally be siding with him in this matter." He paused. "But you would be wrong to assume that." Joanna dug her fingernails into my forearm. I hoped the pain might provide some distraction from whatever my father was about to say. "As I'm sure he would tell you, Andrew and I have disagreed about many things over the years, including his choice of professions.

"But say what you want to about him—and believe me, I've said a great deal, much of which has not been complimentary—anyone who would question Andrew's commitment to his students would be making a very serious mistake. And to those who would criticize him for not allowing their personal religious beliefs to influence classroom instruction—I would ask, what about other people's beliefs? Are you as committed to protecting their spiritual views as you are to advocating your own? In a class not about theology but about science.

"The fact is, there is not just one religion or a single view of God. There are many, and they all have their place, be it in a church, temple, mosque, or any other house of worship. But not in a school that was never meant to serve as the mouthpiece of a single faith. The classes that my son teaches here are not intended to shape his students' spiritual view of the universe but to inform their scientific understanding of it. Not because he is opposed to them having a spiritual view, but because that's not what he's here to teach. And, presumably, that's not what they are here to learn."

Del Rio bolted from her seat. "Mr. Chairman, the members of this board are providing governance for a private, not a public school. Therefore, a religious perspective in the classroom is not only permissible but perfectly appropriate. I don't believe any of our board members need a lecture from Mr. Siegel about the separation of church and state."

"That's exactly what they need!" my father fired back. "The two are rightfully kept separate, not because one is more valid than the other but to ensure that neither sullies the other. But that is not the point of these proceedings, and you very well know that. This is about money, greed, and ambition. Nothing more." He turned to the board chair. "Mr. Chairman, let me add in closing—if there is anyone so offended by anything my son has said or done that they would withhold their financial support from this school, I will personally replace any funding shortfall that results. Thank you, Mr. Chairman and members of the board."

And with that, he stepped away from the lectern and walked out of the room.

"We lawyers are pretty damned eloquent, aren't we?" Joanna said, releasing her grip on my arm.

A restless murmur rose from the visitors' gallery. Chairman Davidoff rapped his gavel sharply.

"If Mr. *Andrew* Siegel would care to make a statement," the chair said, "he is welcome to address the board at this time. And we will then adjourn for the evening."

That was my cue, but I needed to take a few seconds after what had just happened. Talk about a holy shit moment. I hadn't expected my father to even be at the meeting, much less make a statement on my behalf. Now, though, I had to put all that aside and focus on my own statement. I leaned forward and stood up, a bit unsteady at first, and began walking toward the speaker's stand with a slew of thoughts in my head that I still hadn't fully stitched together. When I reached the lectern, I stole a quick look at Joanna. She sat straight up in her chair and nodded her head slowly.

It was time.

"Thank you, Mr. Chairman and members of the board, for giving me the opportunity to speak with you tonight. I'd like to take a moment to thank someone who is not with us this evening: Dr. Simeon Marshall, the founder of the Benjamin Banneker School and the man who recruited me to teach here. Without his vision and perseverance, this school would not have been possible.

"I also want to thank Dr. Janet Del Rio for doing what she believes is right. Although Dr. Del Rio and I have not always agreed on everything, one thing I hope we do agree on is that our students must always come first. We are here to serve their needs, not the other way around. I have tried to conduct myself with that in mind every day since I joined the Banneker faculty earlier this year. Obviously, there are some who feel that I have fallen short, and they have brought some serious charges against me tonight. I would like nothing more than to respond to those accusations. But rather than offer a point by point rebuttal, I'd like to ask you to join me and take a step back, so that we might bring some perspective to all this.

"There are many things that we all take for granted—some of them very basic. We expect that the Sun will rise each day and provide us with warmth and light. That there will be sufficient oxygen in our atmosphere for us to breathe. And that the rules and laws of the universe that we trust and depend on will always be here. Of course, even with those rules and laws, we know that there are ongoing threats to this planet and all who live here. Just ask the dinosaurs. Nonetheless, most of us go to bed each night believing that the world will still be here when we wake up the next morning.

"The good news is that, as of *this* morning at least, our world was still here. But the mysterious events of the past several months have left us wondering what may come *tomorrow* morning, or the morning after that. And because no one has yet come up with a credible explanation for those events, we are left with little more than hope that everything will be okay. That this will all turn out to be some enormous cosmic mistake that will somehow correct itself.

"But consider for a moment the possibility that this is not

a mistake—an astronomical aberration of some kind—and that there may, instead, be something that wants to harm us, perhaps in a way that we can't even fathom. Something that operates at a level not only beyond what we know, but what we *can* know. Something that preys upon bewildered humans like a mischievous child with a packet of salt preys upon an unsuspecting snail. And then consider the possibility that this something is not a thing but an energy or a force of some kind. Perhaps a warped and perverse form of what we call nature. What if this version of nature isn't natural at all but something sentient, with thoughts, plans, intent—and a really big saltshaker?

"Based on what we've seen thus far, this force or energy appears to impose its will through the use of electricity—in this case, using it to tease and torment us. First, with mysterious sounds that no one can explain. Then with a twisted form of immortality in which human hearts are reanimated, but the patients never recover. And finally, with an onslaught of tragedy and devastation unlike any we've ever seen.

"The question, of course, is why? Why would it do these things? And why now? Have we done something to anger it? Do we have something that it wants or needs? Or is it doing all this just because it can? Again, think of the child with a packet of salt, who ends the life of an innocent creature merely to amuse himself. It may be that we are simply the designated victims in a vast celestial game or simulation—played by an opponent more intelligent and powerful than any we can possibly imagine, according to rules we can't begin to understand.

"In the 1920s, British geneticist J.B.S. Haldane wrote that the universe is not only queerer than we suppose, but queerer than we *can* suppose. Those words are as meaningful today as they were then—if not more so—as we struggle to make sense of the events that have turned our world upside down since late August. If I have done anything wrong during that time—and I don't doubt that I have—it has not been due to insolence or ego. My sole intent has been to help my students better understand this strange and vexing universe that Haldane so simply but eloquently described. Whether that is enough to save one man's job is unimportant. What is ultimately at stake, not just for me but for all of us, is our very survival. And that is of far greater consequence."

There may have been some scattered applause as I returned to my seat, but that's just a guess because, by that point, my brain had decided to take the rest of the night off. I do recall hearing the sound of the gavel and seeing people file out of the room. My only other recollection is walking into the chill of that December night with Joanna, our fingers tightly interlaced. I had no idea if my words would have any impact on the Banneker Board of Directors. All I knew was that the ordeal of the past few days was over, at least for the time being. In the collision of exhaustion and euphoria that followed, my attention shifted to a solitary figure standing across the courtyard with his back turned.

"I'll be back in a minute," I said to Joanna.

I walked with some trepidation toward my father, who was staring up at the sky with his hands thrust in his pockets. My instinct was to wrap my arms around him, but decades of conflict and mistrust tempered that inclination, so I simply stood alongside him.

"It's a beautiful night," I said.

"Yes, it is."

"Thank you for what you said. It meant a lot."

He turned to me, his breath suspended in tiny clouds of water vapor that disappeared into the darkness. His face seemed to dissolve, its rigid arrogance giving way to a humility that was almost tragic. "I lost one child already," he said, tears pooling in his eyes. "I don't want to lose another."

I felt myself opening to him in a way that I hadn't since I was a child, the resentment of the intervening years evaporating like those misty puffs of breath. We embraced one another tightly and without reservation—two weary adversaries who finally realized there was nothing left to fight about. Apologies and explanations would come later; this was simply a time to reconnect.

CHAPTER 22

JOANNA HAD BEEN unflinchingly supportive that entire week. But the moment we walked in the house, she announced that she had a brief due the next morning and disappeared into the study. I, on the other hand, having just been relieved of all professional duties, had no such obligations and wanted to do nothing more than stare into space for the remainder of the evening. An unopened bottle of Courvoisier in the back of the pantry looked like something that might help facilitate that outcome, but cognac was not on my wife's pregnancy diet, and I didn't want her to feel excluded. So, I decided instead to brew us a pot of her favorite tea, an herbal blend that she had always loved for its alleged calming qualities but that I had despised because it tasted like dirt. Still, I was willing to endure some minor unpleasantness if that nasty concoction could work its tranquilizing magic. Then I took a sip and discovered that it tasted even worse than I remembered. The only solution was to donate the entire pot of steaming serenity to Joanna. From the sound of the rapid-fire bursts coming from her keyboard, she needed it more than I did. When I presented it to her in a scalding ceramic mug, she thanked me without looking up and continued typing, which I took as my cue to retreat to the bedroom.

Sometimes sleep comes gradually; at other times, like on that Thursday night, it crashes down all at once. I woke up disoriented and confused a few minutes after 2:00 a.m. The only thing I felt when I reached over to the other side of the bed was the cool sheen of our quilted duvet. Then I heard Joanna banging away on her laptop, which both established her whereabouts and demonstrated beyond any reasonable doubt that the word *brief* had to be the ultimate oxymoron.

⌇

The muted sound of a distant bell tower echoed through the air, growing steadily louder until it reached the volume of a digital sledgehammer. I pawed at the snooze button several times before the racket finally ceased. It was 6:15 a.m., and my wife—who had apparently given up the quaint custom known as sleeping— had already left for work. I panicked for a moment, thinking I had overslept.

Then I remembered.

I shuffled into the kitchen in my moccasins and sweats with no plans and nothing scheduled. A few minutes later, dark-roast Sumatra was drizzling into the coffee pot, and I was settling in for my first full day of unemployment. Unfortunately, the robocallers of the world were already hard at work. Two calls came in from out-of-the-area numbers before I even had a chance to grab a mug from the cabinet. I let both go to voicemail.

Not to be outdone, the email spammers were out in force as well. There were about thirty more messages than usual littering my junk-mail folder and inbox that morning, most from people I didn't know. I scanned the names quickly and was relieved to see that "Del Rio" was not among them. I was determined to hold off on reading emails until I'd had some coffee, but there was no stopping the phone calls. My cell rang yet again with an outside area code, but this time a name popped up that I actually recognized. I had no idea why Marty would be calling at this hour, but hopefully he wouldn't be trying to sell me something.

"Hey, you're up early," I said, stifling a yawn.

"Yeah, right. I've been at work since five."

"Ouch. What's going on?"

"Just wanted to offer my congratulations."

"For what?"

"You did a good job last night."

"I did?"

"Yeah. I was actually proud of you."

Another yawn. I really needed that caffeine.

"What are you talking about?"

"The board meeting, dingus."

"Oh, that."

"Was there something else you did last night that I should be congratulating you for?"

"Not that I know of. How did you find out?"

"I'm guessing you haven't been online this morning."

"No, I slept in."

"Must be nice. Some of us still have to work for a living. Anyway, I gotta run. Talk to you later."

Marty could be an occasional pain in the ass, but I had never known him to be intentionally cryptic. I finally poured myself a cup of coffee just before a string of congratulatory texts came in from several of my Integrated Science students. It was at that point that I decided to check my Twitter feed. There were dozens of tweets, retweets, and direct messages pertaining to the meeting, most from total strangers. Several of these included the link to a YouTube video titled "California Teacher Battles School Board."

Once I got over the shock of seeing a mini-documentary about the board meeting that looked like something out of *60 Minutes*, I started to think about who could have produced it. My initial thought was that David Phan might have been responsible. He had stood up for me at the meeting, plus he had a technical background, which meant he was probably capable of putting something like that together. That made him the prime suspect, until I got to the part where he was at the lectern talking. I was trying to figure that out when my phone rang again. I picked up without thinking.

"Hello."

"Burn in hell, child killer," the male voice on the other end said with all the emotion of someone ordering a pizza.

That was harsh—not to mention inaccurate. No one had died on my watch. Unfortunately, the caller hung up before I'd had a chance to register my complaint.

Within seconds, the landline rang for the first time in weeks. After what I'd just been accused of, I probably should have ignored it. But the old school ring tone sounded so comforting that I took the call—although in a somewhat more business-like manner.

"Siegel residence."

"Hello, I'd like to talk with Andy Siegel, please."

I never used that nickname, but at least the caller, who iden-tified himself only as "Edgar," addressed me as something other than child killer. For some reason, Edgar believed we needed to converse about an arcane aspect of unified field theory that he attempted to explain. The good news was he didn't call me any nasty names. But that was also the bad news because it made it more difficult to end the call midequation, which I ultimately had to do. There were two more calls on the landline in the next few minutes. I didn't answer either, for fear that Edgar might be calling back with breaking news from the unified field theory front.

The landline rang again about ten minutes later, and I decided to take a chance that the caller wasn't a frustrated scientist or an unhinged nut job. My instincts turned out to be correct—she was a sweet old lady named Mildred Jamison. After complimenting me on my public-speaking skills, Mildred asked if I might be available to deliver a motivational speech at a furniture-polish convention the following month in Iowa. I was relieved that she didn't want to discuss particle physics, but I politely declined, citing schedule conflicts.

I ignored several more calls, most of them on my cell from unrecognized locations, until one finally came in from the 212 area code in New York City. New Yorkers probably make as many crank calls as people anywhere else, but I decided to pick up anyway.

"Hello?"

"Hi, is this Mr. Siegel?" The voice belonged to a young female who sounded reasonably sane.

I almost blurted out "yes," but a childhood lesson from Mother kicked in.

"Who's calling, please?"

"This is Sarah Chadwick. I'm calling from the *Today Show*."

In less than an hour, I had gone from an accusation of juvenile homicide to a call from a television institution.

"Speaking. What can I do for you?"

"I'm one of the bookers on the show. We'd like to know if you might be able to fly to New York on Sunday for an in-studio interview Monday morning."

"You want me to appear on the *Today Show*?"

"Yes, if you're available."

"This coming Monday?"

"Yes."

This was turning out to be a morning of unexpected happenings. I told Ms. Chadwick that I would think about it but couldn't commit without first talking to my wife. I needed to talk with Joanna anyway. She had stood by me during this entire mess, and I wanted to do something, however minor, to acknowledge that. I called her at work to discuss dinner possibilities.

"Funny that you called," she said. "I was about to call you."

"Oh really? About what?"

"You first. You called me."

Joanna had always been a big fan of curry, so I suggested that we try a new Indian restaurant I'd heard good things about. She pleaded extreme fatigue and asked if we could stay home instead and make something simple or order takeout. We were about to end our call when she mentioned between yawns why she had planned to call me. In her bleary-eyed state that morning, she'd forgotten her laptop and asked me to email a file to her office.

As soon as we hung up, I realized that I, too, had forgotten something: I never told her about the *Today Show* invitation. Oh well. That would give us something interesting to talk about during dinner. I tracked down the document she needed and sent it off. While I was doing that, I noticed that there were several emails in her inbox that had been sent late the night before and early that morning by somebody named "Charles Harper." I was puzzled at first. Then it dawned on me that the mystery emailer was Charley, my Integrated Science student. The title of the email thread in question was "Board Meeting." I thought back to Joanna adjusting the settings on her phone just before the meeting began, and suddenly the mystery about how I'd become an overnight internet sensation had become a little less mysterious.

With Joanna's email request taken care of, I turned my attention to dinner. I had a cooking app on my phone that creates recipes based on whatever ingredients are available, but I'd never tried it. When I typed in what we had, the app suggested something that was far more challenging than my usual throw-a-slab-of-meat-on-the-grill attempts at cooking. But it was something I knew Joanna liked and would appreciate, assuming I didn't butcher it beyond recognition.

When she got home that night, the aroma from my kitchen extravaganza was wafting through the house, and two glasses of her favorite Oregon pinot noir were sitting on the dining room table. "I'm not sure what that is," she said, taking note of the scent in the air, "but it's definitely not barbecue."

"Would you believe *coq au vin*?"

"I'm occasionally gullible, but I'm not stupid."

"As Largo is my witness . . ."

"No way."

I handed her a glass of wine and raised my own. "To my amazing wife, who not only puts up with me but sticks around when I go fully off the rails. I love you more than you will ever know and hope that tonight's dinner will in no way diminish your appreciation of French cuisine." We clinked glasses, and I took a sip of wine.

I noticed Joanna had not joined me.

"It's your favorite pinot noir."

"I know. The aroma is wonderful."

"From Oregon."

"Best pinot anywhere."

She rubbed her stomach in a circular motion.

"Oh shit. I totally forgot. You can have one glass, can't you?"

"Assuming you didn't make tonight's dinner with grape juice, I probably shouldn't."

"I am such an idiot."

"I've been telling you that for years." I laughed at the reminder. "It's okay, I'll avoid the sauce."

"But that's the best part."

"No, the best part is that you made it." We put our glasses down and kissed. "You know, just because I can't drink doesn't mean you can't indulge me in other ways."

"And what exactly did you have in mind?"

She pulled out a chair and sat down. "Well, this was an exhausting day. I barely slept last night. And my neck is so stiff I can't turn my head."

She pivoted her entire body left and then right to demonstrate the problem. I walked behind her and placed my hands on either side of her neck. My fingers dug in, settling into a slow rhythm. I could feel her begin to relax.

"Oh wow. You should work at a day spa."

"All future employment options are on the table. Speaking of which, did you happen to see anything online today about your favorite masseur's appearance at a school board meeting last night?"

"Something online about last night's meeting?"

"Mm-hmm."

"At Banneker?"

"Yes, that's where the meeting was held."

"I didn't, but I'm not surprised there might be something. I mean, it is kind of a big deal. You know, academic freedom and all that."

I circled around in front of her and leaned forward. "You are the most beautiful, brilliant, and talented woman I've ever known. But great acting is not one of your skills."

She looked away for a moment and smiled. "Sorry. I thought it was a story that needed to be told." We agreed to put off further discussion of the video until later, and I resumed my new job as in-house massage therapist. "That feels so good, I might fall asleep right here."

"And miss dinner?"

"How about you just rub my neck while I eat?"

I brought the feast in from the kitchen, along with two glasses of apple cider.

Joanna took a sip and nodded her approval. "Not a great vintage but acceptable." I spooned a bit of the *coq au vin* onto her plate. "I didn't know this was one of those restaurants where the portions are fit for a doll," she said.

"Which you are."

"Attempts at charm will have no influence on my assessment of your cooking talents."

She cut a piece of chicken off the bone and popped it in her mouth. After the first few tentative moments, a quizzical look formed on her face. "I may have to keep you around for a while," she said.

"Maybe I should forget the day spa and get a job as a chef."

"Or maybe even go back to teaching. Any word from school?"

"Only if you count the texts from my students. And did I mention that I spent most of the day taking calls from half the world's crazies who'd seen your video?"

"Whoops."

"I did get one very interesting call I forgot to tell you about when we talked earlier." In between bites of chicken washed down with non-vintage apple cider, I told her about the *Today Show* call.

"Wow, from science geek to media superstar," she said.

"I owe it all to my wife."

"Which I expect you to mention during the interview."

"So, you think I should go?"

My phone chose that moment to chirp at us.

"Tell whoever it is that they're interrupting culinary history."

I glanced down at the text. "It's the LA Times."

"They probably want to schedule an interview for the food section."

I read the message again and turned on CNN.

". . . marking the first time that unexplained booming sounds have been reported outside the United States," the news anchor said. A world map filled the screen, and digital markers appeared at locations as they were announced. "Confirmed locations include: Meyrin, Switzerland; Sudbury, Ontario in Canada; Bonn, Germany; Gran Sasso, Italy; Sichuan, China; and Hida, Japan."

"That's a pretty random bunch of places," Joanna said.

"Yeah, except for the fact that every one of them has a lab where scientists are studying dark matter."

"There are no other details at this time," the anchor continued. "Should any additional information become available, we will bring it to you as soon as we get it. Again, booming sounds have now been reported in—"

Joanna tapped the mute button on the TV remote.

"So, to answer your question: Yes, I think you should go to New York."

I knew she was right, but part of me just wanted to get back to the simple existence that used to be my life before I became a YouTube phenomenon.

"It's kind of cool that they asked, I guess, but I'm not really sure I need to go."

"Why do you say that?"

"Because the government or somebody is eventually going to figure all this out."

"You're kidding, right?"

"No. I mean, it might take a while, but at some point, they're bound to get to the bottom of this."

"Andrew, our government doesn't even want to acknowledge that there's a problem. Maybe because they don't have an answer. Or maybe they do, but they don't want to scare everyone. All I know is—this might not be a job you were looking for, but it seems to have found you."

∽

An airport shuttle was scheduled to pick me up Sunday morning at 7:45. I set the alarm for 6:00 but was showered and dressed long before that. There was an odd sense of unease in the air, like the feeling when it's about to rain and you just want it to start. When Joanna woke up, I offered to make eggs Benedict, which had always been one of her Sunday morning favorites. She said the thought of eating Hollandaise sauce sounded disagreeable—a euphemism that required no further explanation—so we settled on scrambled eggs and toast.

We picked at our food without much enthusiasm and tried to figure out how the interview would go. "Obviously, they'll want to know where things stand between you and the board," Joanna said. "And then they're going to ask you the same two questions that everybody is asking, but that nobody in Washington wants to talk about."

"And what would those be?"

"Number one: do you know why all this is happening?"

"Nothing beyond what I said at the board meeting. And number two?"

"Do you have any idea what we can do about it?"

"By the time we get to that point, they'll be bringing out some fitness expert or personal finance guru." I cleared the table and headed into the kitchen to wash the dishes.

"But just in case they don't, what will you say?" Joanna called to me.

"I'll tell them that it's probably a long shot, but I do have an idea that might be worth thinking about."

"I didn't know that. Why didn't you say something?"

"It's kind of vague at this point. Just something that occurred to me in Wisconsin."

"Well, don't keep me in suspense. What is it?"

A pair of shrill blasts from the driveway signaled the arrival of the shuttle and guaranteed that everyone in the neighborhood was now awake. I turned off the water and walked back into the dining room. "Maybe you should just tune in to the *Today Show* tomorrow morning and find out for yourself."

"I might just do that."

We walked to the front door, where a hulking, four-legged beast had stationed himself.

"You take care of things while I'm gone, mister, you hear?" I said to Largo, who offered a sloppy kiss in the general vicinity of my nose. Joanna used her sleeve to dry me off.

"It seems like we just did this," she said, draping her arms around me.

"That's because we just did."

My normally tough-as-nails wife let her guard down just long enough to blink back a stray tear. "Just promise me you'll come home safe."

"I promise."

The shuttle honked again.

"You better go."

"Sorry to leave you with such a mess in the kitchen. I didn't get very far."

"It's okay. I think I know someone who'll help with cleanup." She glanced over at Largo.

I reached down for my bright-blue suitcase and pulled out the handle. It snapped into place with a crisp click.

"Thanks again for my birthday luggage."

"You're welcome again."

"See you tomorrow night."

Joanna patted the back of Largo's head. "We'll be here."

CHAPTER 23

THE PASSENGER CABIN of the wide-body jet was bathed in the soothing pink and purple glow that had made this airline famous. A gentle mix of chimes and rustling leaves provided the perfectly matched soundtrack. When I walked up the aisle, I felt like I'd entered a cocoon, which reduced but did not entirely eliminate my usual preflight anxiety. I still found plenty to worry about on the way to my seat, like would there be enough overhead space for my carry-on, and would I be stuck next to an insufferable blowhard determined to be my best friend for the next five hours. As it turned out, there was plenty of room for my bag, and the person seated next to me—a fortyish woman with big hair and even bigger headphones—had no more interest in social interaction than I did. In fact, she never even looked up from her hefty paperback when I slid into my aisle seat. I felt like I had just won the aeronautical lottery; the seat-assignment gods had placed me beside an unsociable curmudgeon, and I couldn't have been happier.

Moments after takeoff, I was sealed away in blissful isolation, courtesy of my own noise-canceling headphones and a novel I had been trying to get through for months. The story concerned an eclectic group of characters, each of whom had some connection to a jewelry box that had made its way across continents and generations, its contents shifting through the years like a mercurial time capsule. It was a clever conceit, but the pacing was ponderous. Clearly, my neighbor's book was far more compelling. I couldn't make out the title, but the back cover was striking, with its wavy bands of silver and blue that reminded me of a giant slide at a county fair.

I put my book down after yet another failed attempt to read more than five pages at a single sitting and turned my attention to the pricey packet of snacks I had bought on the way to the gate. Unfortunately, what had looked so appealing at the time of purchase lost its allure the moment I peeled off the ice-blue cellophane wrapper and bit into a very stale cashew. So much for passing the time with books or food. I considered watching a movie, but the in-flight entertainment alternatives were equally bleak. With no other options available, I returned to the simple solitude of my headphones and drifted off to sleep somewhere over Colorado.

When I woke up several states to the east, I took a sip of cranberry juice and booted up my laptop. It would be another hour and a half before we reached New York, and I wanted to organize my thoughts for the next day's interview. A recurring idea had been percolating around my brain since Wisconsin, when Amy mentioned that her father had said that everything has a distinctive signature, which he compared to a chemical or electrical fingerprint. I wondered if that might apply not only to small things like the snails I had dreamt about but to much larger things, like planets. This was more than just an idle academic question. If the force or energy source tormenting planet Earth used electricity as its means of expression, maybe it also used electricity to track this planet via our electrical signature. If we could somehow alter that signature, perhaps we could disguise our location.

I had no idea how we might actually do that, but it seemed like something worth thinking about. At that moment though, I couldn't seem to focus on anything but my cursor blinking back at me. Hopefully, I'd be more productive at the hotel. At least that was the convenient rationalization I allowed myself when I powered down my computer.

I rummaged through the seatback in front of me and pulled out a luxury lifestyle magazine, losing myself in its elegantly mounted fluff about five-star hotels, fine motorcars, and other spoils of unfettered affluence. I had just started an article about the world's best restaurants when the plane vibrated and bounced three times in succession. An infant, who clearly did not appreciate being jostled, registered its noisy displeasure a couple of rows back. A pair of pinging sounds followed over the intercom, and a member of the flight crew made the usual cautionary announcements.

We entered a tunnel of puffy clouds that looked like cotton candy. I glanced over at the lady in the next seat, who was still immersed in her book and didn't seem the least bit concerned about the minor hiccup we had just experienced. If she wasn't worried, I thought, why should I be? There are random noises and vibrations on every flight. All things considered, this one had been quite pleasant. Or so I thought until the aircraft shimmied from side to side and shuddered—a labored, heaving groan—before plunging into a brief freefall. The unexpected drop triggered gasps from around the cabin, as polite civility got a sharp nudge from budding unrest. A flight attendant announced that we were entering an area of turbulence and told passengers to stay in their seats and fasten their seatbelts.

The clouds that had been white and welcoming were now gauzy patches of gray. Drops of moisture began to trickle down the outside of the window. A dim flicker of lightning flashed in the distance, followed by another just above the wing. The plane bobbed up and down several times, and my chest tightened. The flight attendant, who had sounded so measured and assured just moments earlier, barked at a slow-moving passenger to get back to his seat.

Seconds later, oxygen masks deployed. I'd sat through countless safety demonstrations over the years and paid very little attention to any of them. It seemed almost surreal that this was actually happening. It took me a few seconds to figure out that I needed to put the damn thing on, and I struggled at first trying to tighten it. The lady next to me had no such problems, continuing to read what was apparently the most gripping novel ever written, while slipping the mask over her face like it was part of her nightly beauty regimen.

I looked out the window and noticed that the raindrops were larger than normal, almost like bubbles. Watching them fall in lazy slow motion was hypnotic, like staring at an aquarium screensaver. But the tranquility was fleeting. The plane lurched to the right and dove downward, gaining speed by the second as it hurtled through the clouds. Neatly stacked plastic trays on food carts were slung to the floor. Overhead bins flew open, dumping backpacks and garment bags on the ashen-faced passengers below. Some sat in stony silence; others shrieked or chanted in a desperate cacophony of prayer—in multiple languages, to myriad deities.

I could no longer feel the normal passage of time. Each moment stood disjointed and alone, an island of dread unto itself. I found myself in the middle of the aisle, hunched over with knees bent. A roaring sound bellowed up from some primordial place deep within me. Then I was back in my seat as if nothing had happened. The people around me were frozen in place, glowing like luminescent x-rays. A fusion of screams, vibrations, and shearing wind grew maddeningly loud, merging into a single point of deafening static that sliced through my brain like an ice pick, before resolving into absolute silence.

An immersive stillness enveloped the cabin like a shroud . . . and all motion ceased. The plane was still in the air, but it was no longer moving.

The woman in the next seat took off her headphones and put her book down.

"I'm sorry," she said with a gentle smile. "I should have introduced myself. I'm Katherine."

There was a soothing quality to her voice that I found comforting, even if we were suspended miles in the air like a drop of dew.

"I'm Andrew."

"Yes, I know."

I wanted to ask how she knew, but my brain veered off to another track. "Did you hear the chanting?" I asked. "Everyone praying in a different language to a different God."

"Many languages. One God."

"Who doesn't seem to be anywhere near this airplane."

She looked at me with the serenity of a wise elder.

"God is everywhere. Even here."

"Yeah, well, I've never been able to find Him."

"You don't need to find Him. God is inside of you. Inside all of us."

Katherine's New Age mumbo jumbo was interrupted when the skin covering her face cracked like a sheet of glass and began to pull apart. She was shedding years before my eyes, going backwards in time from the wrinkled mask of middle age, to the slight imperfection of young adulthood, to the effortless glow of youth. I realized then that the person sitting beside me was not a stranger I had just met on an airplane.

"Katherine—my God. You're Katie. You're my sister." Joy and sorrow were bleeding together, flowing through me like a churning river. I struggled to process a flood of emotions I could neither explain nor contain. Some kind of internal circuit breaker kicked in, and I began to cry.

"It's okay," she said. "You're going to be alright."

"How is this even possible?" I asked on the verge of hyperventilating.

"Don't worry about that now. Just breathe."

I inhaled deeply several times and tried to make sense of what I was seeing. Katie, or at least the version of her seated next to me, looked very much like the sixteen-year-old girl I remembered. But her skin, which used to run toward olive, was now pale yet luminous, as if it were glowing. Beads of light danced through her hair in shimmering hues that flickered as she moved, like sparklers on the Fourth of July.

"Did you see the circles?" she asked.

I wiped the last remaining tears from my eyes. "I don't . . . I'm not sure what you mean."

"They might have looked like very large raindrops or bubbles."

I remembered staring out the window and seeing oversized drops of rain that appeared transparent. "Oh, yes, I think I did. I've never seen anything like that before."

"Actually, you have. But you've forgotten what the view is like from the edge of this universe."

"*This* universe?"

"Yes. Each of those circular structures is a universe unto itself, although they are all connected."

Images of interconnected circles flashed before my eyes. The Olympic rings on the poster Katie had made for my tenth birthday party. The rings on the grill of Marty's Audi, which I had noticed when he pulled out of my driveway. Both images were seared into my memory, but I remained unconvinced.

"How could they possibly be universes?" I asked. "They were big for raindrops but still very small."

"Universes come in all sizes—some a thousand times larger than this one, others so small we call them microverses."

"And why do they look like transparent spheres or bubbles?"

"Circles and spheres are at the core of everything. From ripples in a pond to gravity waves. From the water cycle to the flow of time. From the smallest particles of matter to stars, planets—and universes. Everything is based on circles."

"I've always heard that there are no perfect circles anywhere."

Katie considered the idea for a moment.

"I guess that depends on your idea of perfection."

We sat for a while in silence. I stared at the dormant figures around us, trapped in place like statues. Then the plane began to fall again, barreling through a spinning, swirling vortex that sucked us down until the passenger cabin tore apart, and everything in it—every person, every seat, every scrap of paper—exploded in all directions. The wind ripped at my skin. A low frequency hum rose sharply to a screeching pinnacle of sonic pain. Another blade of static tore through the maelstrom and thrust me into a place that was dark and silent.

From this blank slate of nothingness, faint, blurry shapes began to emerge. I was sitting up in bed in my childhood bedroom, and everything was just as I remembered it: the maple dresser with my first baseball glove on top, my little student desk, the bookcase filled with my favorite children's books, and dozens of glow-in-the-dark stars and planets that covered the ceiling and bathed the room in a soft, glimmering blush. But the most reassuring sight of all was my sister sitting next to me on my straight-back, wooden desk chair. I had nightmares a lot when I was a kid. If Katie was still up, she'd usually come into my room, pull up that chair and sit with me until I fell back asleep. Now she was beside me once again. We spoke without using our voices, the words flowing between us through a telepathic process she called "merging."

"Can you tell me where I am?" I asked.

"You are everywhere."

"I don't know what that means. Am I alive or dead?"

Katie took a moment before she answered. "You have learned to experience life through a binary lens. On or off, true or false, alive or dead."

"Is that wrong?"

"Not wrong—incomplete."

I had more questions but was distracted by a crush of sensations—a mix of rushing liquids and firing synapses—tissues, muscles, and organs, all pulsing and beating inside of me. I must be alive, I thought, as I struggled to follow the arc of Katie's argument.

"How is it incomplete?" I asked.

"Binary is a myth. A single particle can be in two places at the same time."

"As long as you believe in quantum entanglement, or as Einstein called it, 'spooky action at a distance.' He was not a big fan."

"Einstein was brilliant, but he missed a few things every once in a while."

Katie was drilling down, exploring the deep furrows of physics and metaphysics. I was experiencing something much more basic—the sensory bliss of life surging through my body. It was a feeling more powerful than any drug, and I wanted it to continue. But the lure of the person seated beside me—this woman-child I had once known better than anyone else—tugged at me like a magnet.

"You're talking about subatomic, impossibly small particles," I said.

"Combine enough small particles, and you can make something really big."

"As big as a person?"

"As big as a universe." Katie's mind was taking great leaps, while I struggled to take baby steps. "What you see as either one thing or another is not a choice between two opposites but two points on a continuum. What you think of as death is the evanescent transition from one of those points to the other." Her words wove an intricate web, yet critical strands remained dangling and disconnected. She could sense my confusion. "Think of the focus ring on a camera," she said. "When it turns, some objects blur, while others come into sharp focus. But nothing disappears. Your physical form and location may change, but your essence remains the same. It is continuous and everlasting. And it has never shined brighter."

The logical, analytical part of my brain would have normally rejected that sort of flower-child babble, yet her words resonated. I let the moment settle and work its way through me. But there was more I needed to know.

"Are you still my sister?" I asked.

"I have been your sister before, and I will be again. But our connection is not always the same. At times, like this one, I have been your guide. At other times, it is you who guides me."

A whisper of sadness welled up inside me. "Now that I've found you again, I don't want to lose you."

"I have always been with you and always will be."

Her words flowed over me like a gentle wave.

"Do you know who Joanna is?" I asked.

She smiled. "Yes, of course."

"I don't want to lose her, either. Where is she in all this?"

"She, too, is on her journey and will be with you always. And there will be others, some of whom you have not yet met in this life. They are from what you think of as the future. One of them is your child."

My child. Suddenly nothing else mattered.

"What do you know about that?"

"I know that you will meet her very soon."

"Her?"

"Yes. And she, too, will be with you forever."

I felt a surge of exhilaration, tempered by confusion. What kind of world would my daughter inherit? Would it be a safe and welcoming place like the room in which we were sitting? Or would it be a cauldron of chaos and fear like the world we had been living in the past four months?

"Do you know what's been going on since late August?" I asked. "The accidents and everything else?"

Katie nodded. "Yes, I do."

"Can you tell me why it's happened?"

"I can tell you that you were right to focus on the particles you call dark matter."

Her response startled me.

"Someone who knows a great deal about dark matter told me it couldn't possibly be responsible for everything that's happened."

"Not directly. But there is a link."

"What . . . what kind of link?"

Katie paused for a moment.

"Those particles are like breadcrumbs that show the way from one universe to the next. A roadmap in spherical form with no beginning and no end. Where distances span not miles but dimensions."

If I needed proof that J.B.S. Haldane was right, maybe this was it. The reality Katie described was stranger than any I could have imagined.

"You speak easily of things that unfold on a cosmic scale. I'm still trying to figure out what's happening around the United States."

Katie hesitated again, as if she didn't want to tell me something but knew she couldn't *not* tell me.

"You only need to look at what's been going on at the underground physics lab in Minnesota."

My body tightened. "I don't understand. What do you mean?"

"The scientists there and other places are close to learning the truth about the particles you think of as dark matter. And that has triggered a response."

"A response that includes booming sounds, accidents, and hearts that beat for no reason?"

"Yes."

"Who is it exactly that's responding? And for what reason?"

"The particles that connect universes are very important, very powerful. There are forces in this universe and beyond that don't want those connections to be revealed."

"If their goal was to stop dark-matter research, their response makes no sense. It has done nothing but bring unspeakable pain to people who had no involvement with the work being done in Minnesota."

Katie looked away, her eyes avoiding mine.

"The forces I'm talking about are comprised of electric energy in its purest form. They use electrical vibrations for everything. To perceive what goes on around them, to communicate—and to take action. Sometimes during that process there are certain . . . what they think of as inefficiencies. Things that we might call mistakes."

"Like the events of recent months."

"Yes." Katie turned to me. The barest hint of a smile creased her lips. "It is my understanding that those are always corrected."

"So, does that mean these things are going to stop? Or will they just be carried out in a more efficient manner?" A tear slid down Katie's cheek, but she didn't answer. "Katie, I need to know. Is all this going to come to an end, or will it keep happening?" Still no response. "Katie, please—"

The room and everything in it started to move, slowly at first, like a train pulling out of a station. Then we began to accelerate. The objects around us flowed into one another, their shapes and colors blending together. The features on Katie's face began to wear away as if by erosion, until she was unrecognizable. I glanced down at my hand; it was frayed and distorted. I knew in that moment that it was no longer *my* hand. I didn't own it, any more than one can own a blade of grass. I looked up, away from myself, away from Katie. We were moving at a velocity that was beyond my capacity to comprehend, faster even than the speed of light.

It was the speed of infinity.

The sound of static blistered the air. Katie was gone, and I, too, was somewhere else, lying in a thick haze inside a transparent dome-like structure. Something soft and pillowy cradled me from below; a warm liquid sloshed up against me. I looked beyond the watery membrane surrounding me and saw another aqueous structure, one that contained what looked like a duplicate form of myself. I raised my right hand and moved it in a circle. The alternate image of me mimicked that motion. I put my right hand down and raised my left, and made another circle. He did the same, tracing my movements with his own. We were moving in parallel—a single entity in two places at once, just as Katie had described.

I wondered how similar my doppelganger and I actually were. Was his life the same as mine, populated by the same people doing the same things at the same time? I closed my eyes for a moment. When I opened them again, the other structure had vanished—and with it, the other version of me. I was surrounded by faint, shadowy figures, who glided through the haze like animal characters on a merry-go-round, their voices rising, falling, and overlapping.

There was a chill on my skin and a feeling of slight pressure on my chest. I heard a series of crisp, popping sounds followed by static and a massive shock of electricity that coursed through my body. The shadowy figures were gone. The pressure on my chest lifted, and a brilliant white light illuminated a young child who hovered in front of me. She looked about five years old, with golden curls that framed her sweet, radiant face.

"I love you, Daddy," she said.

Her words filled me with a joy unlike any I had ever known, but it was short-lived. Another withering blast of static discharged through the air, and I was alone again. I closed my eyes for a scant instant. Every event, every thought, every emotion—from my tenth birthday party to that ephemeral moment with my daughter—rippled through my brain. In the split-second it took for my life to replay, the past caught up with the present.

And I was back.

CHAPTER 24

THERE'S A DULL, throbbing pressure behind my eyes and a heaviness that extends across my forehead. A woman's muffled voice drones on in the distance, its cadence relentless, like a metronome. A loud crack of static whips through the air, followed by what sounds like gears grinding and then meshing into place.

My eyes open slowly.

The woman's voice is now clear.

". . . with connections to London at Terminal 4, Concourse A, Gate 2; Paris at Terminal 1, Gate 5; Frankfurt at Terminal 1, Gate 7; Athens at . . ."

I think I slept too long; it feels like somebody poured a cup of sludge into my brain. I can't tell if the flight attendant is reading the list of gate assignments or if I'm listening to a recording. One thing I do know: the bookworm seated next to me is still reading, although it looks like she might have switched to a different book.

The intercom clicks on, and the pilot introduces himself in the flat, authoritative monotone of pilots everywhere: "Good evening, ladies and gentlemen, this is Captain Henderson. On behalf of the entire flight crew, we'd like to thank you for flying with us today. We do want to apologize for the turbulence along the way. Some unexpected electrical activity briefly interfered with our instrumentation, which caused a momentary drop in cabin pressure and altitude. Fortunately, we didn't lose any time. We'll be arriving in New York City at 8:05 p.m. local time."

I'd almost forgotten that the plane bounced up and down several times at one point before it caught its balance. A murmur of relief ripples through the cabin when we break through the cloud cover, and the sight of highways and bridges comes into view. The jarring bump of the wheels touching down at JFK a short time later prompts some scattered applause. Everything is happening by the numbers now: the plane searching for a parking place, the flight attendant warning about overhead items shifting, and a cabin full of weary passengers gathering up their belongings. But there is one surprise. After a five-hour, silent stalemate, the lady in the next seat has just removed her headphones and put her book down. She glances over in my direction and flashes a quick smile. We've had zero interaction to this point, so I guess that's progress. She actually looks kind of familiar. Probably just has one of those faces.

"Nothing like a little turbulence to make things interesting," she says.

"When it comes to flying, I'll take boring over interesting anytime."

"Seriously," she says with a chuckle. "You from New York or just visiting?"

"Just here on business for a couple days."

"Oh, same here. Well, enjoy your stay."

"Thanks. You too."

She seems friendly enough; I probably would have enjoyed

talking to her. But I'm already thinking about other things as we step into the packed aisle and prepare to go our separate ways.

❧

I think there's a car that's supposed to meet me, but I realize walking out of the jetway that I'm not exactly sure where. I'm just following the crowd and enjoying the children's artwork that's pasted up on the walls. It's a nice touch amid the usual propaganda promoting hotels, Broadway shows, and tours of the city.

People are lined up three-deep to greet us when we spill out into the arrival area. I don't think I've ever seen so many anxious faces at an airport. A shoving match breaks out up ahead between a TV crew and airport security trying to clear a path for the arriving passengers. There are random cardboard signs scattered throughout the area, including one with "Segal" written on it that I assume is meant for me. I can live with the misspelling; I'm more concerned that the guy holding the sign looks barely old enough to have a driver's license.

"Excuse me, I think you're here for me."

"Are you Mr. Siegel?" he asks with a New York accent as thick as pea soup.

"Yes, I am."

"Mr. Andrew Siegel?"

"That's me."

"Excellent—I'm Eddie. Let me get that for you," he says, reaching for my carry-on. "Did you check any luggage today, Mr. Siegel?"

"Yeah, unfortunately I did."

"Not a problem."

"Tried to fit all my stuff into that thing last weekend," I said, pointing to my bag. "Wasn't going to make that mistake again."

"No worries, we'll be out of here before you know it." With Eddie leading the way, we push through the mass of humanity in front of us and head toward the baggage area. "So, you do a lot of travelling for your job?" he asks.

"No, not usually. Just kind of worked out that way the last two weeks."

"Yeah, tell me about it. I been packing on the hours like you wouldn't believe. When it rains, it pours. You know what I'm saying?"

"Yep, I sure do."

"Speaking of rain, I hear you ran into some turbulence up there. Was it a weather-related thing?"

"You know, I'm not really sure. I think they said it was electrical interference or something like that." A guy with a serious camera rig has just gotten past security. Reporters are sticking microphones or cell phones in every face they can reach. "So, just out of curiosity, do arriving passengers usually get this kind of reception here?"

"On a day like today, I guess they do."

A sliver of open space splits the crowd ahead of us, and we dart through it.

"What do you mean, 'on a day like today'?"

He leans toward me as we walk, like he has a secret to share. "Well, not to scare you or anything, but four planes have gone down in the last two and a half hours."

I stop short, almost getting run over in the process. Eddie takes another step or two and pulls up. We're blocking traffic like a fender bender at rush hour.

"Four planes where?"

"One was going to Newark. One to La Guardia. And two were coming here."

"Jesus."

People are speeding past us like we're invisible.

"And if that's not freaky enough—all four of them were coming from L.A."

It feels like all the blood is draining from my head, like I'm going to pass out. I'm looking for something to grab onto, but there's nothing—just the twitch of bodies rushing past.

"You okay, Mr. Siegel?"

"Yeah, I'm alright."

"You sure? Your face is looking a little gray. Can I get you some water or maybe a soda?"

"No, I'm okay. Just need to get some air." I force down a couple of breaths, and we start walking again.

"So yeah, there's a lot of rumors out there. Computer failures. Terrorists. Crazy weather. Maybe an outage of some kind. Nobody knows what the hell's going on."

"Anything happen outside of this area?"

"Not that I know of." The throng of people in front of us grinds to a halt. Looks like half the city is trying to squeeze into the baggage-claim area. "Can I ask you a question, Mr. Siegel?"

"Um, sure."

"Are you a religious person by any chance?"

"No, not really. Why do you ask?"

"Well, something kept you safe today, that's for sure. Maybe it was the man upstairs. Maybe it was just good luck. Whatever it was, I'd think about buying some lottery tickets if I was you."

Not sure if it's luck or providence, but we're moving again. It occurs to me that Joanna might have heard about all this. I pull out my phone and there are three missed calls from her. The lottery will have to wait.

"I'm going to go call my wife. I'll meet you over at the baggage claim."

"Not a problem. You take your time."

The sound in here is more annoying than loud—a constant hum punctuated by flight announcements and the occasional cough. There's a deserted electronics kiosk up ahead on the right that looks like it's closed for the night. It's probably as quiet there as anywhere else. I duck behind it and make the call, but it doesn't go through. Try again, same thing. My phone is showing two bars, so I'm not sure what the problem is. Maybe the circuits are overloaded. At least the crowd on the way to the baggage area is starting to thin out. I make it over there just in time to see the luggage from my flight come tumbling down onto the conveyor belt.

Twenty minutes later, the only bags left are a bashed-in shipping box and an oversized duffel bag that circle around like unwanted orphans My super-fancy, hard-shell beast—the one that Joanna promised I'd always be able to spot—is nowhere to be seen. Which means there's an excellent chance I'm going to end up on national television tomorrow looking like I slept in my clothes because I actually did. Maybe if my bag shows up, they can drive it over to the hotel before morning. That's what I tell myself, anyway, on the way over to the office where they deal with missing luggage and other assorted complaints. I'm about to walk in when I hear someone whistle behind me. I look over my shoulder, and there's Eddie, standing in front of the baggage carousel, waving his arms. It seems my birthday bag and a few other last-minute stragglers have finally shown up.

"Yo, Mr. Siegel. Is it one of these?" he shouts.

"Yeah, it's that one over there." I yell, pointing to it on my way back to the carousel.

"This one?" He motions to a vinyl relic with a cracked handle.

"No, the one behind it. The blue one."

Eddie hustles around and pulls the iridescent-blue behemoth off the conveyor belt. "This is definitely one you're never gonna lose," he says, even though I almost just did.

With that problem solved, we take our place at the back of a long line waiting to get out of the terminal. Security people are checking IDs, which is slowing things down.

"They usually don't even check the bags at LAX, let alone IDs," I tell Eddie.

"Probably just being extra careful because of everything going on today."

We finally make it outside, where a light snow is falling, and Eddie heads off in search of his limo. I try Joanna again, and this time the call goes right through. She picks up midway through the first ring.

"Hi, baby," she says.

I can tell she's freaked out because she never calls me that.

"Hey, sorry I couldn't get through before this. I think something's up with the phone lines."

"Are you okay?"

"Yeah, I'm fine. Just really tired."

Joanna starts to say something, but an armada of honking horns drowns her out. "What'd you say?" I shout over the racket.

"You heard about all the crashes, right?"

"Yeah, I just found out. Everybody here is hugging or crying—or a little of both."

"I can't even imagine. I'm just glad you're okay."

"What about you? You alright?"

"Other than having a heart attack every time they announced

another plane crash, I'm fine. I'm thinking maybe you should take a train back."

"I'll be ok. Don't worry." Eddie swoops past a line of cars and pulls up in a black Town Car. Before I know it, he's got my bags loaded in the trunk. "Hey, I kind of gotta go. My driver's here with the car."

"Listen to you, mister celebrity, with your driver."

I know Joanna's feeling better when she starts poking fun at me. "Can you call my parents and let them know I'm okay?"

"Yeah, of course."

"I'll call you when I get to the hotel."

"Okay. I love you."

"Love you too."

Eddie swings the front passenger door open, and I slide in. I'm feeling so drowsy, it's hard to keep my eyes open. I put on my seatbelt and lean back; my eyes flutter a couple of times and close for a moment. When they open again, I'm in my seat on today's plane, and we're plunging down through the clouds. I unbuckle the seatbelt and leap into the aisle, landing hunched over and roaring like a jungle animal.

The thud of Eddie's door slamming shut snaps me back to reality. I'm not sure what just happened. It was almost like a flashback of some kind. Either that or the strangest, shortest dream ever.

Once we get away from the airport, Eddie is in his element—left hand on the steering wheel, right hand tapping out commands on a touchscreen that looks like it could launch the space shuttle. The snow has stopped, but there's a fine mist covering the hood, and the road is slick. Eddie pumps the brakes every so often to make sure we've still got traction.

"So, I can take you straight to your hotel. Or, if you're not in a rush, we can do the scenic route. Might be a good way to get your mind off everything."

"You gotta be the first airport driver who actually admitted he takes people the long way around." We both laugh. "Listen, if I didn't have work to do, I'd take you up on that."

"Well how about I at least turn on the radio for you? We just upgraded the speakers in here."

"Sounds good to me."

"What kind of music you like?"

"Country, if you've got it, but really anything besides opera."

"No worries there. I'm Italian, but I think I missed out on the opera gene." Eddie turns on the radio, which is tuned to a death metal station. "Whoops—sorry about that, boss."

He taps the screen, and the station changes.

". . . are now being told that President Martell will address the nation at ten o'clock tonight," the news anchor says.

"You want to listen to this?"

"Yeah, I kind of do, if you don't mind."

"Not a problem."

"Apparently the text of the president's speech is still being finalized," the anchor continues, "but we do know that he will be speaking about the plane crashes that took place in the greater New York area earlier this evening. Again, that will be coming up at the top of the hour at 10:00 p.m. In the meantime, we now return to our program about the mayor's initiative to—"

Eddie turns off the radio.

"Too bad you had to come here at a time like this, Mr. Siegel. This is the greatest city in the world when there isn't all this goddamned craziness going on. Sorry about the language."

"Apology accepted but not necessary."

"I'll give you my card when we get to the hotel. Let me know if you need a ride back to the airport for the trip home."

"Thanks, I'll do that."

༄

Eddie drops me off about forty minutes later at my hotel a few blocks from Rockefeller Center, where they film the *Today Show*. With its tasteful blend of marble, wood, and brass—not to mention a ton of people buzzing around the lobby—this place is a long way from the Hometown Inn in Eau Claire, Wisconsin. Piped-in Christmas music and a perfectly decorated Christmas tree with perfectly wrapped gifts beneath it set a festive holiday mood. You'd never know that four planes crashed near here just a few hours ago.

I get in line at the check-in desk behind a pair of businessmen, who are standing behind a frazzled mom and dad and their two kids. I'm not thrilled with the delay, but I am impressed with the young lady behind the desk, who is doing her best to keep things moving and make everyone happy. Not an easy task when the irate mother won't stop arguing for an upgrade she insists she was promised online.

I finally get up to my room on the twenty-second floor a few minutes after ten. It's like something out of an interior design magazine in here, with cove lighting, teak furniture, and a pedestal sink in the bathroom that looks like an abstract sculpture. But all I really care about, as I swing my suitcase up on the bed, is what the leader of the free world has to say. It takes a few seconds to figure out the user-unfriendly remote, but I finally get the flat screen on the wall to cooperate midway through the president's speech from the Oval Office.

". . . most believed, including your president, that the

unusually large number of tragedies that have occurred in recent months were simply random accidents linked by pure coincidence. What happened in the skies above New York and New Jersey today was something else, something very different. And unfortunately, the carnage didn't end there. A massive electrical explosion destroyed a world-renowned, underground physics lab in Minnesota tonight, killing more than a dozen people, including the lab director.

Sweet Jesus.

"While we are still in the process of gathering information about all of today's events, we believe that they were intentional acts of terror, carried out in a carefully orchestrated and calculated manner. Whoever the perpetrators were—be they violent terrorists or military forces directed by rogue dictators—they have vastly underestimated the will and resolve of the American people.

"My fellow Americans, these are perilous times, and the stakes are high. No one should underestimate the challenge we face. But make no mistake: we will rise to that challenge. We will identify those responsible for these heinous acts, and we will bring them to swift justice. The evil that was perpetrated today may have shaken us to our core, but it has not shaken our core beliefs in this country and what it stands for. Thank you. God bless you. And may God bless the United States of America."

NBC is sending a car for me at 5:15 a.m., and my wake-up call will come before I know it, so I decide to forego the post-speech analysis from the network pundits. I do want to try to get in touch with Rich and make sure he's okay. I grab my phone to call him and see that there's a text from Marty, who says he's heard from Rich and that he was off-site at the time of the explosion. So, that's at least good news. What's not so great is that

President Martell seems to be completely unhinged from reality. I mean, I agree with him that these were premeditated attacks. But by terrorists or rogue dictators, Mr. President? After everything we've been through these past months and all the resources at your disposal—that's the best you can come up with?

When Mike Martell was elected, many of us hoped that his presidency would mark a new era in American politics—one based on intelligence, honesty, and common sense. The president's plans, regrettably, appear to contain none of those things. He is either delusional or, in the face of plummeting approval ratings, incapable of resisting the lure of political expediency. Whatever his motivation, President Martell has apparently decided not to confront an enemy he can't comprehend and instead engage a more conventional opponent. Even if it's one he must fabricate from the ghosts of battles past.

Before I do anything else, I need to charge my laptop, which tapped out somewhere over Pennsylvania. The phone rings while I'm crawling around under the desk in search of an outlet, and I realize I never called Joanna back, as she's probably about to remind me. It turns out that the caller is not my wife but *Today Show* booker Sarah Chadwick, who wants to make sure I got in okay. I assure her more out of habit than anything else that I'm fine. But with four planes from L.A. falling out of the sky today—and a physics lab I recently visited getting blown to bits—I feel more vulnerable than ever before. I'm also a little surprised that my segment is still slated to go ahead as planned tomorrow, but Ms. Chadwick informs me that it is, although likely a bit later in the program.

I brought some physics articles with me that I want to look

over, just to make sure I've got my facts straight before the interview. I reach into my carry-on and grab what feels like my novel, but the alternating bands of silver and blue on the back cover are not what I was expecting. This is not my book, and I have no idea how it got in my bag—but it does look vaguely familiar. Then it hits me. This is the paperback the lady sitting next to me on the plane today was reading. I turn it over and a chill runs through me. The title of the book is *Hide in Plain Sight*, which is also the strategy I hope will protect this planet if we can find a way to change our electrical signature. Maybe it's just another coincidence that a book by that name should end up in my carry-on, but I'll take it as a sign from somewhere that my plan might actually make some sense.

I feel like I need to rest for a few minutes before I read those articles, but I don't want to fall asleep. My compromise is to turn out the lights and lie back in bed without closing my eyes. I'm not sure if what I'm seeing is a reflection from outside or just exhaustion setting in, but the ceiling looks like it's twinkling. I take a closer look and see that it's covered with glow-in-the-dark stars and planets like the ones that used to light up my bedroom every night when I was a kid. Not something I'd expect to see in an upscale Manhattan hotel.

I look away from the starscape above; my eyes drift downward to something even more unexpected. A translucent figure, her skin snowy pale like alabaster, sits motionless on a straight-back wooden chair next to the bed. I'm not sure how to explain this—any more than I can explain why I thought I was back on today's plane, roaring like a jungle cat, when I was actually in an airport limousine—but what I'm looking at is my sister staring out the window with beams of light streaming through her eyes. I don't know if I can trust my vision at this point—or my sanity, for that matter—but she appears ageless, neither child nor adult, in this timeless, fluid place she seems to occupy somewhere between life and death.

Katie has been gone since I was ten years old, but it feels like she never left—like I was just with her earlier today. She turns her head toward me and smiles, her energy wrapping around me like a cloak. I sit up in bed and squint my eyes to get a better look at her—if only to verify that what I think I'm seeing is real—but it's almost dark in here. I reach back to the lamp on the nightstand and turn the power switch until it clicks on. A rush of light floods the room . . . and Katie vanishes, as does the wooden chair, followed by the stars and planets on the ceiling. I turn the lamp off, hoping the darkness might lure her back. Her physical body does not return, but in its place, rotating bands of brilliant white light burst into a torrent of shimmering particles that vibrate like a thousand fireflies and surge through me.

I may not be able to see her, but I know that Katie is with me. Maybe that's what compels me to get to my feet and walk to the window. The iconic image of planet Earth as seen from the surface of the Moon lights up the night on a massive electronic billboard across the street. The caption beneath the picture reads, "It's Your Home—Keep It Clean." This planet looks so calm and peaceful from a quarter million miles away—an aqueous blue gem floating in a silent sea of darkness. But the blue is more than just a color that registers on the retinas of my eyes. It is a reminder of the sadness and despair that will forever roil beneath the surface of this world, despite its tranquil guise.

It feels like several lifetimes ago since that day in late August when I first heard about mysterious booming sounds in a handful of cities whose names I can hardly remember. With everything that's happened since then, it's clear that none of this has been accidental. I'm not sure why I was spared today, but there's no doubt that I was targeted. To whomever or whatever is responsible for that and everything that's preceded it: you appear to be a form of energy, with capabilities that exceed anything we have ever witnessed or even imagined. But apart from that, we know almost nothing about you. There are also things that you don't know about us. We humans are a jumble of contradictions, at times shallow and shortsighted, yet capable of extraordinary courage and compassion. But there is something else that defines us, something I never understood until I saw my sister's transcendent aura shine like a beacon of hope in this room tonight. Whatever we do and wherever we go, we carry God within us. Which means, when you fight against us, you fight against God—the source of all energy, including yours. And that is a fight you cannot win.

∽

The street below is a whirling blur of asphalt and steel. An urban mosh pit filled with dreamers and desperados, wayfarers and wannabes—all racing to get somewhere that offers them something. It is a scene so kaleidoscopic that I nearly miss the stream of transparent orbs drifting this way from some vague point in the distance. I can only guess what these spherical structures that look like bubbles might be. Perhaps an elaborate holiday display that only New York City could pull off. Or maybe my mind is just playing tricks at the end of a very long day.

Whatever they are, I don't have time to dwell on them. There is one thing and one thing only that demands my full attention: a resolute, enigmatic foe who has thrown down a gauntlet of cosmic proportions and challenged me and all of us to respond—with or without the president of the United States. To quote

Joanna, this might not be a job I was looking for, but it seems to have found me. And with the loss of life around this country and my own personal safety now in peril, I have no choice but to answer the call. To do anything less would be to abandon the promise and potential of this glorious celestial jewel on which we live. And that—to borrow from something else my wife once told me—would be the greatest loss of all.

The End

ACKNOWLEDGEMENTS

My thanks to Christopher Hoffmann for his keen proofreading eye and sage editorial suggestions. Thanks also to Kelly Figueroa-Ray for her tireless permissions research work.

I owe an enormous debt of gratitude to the friends, family members, and colleagues who read early drafts and offered insightful feedback and encouragement. I could not have made this journey without you.

And most of all, thank you to my parents, who raised me in a home alive with words and ideas, where curiosity was my constant companion. That companionship continues to this day.

ABOUT THE AUTHOR

 Glenn Kammen wrote his first science fiction story at the age of ten about a man who wanders through a fog-shrouded cemetery and stumbles upon his own gravestone. In the ensuing years, Kammen put his creative writing aspirations on hold and turned his attention to the mastery of essential life skills, like diagramming sentences and memorizing geometry theorems. He eventually paired an interest in science with educational television, writing and producing documentary programs about computer science, physics, oceanography, and earth science. He dragged his young daughters to the Griffith Park Observatory more frequently than any parent should and bought a telescope of his own to scan the heavens. But the lure of fiction continued to tug at him. When reports of mysterious booming sounds began to routinely appear on news websites, Kammen knew it was time to revisit his science fiction roots. *Anomalies in Blue* is the result of that realization.

Made in the USA
Columbia, SC
19 August 2020

16905256R00171